CRASH LANDING ON THE DUKE

The Silver Dukes
Book 6

by

Meara Platt

ARE YOU SIGNED UP FOR DRAGONBLADE'S BLOG?

You'll get the latest news and information on exclusive giveaways, exclusive excerpts, coming releases, sales, free books, cover reveals and more.

Check out our complete list of authors, too!

No spam, no junk. That's a promise!

Sign Up Here

www.dragonbladepublishing.com

Dearest Reader;

Thank you for your support of a small press. At Dragonblade Publishing, we strive to bring you the highest quality Historical Romance from some of the best authors in the business. Without your support, there is no 'us', so we sincerely hope you adore these stories and find some new favorite authors along the way.

Happy Reading!

CEO, Dragonblade Publishing

Additional Dragonblade books by Author Meara Platt

The Silver Dukes Series
Cherish and the Duke
Moonlight and the Duke
Two Nights with the Duke
Snowfall and the Duke
Starlight and the Duke
Crash Landing on the Duke

The Moonstone Landing Series
Moonstone Landing (Novella)
Moonstone Angel (Novella)
The Moonstone Duke
The Moonstone Marquess
The Moonstone Major
The Moonstone Governess
The Moonstone Hero
The Moonstone Pirate

The Book of Love Series
The Look of Love
The Touch of Love
The Taste of Love
The Song of Love
The Scent of Love
The Kiss of Love
The Chance of Love
The Gift of Love
The Heart of Love
The Hope of Love (Novella)
The Promise of Love
The Wonder of Love

The Journey of Love
The Dream of Love (Novella)
The Treasure of Love
The Dance of Love
The Miracle of Love
The Remembrance of Love (Novella)

Dark Gardens Series
Garden of Shadows
Garden of Light
Garden of Dragons
Garden of Destiny
Garden of Angels

The Farthingale Series
If You Wished For Me (Novella)

The Lyon's Den Series
Kiss of the Lyon
The Lyon's Surprise
Lyon in the Rough

Pirates of Britannia Series
Pearls of Fire

De Wolfe Pack: The Series
Nobody's Angel
Kiss an Angel
Bhrodi's Angel

Also from Meara Platt
Aislin
All I Want for Christmas
Once Upon a Haunted Cave

CHAPTER ONE

Gull Hall
Weymouth, England
August 1819

"I SN'T THIS AN intriguing turn of events," Trajan Aubrey, the newly installed Duke of Weymouth, remarked while studying the pair of legs dangling from the leafy cover of a majestic oak tree on his property. The tree was among several comprising a small woodland separating his property from that of his neighbor, Lord Everleigh Frampton, a man who had risen quite rapidly in political circles of late and was viewed by some as prime minister material.

But the lovely pair of legs now before him had nothing to do Frampton or politics, and all to do with his bird-watching nemesis, Lady Florence Newton, a bluestocking who did her utmost to hide a body that could drop a man to his knees in lustful desire.

Not him, of course. He was impervious to her charms…for the most part.

In truth, he did not know what to think of her other than she was one of the few people ever able to outwit him on a regular basis. And that, he had to admit, rankled him to no end.

"Florence, is that you?"

"Aubrey? I don't believe it. *Ugh*. What are you doing here?" Florence began to wriggle and twist her lithe body in an attempt to tug the gown over her legs, which remained indecently exposed.

He grinned, knowing he should not be enjoying her predicament as enthusiastically as he was, nor should he be studying those shapely limbs so avidly. But how could any man with an ounce of sense turn away when she was giving him a delightful glimpse of those exquisite legs? Her every movement was making matters worse for herself. The gown, an ugly brown muslin that he decided was quite unfashionable, now rode up her thighs because the hem was well and truly caught on the protuberance of a branch and would not budge without tearing the fabric, which was not easily torn because it was a very sturdy fabric. She might need a knife to cut it free.

"Stop, Florence," he cautioned her before she gave him an unimpeded view of her pert, rounded bottom. He dared not think what else she might inadvertently expose, but the mere thought of it was making him sweat.

It was already too hot this morning, almost no wind whipping off the cove waters to offer a cooling reprieve. Even the shade provided by the canopy of trees did little good. For this reason he was merely wearing a work shirt and trousers, having forsaken his cravat, waistcoat, and jacket for this more practical attire. "I'll climb up there and help you."

"No! I can do it myself."

Stubborn chit.

"That branch is about to crack and you are going to fall. Stop being obstinate and allow me to help."

"I am not going to—" Florence shrieked as, true to his prediction, the branch on which she had been dangling suddenly snapped, sending her tumbling out of the tree and crash landing atop him.

He yelped as she struck him full in the chest, and the impact sent him reeling backward.

Served him right, fool that he was.

Instead of darting out of the way and leaving her to the bruises and ankle sprains she was certain to receive, he had played the hero and flung himself forward to catch her. Not only did he catch her, but he'd had to twist his body awkwardly in order to ensure she landed atop him rather than under him, where the weight of *his* body landing on *hers* might have crushed her.

That mistake now had him breathlessly knocked to the ground, stunned for a full minute as twinges ran up his side and a wicked spasm coursed unrelentingly along his back.

"Blast it, Florence," he said upon regaining his voice. "What were you doing up there?"

"Did I hurt you?"

"No." Which was clearly a lie, but he was not going to give her the satisfaction, even though she appeared genuinely concerned and gave his cheek a light caress. "I always enjoy having the stuffing knocked out of me while twigs and pebbles poke holes in my arse."

"Why are you being so unpleasant? I did not ask you to save me…but thank you. You were quite heroic and magnificent," she said with a sincerity that melted his irritation.

She took another moment to regain her breath, but could not manage to roll off him just yet. Trying to rise proved too difficult for her, and he worried that she might have truly been hurt in the fall.

"Take another moment," he said, allowing her to remain perched atop him. "You took a bad tumble. Does anything feel broken?"

"No, I'll be all right in a moment. You cushioned my fall."

In truth, he did not mind her using him as a makeshift mattress until she recovered.

However, it did pose a little difficulty, as the entire length of her was stretched across the entire length of him, making it impossible to ignore the sensations aroused by this impertinent little nuisance who should not be affecting him at all.

But who could ignore her hips? Or her fine legs. Or those pert, yet surprisingly ample, breasts that rested on his chest as though he were some convenient shelf upon which to place assorted sundry items.

Not that he minded the slight weight of her on him.

In truth, her body fit his with remarkable perfection.

He grunted to acknowledge her gratitude in his cushioning her fall.

Her mouth was dangerously close to his as she studied him. "Have I maimed you for life?"

"No. I'll recover," he said, managing a small smile. "You're awfully heavy for a little thing."

She laughed, taking no insult at the comment.

He liked the melodic lilt of her laughter. He also liked the graceful curve of her lips.

It would take nothing for him to lean forward and capture her mouth in a kiss.

Wait. No.

Why would he ever want to kiss her?

"What are you doing here, Florence? Why aren't you in London menacing the unsuspecting populace?"

She blushed and averted her gaze a moment before returning her attention to him. "Would you believe me if I told you I was on holiday here because this Dorset seacoast has the best bird watching in the entire south of England?"

"No, I would not. We established that you were a fake bird watcher last year."

"I am not a fake," she insisted. "I am still chairwoman of the Lower Bramble Ladies' Ornithological Society."

"And yet you would not know a cormorant from a kittiwake." He held her fast when she attempted to wriggle off him. "Tell me what you were really doing perched up in that tree, other than delightfully baring the lower half of your body to my inspection?"

"A gentleman would have averted his gaze." She frowned at him when he remained silent. "Are you going to hold me hostage until I confess?"

"Yes." He did not bother to point out *she* was the one who had settled atop *him*, and only then had he bothered to wrap his arms around her. "And where are your spectacles?"

"Oh." She stopped trying to push herself off him and let out a breath. "They're probably crushed now. I had them in the pocket of my gown."

He stared at her, noting the striking flecks of dark amber within her emerald eyes. They even sparkled like gemstones, or perhaps that sparkling effect on those deep green pools was merely a trick of the sunlight beating down on them through the silvery canopy of leaves. "I knew those spectacles were fake, too. Why pretend you needed them?"

"Because I do not want people to notice me. How am I to go about my discreet investigations if everyone is watching me?"

"Who are you investigating now? Not me, I hope."

"No, Aubrey. Nothing to do with you." She was still pressed atop him, stretched quite comfortably, and apparently resigned to remaining in that position for a while. She folded her hands on his chest and rested her chin on them while studying him.

He had not been jesting about the twigs and pebbles that were not only digging into his arse but into his back, as well. Still, he was loath to move out from under Florence before he got his answers. "If it's nothing to do with me, then what are you doing on my property?"

"This is your property?" She frowned again, as though confused. "Does it not belong to the Duke of Weymouth?"

"Yes, it does. You are looking at the new duke. Three weeks to the day since I inherited the title."

"From your father? Who must have inherited it fairly recently himself from the old duke." She inhaled lightly. "Oh, Aubrey. I am so sorry. My condolences. I know you and your father were quite close."

"Thank you, Florence. We were. He only held the title for a few months, and was too ill to do much with it. The added responsibilities were too much for him. I had to take over management of the Weymouth properties along with our Lothmere holdings."

"That is quite a burdensome task."

He shrugged. "I am managing."

"You struck me as a very capable fellow when we first met."

They had become acquainted last year at a house party at Northam Hall, the summer residence of the Duke of Bromleigh and his wife, Cherish, located just outside of Brighton. To the best of his recollection, he had not made much of an impression on Florence, although she had quite intrigued him. Unfortunately, she had spent much of that otherwise pleasant week avoiding him as deliberately as one might avoid rotting fish.

"I'm sorry we did not have time to get to know each other better," she said, completely ignoring the fact that she had been the one to snub him. "But you know I was busy investigating Lady Cordelia Milbury and retrieving those jewels she stole from Lady Wilmot."

"Who are you investigating now?" he asked, gently nudging her off him before he grew too comfortable holding her in his arms.

Because she felt really nice in his arms.

She smelled nice, too, a subtle floral scent reminiscent of summer roses at just that point when their petals unfurled under the warmth of the sun and filled the air with the delicate aroma of rose and citrus.

Refreshing. Soothing. Leaving you wanting to breathe in more of her. All of her.

Right. Enough of that.

He sat up and settled her beside him.

She cleared her throat. "The object of my investigation is Lord Frampton's wife."

"What did she do? Another theft of jewelry?"

"No, this time it is a packet of purloined love letters."

Trajan furrowed his brow. "And you think Lady Frampton stole them? I am assuming they contained something quite embarrassing."

She nodded. "I believe so. I was not given details of their content."

"Are they embarrassing to Lady Frampton or to another lady?"

"Another lady, and it is now feared Lady Frampton's husband will make use of those letters for his own gain."

"Florence, be careful. The Framptons are a powerful and well-connected family."

"I know, and Lord Frampton is dangerously ambitious. I think he was the one who urged her to steal those letters from the wife of one of his political rivals. The rival is a decent and honest man, but he will be made a laughingstock and knocked out of contention for any office of importance unless I get those damaging letters back. I haven't figured out how to do that yet."

He cast her an admonishing look. There were so many reasons why this was a terrible idea. Not only were the Framptons dangerous to cross, they were also his neighbors, and he did not want any unpleasant incidents within days of his moving in at Gull Hall, the grand estate serving as the seat of the Weymouth dukes. "You should not be handling this assignment. Why did your client not leave it to the Bow Street Runners?"

"Because those investigators are most effective in London, and this latest theft has brought me all the way out here."

He dug a twig out of Florence's hair that seemed ready to burst from its pins. Rays of sunlight streamed through the foliage, highlighting the dark-chestnut hues of her silky tresses. "Are you sure these are merely love letters you believe Lady Frampton stole? And from whom did she steal them?"

She glanced around nervously as they heard voices nearby. "May we get away from here? I'll tell you everything once we are safe."

"Safe?" He frowned. "You think we are in danger?"

"Well..." She glanced in the direction of the approaching voices. "Yes, we might be. I'm not sure if Lord Frampton saw the glint of my binoculars in the tree as I spied into his bedchamber."

"You did what?"

"*Hush.* I believe that is him walking over to investigate. Please, he mustn't find out I have been watching him," she said, now whispering.

"Oh, do you think he might just be the littlest bit furious?" he whispered back. "Blessed saints, you are out of your depth here, Florence."

"I am not—"

The sound of a gunshot tore through the trees too close to them for comfort. Trajan drew her closer to him. "Give me those binoculars."

To his relief, she did not argue. Without protest, she reached into a large pocket sewn into her gown and handed them over.

"Thank you," he said, and threw them a good distance into the shrubbery.

"Aubrey, you clot!" she whispered with a mingled gasp. "What did you do that for?"

"He'll know it was you spying on him if he finds the binoculars on you."

"But—"

Another gunshot tore past, directly above them, sending leaves and twigs falling atop their heads.

"Quiet…he's close now, and he is not alone." He grabbed her hand and ran with her away from this spot, for the broken branch that had sent her tumbling out of the tree was at their feet, and would give them away if they were so foolish as to remain at the spot and try to bluster their way out of trouble.

Since he had spent this past week exploring Gull Hall, he was familiar with the manor house and its surrounding land. This thicket of trees offered sufficient coverage as they made their escape. However, they were slowed by the fact they had to crouch down and make as little noise as possible while running along the narrow trails.

Trajan took pains to avoid twigs that might snap under their feet and be heard, but the ground cover offered by the lush foliage was enough to keep them out of sight and their footsteps mostly muffled.

The woodlands on his property tapered to a gentle downhill

slope as the tree line ended, and the slope continued for a short distance to a sharp drop-off onto a sandy beach.

There was another path before the drop-off, and that path led straight back to Gull Hall. Unfortunately, it was open air and not at all sheltered. They could not make a run to the house without being seen by anyone emerging from the woods.

The only sensible plan was to take the stairs that led down to the strip of golden-sand beach and the blue cove waters beyond. He had inspected those stairs only yesterday and knew the wooden planks were sound enough to hold them both.

"This makes no sense," she said between panting breaths as they sprinted down the length of those sturdy steps. "Why are you taking me toward the water? Shouldn't we be running to your house?"

"The house is too far and he will spot us easily on that exposed path. Do you trust me?"

"I'm not sure."

Not the answer he was hoping for. "Well, you should. You and I are to be found cavorting on the beach."

"*Cavorting*? What exactly does this entail?"

He paused once they descended the last step and their boots sank into the soft sand. "Forgive me, Florence."

"What for?"

He circled his arms around her and drew her up close.

"What are you doing? Is this your idea of cavorting? If you think I am going pause midway in our escape to put my arms around you, then you have another thing coming."

"Just do as I say. I am not trying to be amorous."

"Then why are your arms around me and why are you holding my body plastered to yours? Oh, you have nice muscles. What are you planning to do? You—"

"Stop talking, Florence. I need to kiss you."

"Kiss me? What madness is—"

He pressed his mouth down on hers and kissed the daylights out of her.

CHAPTER TWO

F LORENCE HAD NEVER felt anything so exquisitely good in her entire life.

But why was Trajan Aubrey, the former Lord Aubrey and now Duke of Weymouth, kissing her with such possessive heat? Or any heat at all?

Dear heaven.

His mouth felt gloriously good on hers.

Was this meant to be a farewell gesture as Lord Frampton came upon them and killed them? Did Aubrey believe this ambitious lord was so depraved?

Florence's senses were too addled for her to think straight. She tried to run through all the reasons, other than impending death, why Aubrey would want to kiss her, but could think of none.

However, she knew he was no coward, was actually fairly intelligent, and would never meekly resign himself to dying.

Trust him.

He had told her to trust him, and so she did.

When another shot rang out, she grabbed hold of his divinely muscled shoulders and held on for dear life as he deepened the kiss.

Mother of pearls.

Why exactly was he giving her the hottest, most insanely wild kiss she had ever experienced in her soon-to-be-ended life? In truth, this was not saying much, because she had never been seriously kissed in a romantic way before this very moment.

But he was kissing her like a demon, and nothing had prepared her for the conquering crush of his lips on hers, or the relentless—but thoroughly exquisite—pressure of his mouth as it fused with hers, so that she was certain they would have to break the suction in order to draw apart.

They would eventually, of course. Both of them had to come up for air sometime soon.

But not yet, please.

If they were to die, could there be a better way to go?

Heat coiled through her and stirred her in places that she did not know existed on her person.

Was this not the saddest comment on her love life?

She pressed into him, still not understanding his purpose in devouring her, body and soul.

Then it came to her in a sudden revelation.

This was how he meant to convince Lord Frampton she was not the interloper he had spotted spying on his home. This shockingly intimate kiss was meant to serve as her alibi, since she could not have been up a tree, binoculars in hand, peering into his house, while at the same time on this lovely sand beach frantically locking lips with the scorchingly hot Duke of Weymouth.

And since Aubrey had tossed her binoculars into the underbrush, they would never be found on her person should Lord Frampton be so loathsome as to order her searched.

Quick thinking on his part. In fact, all-around good thinking by this clever man. Not only did his action deflect suspicion, but it also made their claim to have seen no one else in the woods believable, assuming Frampton bothered to ask.

An entire army could have marched past them and she would not have noticed a single soldier while this impossibly handsome duke was kissing her with enough heat to melt the icecaps atop the Alps.

For this reason, she went along with the ruse and made not

the slightest protest when his hands began to roam up and down the length of her.

However, those little fires he was setting off everywhere in her body were proving most embarrassing. The cur had to know he was affecting her.

She bit his lip lightly when he cupped her bottom, because this was supposed to be an evasive tactic, not a really, really enjoyable moment for either of them.

Much as she *was* enjoying herself.

Was there a point to prolonging this performance that would earn them a standing ovation if ever reenacted in a Covent Garden theater?

Not that she objected to being seduced and conquered by this golden-haired dream of a man with eyes that were sharp as razors and incredibly seductive. Cold. Clear. Pale-green ice. Eyes that could freeze you and also melt you.

Was it her fault she was melting right now?

Florence needed a moment to regain her composure once he ended their kiss. The cad cast her a smile that promised of torrid nights if he ever got her into his bed.

Oh, gad.

How was she ever going to resist him now? Not only was he handsome as sin, but…who had muscles like his?

Well, medieval warriors, perhaps.

Although warriors were generally built like hefty blocks of granite, while Aubrey was tall and elegant, cutting quite the imposing figure when dressed in formal attire.

Lord Frampton and his cohorts were staring at them from atop the stairs.

"Weymouth, do we get a turn next?" Frampton called out in jest, and started down the steps toward them with a hunting rifle in hand. His lackeys, also carrying weapons, followed him down.

Florence's heart beat faster. She hoped he'd meant the remark as a jest.

She moved closer to Aubrey, who had kept an arm protectively around her. "It'll be all right," he whispered. "Don't be scared."

But she was, and could not stop her heart from pounding through her chest as these unpleasant men drew closer.

Frampton's companions had the look of London ruffians, the vile sort who roamed the London docks at night and would just as soon slit your throat as beg your pardon. They were staring at her too avidly.

Trajan Aubrey—well, she really ought to start thinking of him as Weymouth, since he was now the duke—kept tight hold of her. "Let me do the talking, Florence."

"Fine." At this moment, she could not string two words to-gether.

She took several deep breaths to calm herself. The two of them had to keep their wits about them if they were to fool these ugly fellows.

"I hope you are carrying a pistol," she muttered, wishing she had some sort of weapon hidden on her person that she could whip out to defend herself with.

Aubrey nodded. "I have several on me, but they won't be needed. I promise."

She let out a shaky breath, not nearly as confident as he was. "Do not make promises you cannot keep. Those scoundrels do not look nice at all."

"Yes, rough fellows," he agreed. "They're probably his guards. Frampton is ruthless and must have made many enemies on his climb to the top of the social ladder, many who would like nothing better than to do him in."

As she watched them, Florence questioned her sanity in agreeing to take on this particular assignment. But she'd really had no choice.

She would be forever indebted to Aubrey if he got them out of this scrape.

He glanced at her, no doubt to make certain she was not going to faint.

She wasn't. However, her knees were knocking and her heart was still pounding too hard.

"Be brave for me, Florence," he whispered. "I won't let any of those men touch you."

Frampton and his four lackeys were now upon them.

Florence glared back at these men who were eyeing her with shocking disrespect.

Do not show fear.

Never show fear.

"Weymouth, I was going to ask if you had seen anyone running past you recently," Frampton said, all the while leering at her, "but it is obvious you were otherwise occupied."

The other men chuckled.

"You happened to catch me and Lady Florence in a special moment," Aubrey admitted, sounding surprisingly calm, even joyful. "She has just agreed to become my wife."

What?

Florence tried to hide her panic.

Was this his harebrained scheme to keep her safe?

He gave her hand a warning squeeze. "We had hoped to keep the betrothal quiet until notifying our families, but it seems we are now caught and our secret has slipped out."

Frampton arched an eyebrow. "She is your betrothed?"

Florence found herself nodding. "A love match. Quite the whirlwind romance. But when it is right, you just know. He is completely devoted to me. Isn't he divine?"

Aubrey gave her hand another squeeze, silently warning her not to overdo it.

"Mutual, my love. You are mine now. *All mine.*" Which Florence hoped was his way of conveying to those ruffians that he would slit their throats from ear to ear if they laid a hand on her.

Frampton held up a hand and drew back a step. "Who am I to interfere with the course of true love? Well, I'll trouble you no further. But do me a favor, Weymouth. Let me know if you notice anyone lurking on your property. I think someone is spying on me, and I do not like it one bit. In fact, if I catch the fellow, he will not walk off your property alive."

"That is some threat," Aubrey said, arching an eyebrow. "Just do me a favor and kill him on your property if you do catch him. I would prefer that my good name not be dragged into your disputes."

"Of course. In turn, keep your eyes and ears open."

"All right, although I may be a bit distracted." He winked at Florence and cast her a worshipful smile for good measure.

She wanted to tell *him* not to overdo it, but left the warning for later, since she did not want to say or do anything that might give them away.

"But on a more serious note, Frampton," he said, now frowning, "Lady Florence and I do enjoy bird watching. This mutual interest is what first brought us together."

Florence tipped her chin up proudly. "I am chairwoman of the Ladies' Ornithological Society in Lower Bramble."

Aubrey cleared his throat. "Keep this in mind on the chance you see us walking about with our notebooks and binoculars. But if you are concerned at all, is there anywhere on our adjoining properties that you prefer us not to tread? This matter is obviously of importance to you, and I want to respect your wishes."

Frampton appeared pleased. "Oh, it isn't on the grounds so much. But I sensed this trespasser was peering into my house."

"Into your house! That is outrageous. No wonder you are incensed," Aubrey remarked, sounding sincerely appalled—which he probably was, and she would catch a stern lecture for it later.

"Quite so. This invasion of my family's privacy is a serious offense."

"Rest assured, I will alert my staff and have them notify me the moment they spot any strangers walking around here."

With that said, Frampton and his cohorts climbed the stairs and returned to their neighboring property.

Florence dared not breathe until they were out of sight. "Betrothed? Aubrey, have you lost your marbles?"

"The title is Weymouth now," he reminded her. "But all right, call me Aubrey if you prefer, since this is what everyone has called me for most of my life. Or you could call me Trajan, since it is my given name. Better yet, call me *my dearest* or *my heart's delight.*"

"That is not funny. Now everyone is going to think we are getting married."

"Well, it will upend that betting book taken out on me at White's."

Florence pursed her lips and frowned. "A betting book? Why are they betting on you?"

"You really are socially unaware, aren't you? Have you not been reading the London gossip rags? They are placing wagers on me because I am now a duke. Unmarried. Supposedly rakish. And I have a touch of silver at the temples."

"What? Does this qualify you as a Silver Duke?"

"Apparently so. This is what they are calling me now. You gave me those silver hairs last year," he teased. "I hadn't a single one until I met you."

"I do have that effect on people," she said with a gentle smile. "But you are barely in your thirties. Aren't you a little young to be considered a Silver Duke?"

He shrugged. "I thought so, but that betting book was opened on me anyway. They did the same to the Duke of Durham last year, as you well know, and he was nowhere near forty years old either. It is shocking how they have lowered their standards. Seems any unmarried duke with a touch of silver in his hair now qualifies."

"Yours is hardly noticeable." She lightly touched his temples, running a gentle hand through his hair. "I suppose it is because the silver is so easily hidden among your golden strands."

He shrugged again. "Doesn't matter. Even one graying strand is enough to send the *ton* into a frenzy."

Florence sighed. "What a mess I've caused. Now everyone

will think they've lost their bets because of our pretended betrothal. It was a foolish thing for you to do, but I cannot admonish you for it. Your quick thinking probably saved my life."

"So, I am forgiven?"

She nodded. "Yes, without question. You had no time to come up with a better plan, and I came up with nothing at all. Yours was quite convincing. Brilliant, actually. But now we have to figure out how to get ourselves out of it."

"We will in time, but not yet. You are going to need the protection of my name for a little while longer."

"I hope you are proved wrong," she said with a sigh. "But I fear you may be right."

"I *am* right," he said with conviction. "You mustn't let down your guard, Florence. I think Frampton was not completely convinced by our performance. He continued to eye you too intently. He still suspects you were the culprit peering through his windows, and this worries me."

"Oh, that is not good."

"Well, we instilled a small measure of doubt."

"Enough to keep him from shooting us right here on the beach," she said with little mirth, for those men had all been carrying rifles and would not have thought twice about discharging them into their bodies.

Aubrey rubbed a hand along the back of his neck and nodded. "I shudder to think what would have happened had he caught you alone in these woods."

"He is scary, isn't he? Do you think there is something more going on with him than a little extortion?"

"I don't know." He pursed his lips and pondered the question. "But it is all the more reason to keep away from him. I mean it, Florence. You will end up dead if you poke that bear. More to the point, I have no intention of dying alongside you. All right? So, it is best you just drop the matter of retrieving those damaging letters. Has your friend paid you?"

"Only a retainer for my out-of-pocket expenses. I get the rest of the reward once the job is done."

"Then give her back the advance," he said with authority. "I will reimburse you for whatever you have spent. But this has to end now."

He was right to be concerned, but was this not for her to decide?

And what if Frampton was plotting something really serious, such as the overthrow of the monarchy? Should this not be investigated and proof brought to the attention of the Home Office?

"Bloody hell, no!" he cried when she mentioned the possibility.

"But he might be a traitor."

"I would not be surprised, but this is something to be investigated by the Home Office, *not* by you."

"Then by you, perhaps?" She cast him a brilliant smile. "You are quite talented at this sort of intrigue. Clever. Fast on your feet. You were magnificent in the way you tricked Frampton into revealing exactly where he wanted us to keep away. I was certain those letters were hidden in his house, and he has now confirmed it."

Sunlight shimmered on his hair as he raked a hand through those splendid golden waves and eyed her warily. "You aren't going to break into his home, Florence. I forbid it."

"Would you consider doing it?"

He emitted a bark of laughter. "Are you mad? No!"

She cast him a stubborn look. "Then I will have to do it."

He folded his arms across his chest. "You are mistaken if you believe I am going to allow you to risk your life over some stupid letters. Whose are they? You never told me who you are working for."

"Nor will I tell you now," she said, loath to defy him after he had certainly saved her life, but she cast him an impudent look and tipped her chin up. "The matter is sensitive and private."

"Not if it is about to get you killed." He took her by the hand once more and marched her up the beach stairs.

"Where are you taking me?" she asked as they climbed.

"Back to my house."

When they reached the top step, he led her along an unshaded path away from the beach and woodlands.

"I suppose it is quite grand and beautiful," she remarked, deciding to engage him in harmless chatter in the hope he might calm down. He was still angry with her.

Not that she blamed him.

He sighed and glanced at her. "It isn't so much a house as a palace. It is disconcerting to rattle around on one's own in a place of that size. But since we are now betrothed, I—"

"*Fake* betrothed. The arrangement is only temporary."

"But it cannot look fake to anyone. For your own protection, we must be *convincingly* betrothed. So it should not raise disapproving eyebrows if you now move into my home."

"Why would you want me anywhere near you?"

"Because I dare not leave my blushing bride-to-be on her own to run amok. Need I remind you that the next time Frampton catches you anywhere near his property, he will shoot you dead?"

"I do not need that gentle reminder."

"Good. Our living arrangements will be respectable, of course. Who is your chaperone? You must have brought one along with you."

"I did, but only because I would not have been given a room at any inn of good repute if they knew I was traveling alone. My maiden aunt, Hermia Newton, came with me."

"She will join you here, of course. There's plenty of space to accommodate you both. I have so many bedchambers, I can give each of you an entire wing and still have bedrooms left over for other guests."

"Is it that enormous a house?"

He nodded. "But I think I need to rename it. Gull Hall simply does not suit."

After several minutes, the massive chimney stacks of his

home came into view. Florence tried to slip her hand out of his, but he insisted on keeping firm hold of her.

Did he think she was going to run away?

And did his plan to bring her here not have a dangerous flaw? Why move her into his home that was so conveniently, and temptingly, located next door to Frampton? Well, she supposed it was the easiest way for him to keep track of her movements. By the angry look of him, he intended to trail after her like a bloodhound on the scent.

Obviously, he did not trust her to end this assignment. "Trajan…oh, may I call you that? Or should I call you Weymouth now?"

He nodded. "I haven't quite wrapped my head around becoming the Duke of Weymouth yet. Not sure I am ready to be referred to as Weymouth. Nor am I Lord Aubrey anymore. Trajan will do nicely. Yes, I would like it if you called me by my given name. You earned that privilege after our intimate kiss."

She cleared her throat. Yes, it was quite a kiss.

"Just how many chimney stacks does Gull Hall have?"

"At least a dozen. Do you see what I mean, Florence?" He pointed toward his imposing manor. "Who can heat a house of this size in the winter? Calling this sixty-room monstrosity Gull Hall conjures the image of a cozy retreat near the water where nesting birds abound, not a residence fit for a king and his royal entourage."

"Does your family have any plans to join you here?"

"Not this year. Probably never," he said, suddenly turning pensive. "I might write to my mother and ask her to visit while you are here with me. I think she is in London, although she might be with my sister, Persephone, and her husband, the Marquess of Rathburne. He's also fairly new to his title, and was known as the Earl of Hawley until last year. But now he is the marquess and will need Persephone's support more than ever because he's a little dim in the brains department. Do not comment on my sister's name or mine. Our parents were obviously drunk when they named us."

"Trajan and Persephone? I rather like both. They are distinctive and distinguished. Would Persephone and her husband consider visiting you?"

He grunted. "No, they are comfortably settled in Somerset and busily working on producing heirs. Rathburne's a bit of a dolt. As I said, he's a little light in the brains department. But Persephone is quick-witted enough for both of them. I hope their offspring inherit her brains. Surprisingly, theirs seems to have turned into a happy marriage."

"A good match? I think that is lovely. If I were inclined to marry, this is what I would want. A love match." Florence was sincerely pleased for his sister and told him so. "However, do not trouble your mother. She's just suffered the loss of your father and deserves the right to grieve him without distraction."

"I don't know. Getting her out of London and away from all those memories of him…"

"No, they might bring her comfort. It is her choice to make. She'll know when she is ready."

He raked a hand through his hair. "Yes, you are probably right. I'm not good at this sort of thing. Persephone is far better at offering comfort, and will probably have my mother stay with her and Rathburne for the next few months."

"That is a good idea. Besides, I won't be here more than a few days. I cannot imagine it taking longer to complete my mission."

She bumped into him when he came to a sudden stop and turned to her with a growl. "Put that notion out of your head at once, Florence. Are you purposely trying to rile me? I am not having you and your chaperone move in with me so you can more easily snoop on Frampton."

"I know your purpose in moving me here. You want me where you can keep a closer eye on me."

"Bloody hell, yes. You obviously need to be reined in and kept under constant guard. I'll be doing just that until such time as I can return you to London, and that will be as soon as possible. Unfortunately, I require about a week here to settle some Weymouth affairs."

"But—"

He growled again. "As soon as we arrive in London, you are to give your friend back her retainer. She can get herself out of her own mess. Can you keep out of trouble these next few days? I really need you to behave."

She opened her mouth once more to protest, but he laid a finger upon her lips. "There is a dungeon in that monstrosity of a manor house, and I will keep you locked in it if you dare step onto Lord Frampton's property or spy on him through the shelter of my woods again."

"But—"

"No, Florence. End of discussion."

Fine, if he wanted her and her dotty maiden aunt to reside with him in his monument to aristocratic excess, who was she to argue?

Besides, it would be much easier to sneak out of his residence to spy on the Framptons than to make these clandestine trips daily from their lodgings at the Weymouth Inn. The thought had barely popped into her mind when he said, "I shall be watching you day *and* night while you are here. Got that?"

Annoying man.

"Or it shall be the dungeons for me?" she grumbled. "You never would confine me. You are not that cruel. Besides, only castles have dungeons, not fine houses like Gull Hall."

"I'll have one built just for you."

She sighed. "Surely there is a compromise to be reached here."

"I am not compromising with your safety. Do not test the extent to which I will go to protect you, even if it is from your own misguided self. However, I do trust your honor. I will consider allowing you to roam freely if you give me your oath to stay away from Frampton's property and forget searching for those letters."

"And if I agree?"

"First, I shall insist on having that oath in writing, and you must sign it."

"A *written* oath? Gad, you are insufferable. What next? Are you going to tie me to your bed and hold me at your mercy?"

He grinned. "Do you want me to?"

Her eyes widened and the breath caught in her lungs. "Ugh, you are a devil's spawn. Why can you not leave me alone to do my job?"

"Because it is not a job but a death wish. Let your friend retrieve those letters herself, if they are so important. Is she the one who wrote them? Secret notes to herself as a sort of diary? Or was it a careless lover who put his thoughts in writing and she was foolish enough to hold on to them?"

His manor loomed quite large, looking enormous as they approached it.

"You know, two can play at this game," she muttered.

He arched an eyebrow. "What do you mean?"

"Lord Frampton heard you declare we were betrothed. Seems I have done quite well for myself, assuming I hold you to *your* vow of marriage."

He shrugged. "Do you think marrying you scares me?"

"Shouldn't it?"

He chuckled. "Yes, I suppose it should. Surprisingly, it doesn't."

"Are you jesting? You would take me as your wife? With all the *ton* diamonds and other rich, beautiful, well-connected ladies to choose from throughout the whole of England, you would be content to settle with me?"

"Why not? Life with you would never be dull."

"That is an understatement." Her own family had little tolerance for her independent nature. Her father, whom she loved dearly, would give Trajan an earful about all the ways she had disappointed him, were he ever to ask.

Her mother had not hugged her in years. In truth, she could

not recall ever being embraced by this woman who had given birth to her. Perhaps she had been a little difficult as a child, but she could not recall ever doing anything that warranted her mother completely cutting her off from all affection. Her brother disliked her, too. Her father, who ought to have defended her, remained completely indifferent and never raised a finger to help her.

And yet whenever she and her father were alone, he was kind and sometimes complimentary.

The only one who had ever shown her consistent kindness and warmth was Hermia, her dear aunt.

What had she ever done to her parents or brother to make them dislike her so much? She had often asked, but no one would tell her.

Was there even a reason? Or was it something deep and primal that offended them?

If only they would give her a hint. She would move heaven and earth to repair the damage.

And now, her father had cut off her allowance. He had done it upon her mother's orders, for her mother had wanted to bring her to heel and accept a marriage proposal from the odious son of a family friend. The son was an utter toad with absolutely no prospects, but no one seemed to care.

Florence had refused. She did not need her father's money, for she was quite resourceful and managed to make a decent living handling investigations for her friends.

They trusted her and knew she would never reveal their secrets.

Of course, this frustrated her family to no end, since they hoped she would come crawling back to them and agree to marry that simpleton they had chosen for her. True to form, her father, who loved her, buckled to his wife's demands and insisted she marry the toad.

Perhaps he thought they might grow to love each other. More likely, he did not consider love a necessary factor at all. His idea of a good marriage did not comport with hers.

"I think we would get along well if we married," Trajan remarked, regaining her attention as they reached the courtyard of his manor. "Even our nighttime engagements would be quite pleasant. That kiss we shared was nice, wasn't it?"

What?

Their earlier kiss that still had her body thrumming and her lips tingling…not to mention the hidden places that were still vibrating because his touch was unforgettable. "Oh, did we share a kiss? It must have slipped my mind."

He burst out laughing. "Florence, you are an utter fraud. I might believe you if your cheeks were not on fire."

"Because I am hot," she said as they entered the house and he marched her through the exquisite entry hall. She noted the beautiful Italian marble flooring and magnificent crystal chandelier that emitted prisms of light, as the sun happened to strike it at this late morning hour.

He led her through an equally elegant parlor with massive glass doors that opened onto the terrace, and then paused once they were on the terrace to cast her an irritatingly smug grin. "You like me. Your cheeks are still a deep shade of pink."

She looked up at him and frowned. "Because I am *temperature* hot. Summer-heat hot. Sun-beating-down-on-me hot. *Weather* hot and nothing more."

He led her to a shaded arbor and settled her in one of the cushioned chairs positioned around a delicately patterned wrought iron table. "Admit it, I am the one who brought the heat and scorched you."

"I think the heat has scorched your brain." She frowned again. "But I am thirsty and would love a tall glass of lemonade."

"Yes, I'll order refreshments for us while we sit out here and enjoy the view. However, the fact remains that you are thirsty for me, too."

"Hah! You are deluded."

"See, you are blushing again. You are not a good liar, are you?

The drink may cool you down, but I heat you up." He cast her another smug grin. "Good to know."

"You are so full of yourself, *Your Grace*. Stop smirking at me. You will never control me with kisses, even if I happened to like them."

"Ah, an admission from your lovely lips."

They said no more as his head butler, no doubt anticipating his master's orders, brought out a pitcher of lemonade and two crystal glasses.

"Timmons, you are a wonder. I was about to summon you, but you have anticipated my very wish. This is exactly what we need."

The man cast Florence a kindly glance and nodded. "I thought you and your guest might be in want of a libation."

"As for my guest, this is Lady Florence Newton. Isn't she lovely? You may hear rumors abound that we are betrothed."

The staid butler's eyes widened, and he smiled. "Are you, Your Grace?"

"Yes." He then properly introduced Florence to his ever-reliable servant.

"May I offer my congratulations to you and the young lady, Your Grace?"

"No, you may not...well, not yet. I need to write to my mother and sister to tell them the news. So please keep the matter quiet until they receive word."

"As you wish," Timmons said with a flicker of disappointment.

Florence suspected the secret would not be kept for much longer even if Timmons uttered not a word. The butler was never going to risk his position by leaping like a gazelle into the kitchen to report their betrothal to the other servants. He was obviously the reliable sort who would take a secret to the grave.

But would the other servants not notice she and Hermia had suddenly moved in? How was Trajan going to introduce them?

When she pointed out the obvious, he relented. "All right,

Timmons. Let the staff know, and have them prepare rooms for Lady Florence and her aunt. They are going to stay with us for the next few days. Perhaps longer. Perhaps permanently," he said, purposely goading her.

She cast him a smile that reeked of insincerity. "Or not."

"Right, no firm plans yet. And we will need my carriage brought around. Lady Florence and her aunt are presently lodged in Weymouth. Utterly inconvenient. They need to move in here this very day."

The butler sprinted off, delighted.

"I suppose you are right," Trajan admitted once they were out of the butler's earshot. "Frampton would immediately grow suspicious if my own servants had no idea you were my betrothed. We need to keep this ruse believable."

"Yes," she said, but this was going to be a problem for her afterward.

One that might be impossible to overcome.

How was she to break off her engagement to England's most eligible bachelor without completely ruining her reputation once her assignment was accomplished?

CHAPTER THREE

FLORENCE QUIETLY CONTEMPLATED her situation while seated in a shady spot on the terrace of Trajan's grand house. *Trajan.* She liked his given name and had easily stopped thinking of him as Aubrey. He was now Trajan, named after one of the greatest Roman emperors, known for his intelligence and military prowess.

His betrothal scheme had saved her from Frampton, and she would not deny that she had been in a heap of trouble until Trajan's kiss had rescued her. But undoing their betrothal would come with its own perils. Her already-tenuous relation with her parents might never be mended after this.

They would never forgive her for rejecting this perfect duke. Or any duke, for that matter. They would cut her off completely upon learning the extent of his wealth and power.

That he was also handsome and kind did not help. Even she would have thought herself deranged to walk away from their betrothal.

Well, her family had cut her off from their affection years ago. More recently, they had cut her off from her allowance, too. What else could they do to her?

She had never held their love, so there was nothing left to lose beyond the hope of repairing a relationship that had always been damaged and dangled on a very thin thread.

She stared across the lovely view of Trajan's private cove,

admiring its crystal-blue waters.

Trajan had kissed her on the beach in that cove.

She dared not tell him just how much she would treasure their kiss.

Unaware of her turmoil, he sat back comfortably in his chair and grinned. "Nice, isn't it?"

Yes, it was.

"And can you believe the size of this house, Florence?"

His smile held such pride that she could not resist smiling back at him. "It is quite impressive, and also beautifully decorated. Surprisingly tasteful and welcoming, considering its enormity."

She could manage a house of this importance, for her schooling had trained her for this very thing.

It saddened her to know she would never become duchess of this grand home. Trajan could not possibly be serious about their betrothal.

"Can you see yourself here?" he asked, his voice quite gentle as he spoke.

She did not bother to respond.

Did he often rescue young ladies with a remarkable kiss? He needed to stop believing this pretense before he said something that could not be taken back.

Well, had he not said too much already?

She did not blame him, for she had gone along with his every word and made no effort to contradict him. However, they needed to coordinate their lies in order to keep others from catching on to their farce.

He noticed she had finished her lemonade. "Would you care for more, Florence?

Then he smiled and added "dearest" because he found the idea of their betrothal quite amusing. He was only thinking in the moment and not further down the road, when this lark would come to its inevitable end.

Ugh.

He should not be milking every last drop from this situation. It would serve him right if she held him to his word and he was forced to marry her.

But this was a card she could hold in reserve and threaten to play if he insisted on interfering with her mission.

Yes, she fully understood that spying on Frampton from a treetop was no longer a viable plan. She also understood that she would be shot if ever she were caught sneaking into his residence in the middle of the night.

She would have to come up with another less dangerous idea.

In the meanwhile, she had no choice but to go along with this betrothal nonsense.

Well, it wasn't really *nonsense*. It was nice to pretend she had snared England's prize bachelor, and it had nothing to do with his being a rich duke. She liked him because he was intelligent, witty, and wonderfully protective.

It did not hurt that he was also strikingly handsome.

But was it not odd that he appeared so comfortable with the idea of marriage? Perhaps his Silver Duke friends were not off the mark when deciding to open their betting book on him.

However, he did not kiss like a man ready to be domesticated. That kiss had been exquisitely wild and untamed. She had yet to stop tingling from it.

"Florence," he said as they sat in their cushioned chairs and enjoyed the shade of a floral arbor, "you are turning moon-eyed. Thinking of our kiss again?"

"I am doing no such thing," she replied, sounding like a petulant child.

"I might believe you if your face were not in flames again," he teased, certain he had caught her in a guilty pleasure…which he had.

However, she was never going to admit it to him. "You are a most irritating fellow. Did you know that, *Weymouth*?"

"Ah, you are peeved with me. I prefer that you call me Trajan. We are lovebirds, after all. You like me and hope I will kiss you again."

"Gad, you are irritating. Need I remind you it is hot outdoors?"

"Ah, yes. *Weather* hot. *Temperature* hot."

Florence nodded. "Exactly."

"Liar." He leaned so temptingly close that she caught the fresh scent of sandalwood on his skin. "You find *me* hot and are desperately trying to figure out what to do about it."

"Your conceit is unmatched, *Weymouth*."

He shook his head and sighed. "Still peeved."

"Since you have brought up the matter of our so-called attraction to each other, yes. What in the name of heaven were you thinking? You should have come up with something other than a love match betrothal."

Or that insanely delicious kiss.

He shrugged. "I thought it was a brilliant idea at the time. And I am still liking it. Need I remind you, the kiss and our betrothal served their purpose in keeping you alive. You thought so, too. A scorching kiss and the benefit of my protection, all in one. No one is going to touch you now that you are my soon-to-be duchess. They will have to face my wrath if they dare try. I am a bloody duke, and a powerful one at that."

"Do you think this will stop Frampton?"

"Yes, assuming you behave. He knows one word from me would crush his ambitious rise to the top."

Florence waited until Timmons had brought out cakes to go along with the lemonade, set them on the table, and then retreated into the house before she responded. "Oh, so you think he is afraid of you? Do not get too caught up in the power afforded to a duke. If he were to shoot you, you would still bleed like the rest of us."

"How sweet of you to worry about me. If you really care, then just stop whatever it is that you are doing. Frampton will leave you alone so long as you leave him alone."

"What if he doesn't?"

"Then he is a fool and I will see him destroyed."

Florence wished the matter were that simple. "Do not mistake him for a fool. Will you promise me that you will always keep your guard up around him?"

"Me? I am not the one who fell out of a tree while spying on him," he said, reaching over to give her hand a light squeeze. "But I plan to exercise extreme care around him. So must you."

She nodded. "I will. You mustn't worry about me. I am experienced when it comes to these delicate investigations and can take care of myself."

"That is utter rot." He drank the last of his lemonade, finishing it in two easy gulps, and then set the glass down on the table with a *thunk*. "Had I not come upon you first, he would have found you and strangled you with the cord of your own binoculars, then left you for dead in *my* woodlands for one of *my* workers to find. And that's another thing."

"What other thing?"

He leaned forward again, close enough so that their lips almost touched.

He really had to stop doing that, because his mouth was incredibly tempting and she would never stop tingling if he insisted on ravaging her senses like this.

"You are a friend and former schoolmate of Jocelyn, Duchess of Camborne, which means you come from a family of means. That finishing school for young ladies was an elite institution whose curriculum was designed to teach sweet young things like you to become wives to England's aristocratic hierarchy. Yet here you are taking *work* from your friends and acquaintances."

"And your point?"

"Why are you doing this? And what do your parents have to say about it?"

"Assuming they knew, they would disapprove...just as they have disapproved of everything I have ever done in my life."

The remark obviously surprised him.

Did he think her family adored her?

Florence managed to shift the conversation, avoiding his questions for now. But she knew by his daunting stare as they rode to Weymouth together in his magnificent ducal carriage a short while later that he had no intention of letting the matter drop.

She cleared her throat. "Lovely view."

He arched an eyebrow, refusing to engage her in idle chatter. Instead, he studied her as a predator might study his prey, all the while seated on the nicely cushioned leather bench opposite hers. It was slightly disconcerting the way his gaze raked over her, so she stared out the window and pretended to take in the passing countryside.

It would take them an hour or more to reach the seaport town and its namesake Weymouth Inn, where she had taken rooms with her aunt. She estimated it would take another hour to get her and her aunt packed and checked out of the inn. They had each brought one trunk and several smaller bags, not needing dozens and dozens of gowns as one might for a house party or other social occasion.

She had brought along eight gowns for the various occasions, and her aunt had brought along an equal number for herself. But Hermia was one to move slowly and could not be rushed.

It would take another hour or more to ride back to Gull Hall, and hopefully they would reach Trajan's residence well before nightfall, a task easily accomplished if they kept to a moderately efficient schedule.

She turned from viewing the scenery to glance at him. He was no longer staring at her in predatory fashion but regarding her oddly.

"What's wrong?"

"How stupid of me," he muttered as though struck by a sudden thought. "Gad, how could I have overlooked this? Florence, how did you get here? You could not have walked the entire distance from your inn lodgings to my home."

"I hired a carriage and driver to bring me out here."

"And where is the hired hack now? Why did you not tell me you had someone with you? What if Frampton's ruffians got to him?"

"They didn't." She pinched her lips together. "The bounder took my fare and then refused to wait for me. Can you believe it? He barreled off, laughing at me."

"Yes, because you are a naïve little dove."

"I am nothing of the sort. Is there no honor among thieves?"

He arched an eyebrow. "Apparently not, which is a lesson for you to learn. You may be clever, but you are not *street* clever."

"And you are?"

"Who, me?" He shook his head. "No. However, I know my skills and limitations, and I try never to underestimate my opposition."

"Am I your opposition?"

"No, Florence," he said with surprising gentleness. "You are mine to protect."

That sounded wonderfully apish. Her heart did little flips, for when had anyone ever felt this way about her?

She cast him a soft smile.

He let out a breath. "And I shall protect you for the duration of our ruse."

She almost wished their hastily cobbled-together betrothal might last longer, but it was never going to happen. Trajan might appear comfortable with her, and may even have liked their kiss, but he would never love her. Everyone knew his heart belonged to the Duchess of Lynton, the former Lady Eden Darrow. Florence had met her last year and liked her very much. She was charming and lovely—and also deeply in love with her husband, the Duke of Lynton, who came with three adventurous children and a meddling mother, all of whom adored Eden.

For Trajan, becoming the Duke of Weymouth must have been a reprieve from his unrelenting heartbreak, since it allowed him to be tossed into the hard work necessary to maintain the ducal properties in their proper grandeur and bring the failing ones up to snuff.

But the work was merely a distraction. His heart was still broken because Eden had chosen to love another. Of course, her husband was an excellent man.

However, were Florence in her position, she would have chosen Trajan without question. The kiss they'd shared still lingered on her lips.

Did it linger on his, too? It truly was a wonderful kiss.

However, she dared not make anything of it. He had kissed her because he needed to rescue her, not because he liked her and meant to share a little of his heart.

Besides, weren't hot, lingering kisses the sort of thing handsome rakes mastered early on in their lives?

Even if he thought her above the string of ladies he'd kissed and forgotten, where would it lead? Certainly not to something meaningful and lasting.

Anyway, she was totally wrong for him. He needed a gentle, nurturing woman who could bring him solace and distract him from his unrequited love for Eden.

Yes, this was the sort of wife he needed. A healer. A comforting companion. They ought to have opened a betting book at White's to wager on who was the lady most likely to provide him those comforts of a happy home.

That fortunate lady would be the one he'd marry, not some icy *ton* diamond or an unlovable bird watcher whose hem caught on tree branches.

Florence knew his choice could never be her. She cared passionately about many things, but often ruffled feathers instead of soothing them. Simply put, she was more likely to irritate and disrupt rather than provide a welcoming home.

Her mother took every opportunity to tell her so.

It was not long before they arrived at the Weymouth Inn, her charming seaside lodgings these past few days. The inn was quite elegant, ranking high among the finer establishments catering to the upper classes on holiday.

The innkeeper, a portly gentleman with an amiable countenance, hurried toward them as they entered. "Lady Florence! Thank goodness you have been safely returned to us. Your aunt was worried sick about you. What happened? You left early this morning and neglected to have a picnic lunch packed for yourself."

"Do forgive me for worrying you, Mr. Goring. I was out walking longer than planned. But as you can see, I have been returned without incident by His Grace," she said, then hastily introduced Trajan as the Duke of Weymouth.

The innkeeper's attention now turned to Trajan, his expression one of all due deference. The introduction might not have been necessary, since the man had obviously recognized the Duke of Weymouth's crest emblazoned on his carriage that was still standing in front of the inn, its black steel frame gleaming in all its impressive splendor. "Your Grace, it is an honor to have you with us. May I offer you refreshments?"

"Not at this time. Lady Florence and I are in a bit of a hurry. She'll need assistance to gather her belongings and those of her aunt. They shall be returning to Gull Hall with me. Where might we find her aunt?"

"Miss Newton is taking tea in the dining room, but…" The man appeared perplexed, no doubt because he feared she was about to cancel the balance of her reservation and then refuse to pay for those canceled days. Well, that could be straightened out later. He would never be so crass as to raise the matter in front of the duke, would he?

However, Trajan seemed aware of the man's concerns. "Have the rooms for Lady Florence and Miss Newton been paid in full?"

"No, Your Grace. Only a deposit. I would not—"

"I know this sudden change in plans has inconvenienced you. Charge the balance to my account and submit the bill to my man of affairs."

The innkeeper released a breath. "Thank you, Your Grace.

That is most generous and appreciated."

Florence eyed Trajan, not altogether pleased he had done this. "You really did not—"

He placed his hand over hers. "We are betrothed now, Florence. It is only right that I take responsibility for my future wife."

She wanted to kick him.

Truly, she did.

The innkeeper was practically floating on air as he led them to the dining room, where her aunt was seated on her own, enjoying the view of Weymouth's harbor and the boats sailing in and out. She had just chosen one of the miniature cakes set on the table before her, but put it aside and smiled as they approached.

"Miss Newton," the innkeeper said excitedly when her aunt turned toward them, "your niece has been safely returned. And you shall never guess her news!"

Florence adored her Aunt Hermia, who resembled a little bird and twittered like one, especially whenever she got excited. She also happened to belong to the Lower Bramble Ladies' Ornithological Society and was one of its founding members.

"Florence, thank goodness! I had grown so worried!" Aunt Hermia's chirps of delight resounded through the dining hall, and now all the diners had their eyes trained on them.

Trajan gallantly bowed over her hand and introduced himself. "I hope our good news will not come as a complete surprise to you, for your niece has had my heart since we first met last year…and now she has accepted to become my wife."

Florence really needed to give this man a swift kick to his backside. Was it necessary for all of Weymouth to know they were engaged to be married?

This also meant everyone would be gossiping and condescending toward her when their betrothal was called off.

Her aunt, of course, regarded them both in utter confusion. "Florence, why did you never tell me about this charming gentleman?"

"Oh, you know I am quite shy about such things. Although I

am certain I went on and on about him. I always hoped, but never dreamed, he had feelings for me."

Trajan looked ready to burst into laughter.

She cast him an admonishing look before turning back to her aunt. "Surely you must recall our speaking of him a time or two."

Or never.

Her aunt twittered and chirped again. "Oh, but of course you have. Please forgive my scattered brain, Your Grace. My dear Florence has spoken often of you with greatest affection. How kind and handsome you are, just as she described you. It is delightful to finally meet the man who has stolen her heart. But you must forgive me, for my mind has been like a sieve of late. What joy! What exquisite happiness you have given my niece. I can see how she looks upon you with the eyes of love. And now, you will give her parents endless delight when they learn you have proposed to her."

Trajan cast her a gentle and patient smile as she twittered and cooed over him at length.

"I look forward to having you at Gull Hall as my guest," he said, finally managing to get a word in when Hermia paused to take breath into her lungs. "Florence has been quite eager to have me meet her family. And rest assured, I look upon her with as much love as she looks upon me."

He turned to Florence and cast her a wicked grin.

She smirked back at him.

"Yes, I think Florence and I knew our feelings from the start," he continued. "But we dared not believe our good fortune, and did not wish to rush our courtship."

"Florence has always been romantically inclined, even as a little girl. She was determined to make a love match for herself, refusing to accept anything less," Hermia said. "And look at how sweetly she is smiling at you. You have her enraptured. How deeply she must love you!"

Gad, would this humiliation never end? Florence's parents would be thrilled because of the advantageous connection they would have to the new Duke of Weymouth, not for any happiness he might give her. And Trajan was now grinning from ear to ear, impossibly smug because her aunt insisted she was gazing at him with the eyes of love.

Utterly ridiculous.

"To be honest, Aunt Hermia, I was not so certain of my feelings for him until I saw his magnificent home, Gull Hall, and hastily reconsidered. Then I said to myself, why not fall in love with an obscenely rich man? So I did."

Her aunt's smile faltered as she tried to make out whether Florence was in jest or not.

Trajan laughed heartily. "Ah, she is such a little minx. She is teasing you, of course. But we can speak more about how we were smitten by Cupid's arrows on our way back to my home. Rest assured, your niece caught one right in her plump, round *der—*"

"Aunt Hermia does not need to hear the details of how and when we fell in love. Rest assured, Auntie," Florence said, mimicking his words, "there were no arrows, neither to his heart nor my *derriere.*"

Her aunt took a gulp of her tea, shook her head, and stared up at Trajan. "We are to visit your home now?"

"Not merely a visit," he hastened to clarify, "but you are to join me for the duration of your holiday as my guests. It would be my honor to play host and serve as your guide as you tour the area."

She clapped her hands. "How lovely!"

Trajan's smile seemed genuine as he mentioned some local attractions that would make perfect day trips for them, and this delighted Aunt Hermia. "We shall have plenty of time this evening to discuss our itinerary, Miss Newton." He took out his watch fob and frowned upon noting the time. "We need to start back before it is too late. I have taken the liberty of asking the innkeeper for maids to assist you in packing."

"Oh, then I must not keep you waiting." Aunt Hermia rose

and skittered out, calling for the innkeeper, who happened to be standing right beside her and now scurried after her.

"You'll need to pack, too," Trajan said.

Florence nodded. "It won't take me but five minutes."

"Fine, I'll wait here for your return."

She was surprised, for she had expected him to insist on following her up to her quarters. "Do you trust me not to run away?"

He nodded. "You would never abandon your aunt. I noticed how protectively you hovered over her."

"As chaperone, she is the one who is tasked with looking after me. Lately, it has been the other way around. It is wicked of me to deceive her, but I dare not tell her the truth about us just yet. We must keep up the ruse in front of her, for she is easily confused lately and might let something slip." She sighed and shook her head. "I won't be long."

"All right. Stay out of trouble."

She laughed softly. "Seriously? I do know how to behave in polite company. Besides, what can go wrong between here and my room?"

"I have no idea, but you'll come up with something," he gently teased.

"Honestly," Florence said mirthfully, marching out of the dining hall.

She was about to start up the stairs when she heard a commotion in the entryway. Curious, she paused to see who had just come in and caused this flurry.

Her heart sank.

Oh, no.

Why hadn't she run upstairs when she'd had the chance?

"Well, if it isn't Lower Bramble's notorious bird watcher, Lady Florence Newton," Lord Frampton said with an air of joviality that thinly masked his menace. "We seem to be running into each other everywhere today."

She glanced over his shoulder to his entourage of ruffians,

who obviously followed him wherever he went and were once again eyeing her too avidly. She found their malevolent stares unnerving.

"Yes, what an odd coincidence. Have you come to dine here with your friends? Kindly remind them it is rude to gawk at a lady."

He gave a casual shrug. "Do behave yourselves, gentlemen. You are oversetting our bird-watcher friend. By the way, Lady Florence, have you lost a pair of binoculars?"

Dear heaven.

He knew.

Could it be more obvious? Two mentions of bird watching and now he was informing her of her lost binoculars. "No, why do you ask?"

"It isn't important. I happened upon a pair in the woods today and thought they might be yours."

"As you well know, I was busy accepting a marriage proposal today and *not* traipsing about the woods in search of birds."

"Speaking of your charming betrothed, where is he now? Has he abandoned you already?"

"Rest assured, he is close by."

Had Trajan seen them yet?

"And since we are pretending to have a polite conversation," she continued, "and asking after our significant others, where is your dear wife?"

He arched an eyebrow. "Why do you wish to know?"

"Oh, I thought I might invite her to Gull Hall for tea with me and my aunt the day after tomorrow. Seeing as I shall soon be the Duchess of Weymouth and setting up residence at Gull Hall with my husband, is it not the neighborly thing to do? Or is there a reason she might decline the invitation? You would not be so cruel as to hold her hostage in your own home," she said loud enough for others to hear, "and deprive me of her lovely company."

He did not look pleased, but managed to maintain his thin

veneer of civility, especially as several guests standing nearby were obviously listening in on their conversation. "I shall let my wife know to expect your invitation."

"Excellent—one of Weymouth's footmen will deliver her a formal invitation first thing in the morning." She bade him a good day and hurried up the stairs to her guest quarters.

She barely had time to open her wardrobe when the door she had left ajar in expectation of a maid's arrival to assist her suddenly slammed open and a furious Trajan stormed in.

Oh dear.

He looked every inch the daunting duke, quite enraged as he cast her the most ominous frown she had ever seen on a man. "By all that is holy…do you have a death wish, Florence?"

CHAPTER FOUR

TRAJAN HAD MEANT it when he said Florence was his now to protect.

But did she have to make it so difficult for him to fulfill that vow? "What were you thinking, inviting Lady Frampton to tea with you and your aunt? And now she will have to return the invitation and invite you into *her* home."

Florence did not appear in the least remorseful, which riled him all the more.

"You have just answered your own question," she said, sounding as blithe as a summer breeze. "How else was I to get into the Frampton house without raising suspicion?"

He raked a hand through his hair. "Without… Dear heaven, Florence. The man has put a big, fat target on your back. And you think to just stroll into his home without a care?"

"I will be with my aunt. I'm sure Lady Frampton will invite both of us."

He rolled his eyes, for she was just too much. Too stubborn. Too reckless. Too achingly beautiful, and this upset him most. How could he possibly be attracted to Florence when all she had done since their unexpected meeting in the woods today was give him fits?

"Oh, yes. Perfect," he shot back. "That frail, old woman is just the one to defend you. I can see how her little bird fists can bring a man down with a single blow."

"I have no intention of snooping around while I am there."

"Do you think I am a witless fool? You are going to give Lady Frampton a tour of *my* home when you have her over to tea at Gull Hall, so that she will be forced to give you a tour of *her* home when you visit *her* at Frampton Court."

Florence blushed. "Is this not what any polite hostess would do?"

He heard footsteps down the hall and expected one of the inn's maids would walk in at any moment. "Gad, how did your family survive you all these years? We'll finish this discussion back at Gull Hall."

He strode out, almost knocking over the poor maid in his irritation. After mumbling an apology, he stormed downstairs.

But he was loath to return to the dining room, since Frampton and his cohorts would no doubt be watching him like a pack of vultures waiting to swoop in for the kill. Yet he did not want to wait for Florence and her aunt by his carriage and risk missing Frampton's next move…assuming he had one.

What was he doing here?

Trajan knew his presence had everything to do with Florence.

He spent the next few minutes pacing in the entry hall of the elegant inn, his mind fixed on how to protect his fake betrothed when she insisted on diving into danger. She seemed to have completely shrugged off their earlier close call in his woods.

"We are ready," Florence said, gaining his attention as she escorted her aunt down the stairs with loving attendance. Behind them were the innkeeper and several of his helpers, who lugged their trunks.

Trajan oversaw the trunks' loading onto his carriage, and then assisted the ladies into their seats. He settled on the bench opposite theirs, trying to keep from fuming over Florence's ill-conceived plan to get into the Frampton residence.

Florence blushed in response to his angry gaze.

Her aunt, blissfully unaware of what was going on between him and Florence, began to chatter. "What a lovely coach this is," she said in a merry, singsong twitter, "such soft leather and exquisitely sprung. One can hardly feel the bumps in the road."

"Unfortunately, it will get bumpier as we ride out of Weymouth," Trajan replied. "But I hope you will not find the ride too uncomfortable."

"Oh, dear boy. I know I shall hardly feel the jolts. Nor shall my niece, I'm sure. She must be floating on air now that you have declared your love for each other. How exciting for you both. Florence, why don't you sit beside your handsome betrothed?"

"I am fine right here, Aunt Hermia. He would only squash me, because his shoulders are quite broad."

Hermia grinned. "Yes, I've noticed."

Florence sighed.

Trajan engaged her aunt in small talk for much of the ride, since he could not pursue any logical conversation with Florence while he wanted to throttle her.

Why was she insisting on rushing into danger? She had been genuinely frightened this morning when almost caught by Frampton, so why continue her perilous assignment?

Her bird of an aunt was finely dressed and wore expensive jewelry, he noted, so the reason could not be about Florence's requiring money. Even the ugly brown gown Florence had on was finely made and must have cost a goodly sum.

Florence herself sat silently as his carriage clattered through the countryside, her nose pasted to the window while she contemplated how best to evade his questions.

How was he to keep her safe?

Well, he would insist on their working it out this very night. Her aunt was going to retire early, no doubt. He and Florence could talk then.

In truth, he simply wanted to lay down the law and insist on her keeping away from the Frampton residence.

No discussion. His edict set forth. After all, he was the duke, and she had to obey his commands.

But she wouldn't.

He glanced at her as she continued to stare out the window. It galled him to think her mind was awhirl, contriving ways to defy him.

But gad, she was softly nibbling her fleshy lower lip as she devised her schemes.

She had the prettiest lips. Plump and perfect.

He wanted to kiss her again. Yes, he ached to kiss her even while furious with her.

He also had to figure out how to protect her. Despite his threats to do so, he was not going to lock her away. Which meant she was going to give him the slip at some point, because she was too clever for her own good.

The thought of her lying hurt in Frampton's clutches tore him up inside. "Florence…"

"Fascinating view," she muttered, continuing to stare out the window.

He gave up trying to gain her attention and instead remained in conversation with her aunt.

But there came a moment when Florence thought he was not looking at her, when she lowered her mask and allowed her feelings to show. He saw it then, a surprisingly raw and open desolation.

The lonely fear. The vulnerability.

But she quickly restored her mask of defiance and covered up these feelings when she realized he was watching her.

Timmons was standing on the front steps in wait for them, along with several footmen, when their carriage drew up in the courtyard. The excursion to Weymouth had taken much longer than anticipated because Hermia moved so slowly, but they still managed to arrive in daylight, the hour nearing eight o'clock in the evening. Trajan realized Florence and her aunt had to be hungry by now. Florence especially, since she had not eaten anything but a few cakes earlier on his terrace. He was also famished, for he had not eaten since then either.

Timmons, capable as ever, came to the rescue. "Mrs. Palmer

has supper warming for you. Shall I have it served in the dining room in fifteen minutes?"

Trajan helped Florence's aunt down from the carriage. "Is fifteen minutes enough for you, Miss Newton? There is no need for us to change into more formal attire, for meals here are quite casual. Most nights, I dine alone."

"Oh, dear boy. How sad for you."

"It is all right, for I usually prefer solitude to the crush of fancy parties."

He next assisted Florence in stepping down, and felt an unexpected jolt of heat the moment his hand touched hers.

She felt it too. Her eyes widened and her plush little mouth formed a perfect *O* for just that instant.

Curious.

His blood seemed to heat whenever he touched Florence. It had been happening all day. To be truthful, the same had happened last year, too.

Were his feelings something real?

Well, it was too soon to tell. However, was this not better than pining for Eden? Come to think of it, his thoughts had not been much on Eden since meeting Florence last year.

Was this mere coincidence?

"Is fifteen minutes long enough for you, Florence?"

She was still staring up at him with her mouth adorably rounded. "What?"

"Fifteen minutes to prepare yourself before coming down to supper. Stay dressed as you are, no need to change," he said, repeating what he had just told her aunt, who had already been escorted inside by Timmons.

"Oh, yes. Perfect."

"Good. I'll show you to your room, since Timmons must have already handed your aunt over to my housekeeper, Mrs. Albright, the most efficient person you shall ever meet. She will have taken your aunt upstairs by now. Mrs. Palmer is my cook, and she is also excellent at her job." He tucked Florence's arm in his and escorted her inside the house. "I'll introduce you to the rest of my staff tomorrow. We'll spend a quiet evening tonight. I've given you and your aunt adjoining rooms, quite apart from mine."

"For the sake of propriety?"

He nodded. "But I vow I shall nail shut your windows and door if you dare take a step out of this house tonight."

"Understood," she replied, batting her eyelashes and smiling at him.

Gad, she was irritating.

But he cast her a polite smile in return. "I'll give you a tour of the house tomorrow, all except my bedchamber, since that is my bastion. My sanctuary. No one trespasses there."

"Why would you show me your bedchamber?" She stopped suddenly and frowned up at him. "I have no intention of joining you in your bed, if this is what you are suggesting."

He cleared his throat. "Um, how did you get that meaning out of my words? Did I not just say I do *not* allow others in there and will *not* show you this one room? However, since you seem to be keen on—"

She gasped. "I am no such thing."

"Florence, you raised it, and obviously misconstrued my words because you were thinking of doing exactly that."

"Exactly what?"

"Joining me in my bed."

She gasped again.

"If you are that eager for it," he said, casting her a devilish grin, "then I will make the exception for you and show you my sanctuary. To be clear, you are welcome in my bed whenever you feel ready."

She pinched her lips together and tipped her chin upward. "Which I won't ever be."

"That is fine, too."

"*Ugh.* Must you be so smug about everything?"

"Yes, it comes with the title," he said, leading her up the

grand staircase.

Knowing Florence, she was going to steal a moment to slide down the railing on her rump when she thought no one was watching.

But this was what he liked so much about her. She grabbed life's adventures and held on fiercely. She was brave and passionate, something he admired even though he was furious with her at the moment for continuing to prod Frampton.

But it was hard to remain angry when he also ached to have her in his bed.

He sighed. That kiss they'd shared was giving him stupid ideas. She needed to be taken to safety, and his bed was no safe place for her to be.

Although it would be an extremely convenient way to keep her close and under his watch during the nighttime hours. If she were amenable, they could—

No, that was a step too far.

Since Florence's aunt was chirping and twittering in delight in the room next door to the one prepared for Florence, he decided to have them stop in there first.

"I hope it meets with your approval, Miss Newton," Trajan said.

"Oh, this is so lovely, Your Grace! I shall be happy as a lark settled in here."

"I'm glad you like it. Florence has been put in the room next to yours. Have you peered out the window yet? You both have views of the Gull Hall gardens and our private cove beyond it. If you find you require anything, just tug on the bellpull and Mrs. Albright will bring up whatever you need."

Personally, he thought the rose-patterned drapery and bed-covers, in addition to the floral-design carpet, was a bit too much. But Hermia seemed enraptured by the soft pinks and greens of the room's colors. Florence's was similarly designed, but in more subdued shades of cream and yellow.

He now turned to Florence. "Care to see yours?"

She nodded, and off they went.

"Oh my." She paused at the threshold and smiled at him. "It is beautiful."

He watched her as she began to walk around the large room, lightly trailing her fingers over the furniture as she took in all the details—the large, canopied bed, the massive wardrobe that was painted in the same shades of cream and yellow as the walls, the floral curtains patterned with yellow daffodils. She paused by the window to admire the view.

"Like it?" he asked, knowing he would not mind her fingers trailing over his body with a similarly light touch.

She smiled and nodded. "Very much so."

"I hoped you would. But I cannot take credit for any of the splendor of this house, nor could my father. The prior duke, a granduncle of mine, had very definite ideas on what he liked. He ran the Weymouth businesses with this same efficiency and eye for quality."

"I'm sure you will, too."

"In time, perhaps. I have quite a bit to learn still. Fortunately, he left most of the properties in excellent shape. Only a few required my immediate attention, and I shall be working on them next. It is more the enormity of the holdings that are burdensome. One man cannot handle it all."

"Well, your granduncle must have had good estate managers and advisors to assist him."

He nodded. "Yes, but many of them are getting on in years now. Two passed away just this year and several more are no longer up to the task. I've asked my cousins to help me out. You'll meet them soon."

"Your cousins? Will they be joining us here?"

"Yes, they should arrive any day now," he said as his footmen brought in her trunk and other small bags. At his nod, two of his maids who had followed the men in began to unpack with practiced care.

Since Florence did not insist on supervising the maids, who

obviously knew what they were doing, he remained engaged in small talk with her while the staff settled her in these new quarters. "My father had a younger brother, who in turn had three sons. They range in age from eighteen to twenty-four, so they are a bit younger than me. The eighteen-year-old will have to attend university in the fall, but the others have already graduated Oxford with honors, I am proud to say."

"So, they are eager to roll up their sleeves and work for you? I am surprised. Most would prefer to be in London indulging in all the excesses it has to offer."

"Well, Andrew, who is the eldest among them and now goes by my former title of Lord Aubrey, fancies himself quite the ladies' man. Then there's the middle brother, Nathan, and the youngest, Sebastian, who are more rakes in training than actually successful in the art of seduction. But they are clever fellows and hard workers. They want the responsibility. We Aubreys are not used to being idle."

"Hmm," she said, somewhat cryptically.

He leaned against the bed's footboard and folded his arms across his chest. "What about your family? Any brothers and sisters?"

She nodded. "One brother."

She seemed reluctant to talk about him, so naturally Trajan decided to probe further. "Older or younger?"

"A few years older."

"Does this older brother have a name?"

She sighed. "Yes…Matthew Isaac Newton."

"Isaac? I ought to have made the connection sooner. Any relation to *the* Isaac Newton?"

"The renowned mathematician, scientist, and astronomer acknowledged to be one of the greatest minds in all of England?" She nodded. "Yes, we are very distantly related. But the name is all he and my sibling share. My brother is… Well, never mind."

What was she going to say? That her brother was no genius? A disappointment? Perhaps trouble? Was this dangerous

Frampton assignment that she stubbornly refused to give up in any way connected to him?

He tucked that question in the back of his mind for now. This was one among many he planned to ask her after supper, but not before her aunt retired to her bedchamber and they could speak without interruption. "I had better wash up myself," he said, leaving her to instruct the maids on where to place her toiletries and other personal items.

He noticed she had only a tiny jewelry box, no doubt holding a pearl necklace and matching earrings, which it seemed every lady of good breeding had to have. Even last year at the Bromleigh party, he had never seen Florence wear anything other than a single strand of pearls or a simple gold locket, or another discreet adornment. She was not one for glittering diamonds or other precious gemstones. He supposed they would not have suited her.

Florence was not ostentatious, always preferring more subdued articles of jewelry. A cameo brooch or necklace. Jet stone from Whitby or amber from the North Sea coast. Tiny gold hoop earrings or pearl ones for fancier occasions.

She was also quite natural looking, if a young lady could be described that way. She blended in with these countryside surroundings. Even her eyes were a reflection of nature. They were a lovely, dark green and flecked with amber. Her hair was a deep, rich brown with some mahogany highlights when the sun shone down upon her head. Even her gowns tended toward the colors of nature, pine-forest greens and earthen browns. He could not imagine her in a frivolous, sunny yellow or pale lavender, although she probably would look beautiful in those colors, too.

Entering his bedchamber, he hastily poured some water into the basin on his bureau and washed up. He could have insisted they all change into appropriate evening clothes, but the hour was already late, they were all hungry, and he did not think Florence's aunt was going to stay awake much beyond the ritual of *après*-dinner port.

As it turned out, he was right.

Hermia struggled to keep her eyes open once they finished their simple meal of trout, potatoes, and cucumber salad. For dessert, they were served apricot tarts and finished with a lemon syllabub to clear the palate.

They had port on the terrace while watching the sunset over the water. The sky was a mix of fiery colors tonight, streaks of reds and yellows slashing across the darkening celestial expanse.

Hermia excused herself shortly afterward. "You are betrothed now, Florence. To a good man, indeed. I do not think you need me to watch over you. But loosen up, my dear. Enjoy this handsome fellow's kisses."

"I have no intention of misbehaving," Florence insisted.

Hermia shrugged. "Sweet girl, you are only young once. Do not waste this opportunity."

Florence's gaze darted toward him, her eyes wide and her expression bordering on panicked. "I am not that young."

"Yes, almost seven and twenty," her aunt said with amusement. "Obviously quite ancient. You shall be considered as old as the fossils found in the Lyme Regis caves by next year's birthday."

"Do I detect sarcasm, Aunt Hermia?" Florence muttered with a chuckle, taking her aunt's comment in good nature.

They exchanged kisses on the cheek, and then Hermia walked out.

Trajan offered to escort her to her bedchamber, for his home was large and this was her first night here. But Hermia insisted it was not necessary, so he did not press her on the matter. One of his servants would guide her if she lost her way.

Besides, he was eager to have his talk with Florence.

"We'll be more private in my library. I can have Timmons bring in coffee or tea for us, or cocoa."

"Oh, a hot cocoa would be lovely."

"Done," he said, and summoned Timmons to give him the instructions. He took Florence's hand, entwining her fingers with his as they walked to his library.

Only afterward did he realize the gesture was too familiar, since they were not yet husband and wife. Nor would they ever be, but no one had to know this yet.

To his surprise, Florence voiced no objection. Good, because he was not particularly keen to let go of her.

Her eyes brightened the moment they walked in and she saw the rows of polished rosewood bookshelves. "I suppose this was your granduncle's doing, too. Look at all these beautiful books!"

He nodded, stifling a smile as she referred to them as beautiful. But he was not surprised, because she truly had the soul of a bluestocking. "I've added a few, but have hardly had time to take full inventory since inheriting the title. In truth, it is all so new to me. I haven't had much time to do anything meaningful yet."

He settled her on a cushioned settee of burgundy-red and emerald-green damask, and sank into the chair of a matching green leather opposite her.

Where was he to start? Her excitement at discovering the marvel that was his library soon wore off, and she now looked defensive and worried.

He took a deep breath, deciding to simply tell her what was on his mind. "Florence, I need to protect you. I won't be able to properly do so unless you tell me the truth about what is going on. I shall keep whatever you reveal to me in confidence." For good measure, he added, "I give you my word of honor."

"This is so unfair to you," she said, now sounding pained. "I never meant to involve you."

"But it is too late now. I was caught up in your plans the moment you fell out of that tree and crash landed on me."

She sighed. "I know."

"There is no undoing what happened. So, now you must tell me everything. What is going on? Who are you working for? It must be someone of importance if you still refuse to give up this assignment."

"I am helping out a friend of the Princess of Wales," she said, releasing a heavy breath. "One of her dearest and closest friends."

This revelation caught him by surprise. "Gad, Florence. A friend of the princess?"

She nodded. "It gets worse. The assignment was at the request of the princess herself. Lady Wilmot must have bragged about my abilities to her, and a few days later I was summoned. So, you see, I cannot simply renege on my promise to retrieve those letters."

His heart sank, for this was far more serious than he had imagined. "Who is the friend in question? Is it Lady Simmons?"

She looked at him sharply. "How did you know?"

"Not too hard to figure out now that you have narrowed the choices down to the princess's inner circle. Lord Simmons is a brilliant man and has a bright future in government, not only on his merits but because his wife has curried favor with members of the royal family. That gives him a leg up, and Frampton is not happy about it because he considers Lord Simmons his competition."

"One among several ambitious men, I expect," Florence said. "But if Lady Simmons was helping her husband climb the social ranks, then why would she involve herself with another man?"

"Because one has nothing to do with the other, although it is not unheard of for a wife to give her body to some old, high-ranking goat in order to further her husband's ambitions."

"*Ugh.*"

"Anyway, Lord Simmons is a very intelligent man, but I am certain he has not a clue how to pleasure his wife in the sack."

"Trajan!"

"Gad, must you be so clueless as to sexual wiles? My point is, she is frustrated in the bedchamber, and for this reason has a roving eye. Her eye roved on me for a while."

"You?" Florence blushed. "You...you..."

"No, I did not bed her. I suppose this is what you wish to know. It took some doing to avoid her, however. My father's illness was the excuse I often used, although he was not all that ill at the time."

"So, she found herself another lover? Who foolishly wrote her those letters?"

He shrugged. "I have no idea when those letters were written. It could have been years ago. Lady Simmons has been frustrated for quite a while, probably since the first week of her marriage. It is an open secret among the Upper Crust."

Florence stared down at her hands, apparently confused.

He reached over and covered them with one of his own. "What is the matter?"

"If it is so well known that she has had affairs with other men, then why are they so worried about those letters?"

"It is all about how one plays these *ton* games," he explained. "They all have affairs, husbands *and* wives. They cheat because these are not love marriages but business alliances, and love is to be sought elsewhere once the wife has produced the necessary heirs."

"All right, this I understand. But it still does not explain the frantic need to retrieve those letters."

"There is a protocol to these affairs. One does not put one's sordid liaisons in writing. That is the true sacrilege, not the cheating itself. This is because letters are hard, solid proof that can be produced in a court of law, or in the House of Lords, or given to a newspaper to publish." He released her hands and eased back in his chair. "Love letters are nuggets of gold, capable of inflicting ridicule, embarrassment, and destruction of one's power and position."

"But these are letters to Lady Simmons. Would not Lord Simmons be viewed upon with pity and admired for his forbearance? Why would those letters destroy his career?"

"You are assuming he is the one to be brought down. What if he is not?"

Her eyes widened. "Are you suggesting Frampton wishes to destroy the man who wrote her those letters?"

"Yes, in all likelihood. Do you have any idea who wrote them?"

She shook her head. "No, not an inkling. All I was told is they were quite…er…um, descriptive, and now they are in Lord Frampton's possession. I just assumed he would use them to make Lord Simmons a laughingstock, if ever Lord Simmons dares challenge him for the position of prime minister."

"That is among the possibilities, but not the only one. No, Florence. I think Frampton not only finds them convenient to curtail any threat to his ambitions from Lord Simmons, but to another he views as a more serious threat. The man he is most likely after is the one foolish enough to have put his sexual exploits with Lady Simmons into those letters in explicit detail. I wonder…"

Florence edged forward in her seat. "Who are you thinking it is?"

"I don't know. Any number of men, possibly even Lord Liverpool."

She gasped. "But he is our current prime minister. Is he one to have affairs? Or be so idiotic as to set down his most intimate thoughts on paper? Could this scandal unseat him?"

"Possibly, who knows? It would certainly weaken him for a time."

"I hope not. He is a good and steady leader. We are all capable of errors in judgment."

"Yes, for certain. But his peers and the public might not be as forgiving, especially if they are of a mind to see his downfall. Scandals, especially involving other men's wives, are the best way to unseat a man as capable and respected as Lord Liverpool. But I am only tossing his name out as a possibility. I have no reason to believe he is in any way involved. In fact, I have a lot of respect for him and would be surprised if he turned out to be the correspondent."

"Then who do you think wrote those letters to Lady Simmons?"

"It could be anyone of prominence."

"Such as Wellington? Or Robinson?"

"Or any number of other men who are much respected and admired. No one is immune to scandal, whether commoner or nobleman. They are all targets to a weaker man who seeks a position of power."

"Or who hopes to hold on to a position he currently holds."

"Yes," Trajan said. "But clearly, Frampton is aiming for high office. He wishes to position himself as next in line for prime minister. So, he is either trying to knock out Liverpool or a likely successor. There are several powerful men vying to be next in line. Lord Simmons is the least likely among them to succeed to those heights."

"I could ask Lady Frampton when she joins me and Aunt Hermia for tea. Is this not a natural topic of conversation, a general discussion of who might lead our government if Lord Liverpool is not able? Let's see what names she tosses out. Or if she makes some cryptic comment."

"Such as?"

"Oh, maybe saying something about Lord Liverpool not being likely to remain in power very long. Or maybe she will give a disparaging snort at the mention of Wellington or another candidate. I don't know. Something. *Anything*. Although Her Royal Highness made it clear it is not my business to read those letters or try to guess who wrote them. I am only tasked with getting them back for her friend."

"Who should immediately burn them if she has a lick of sense."

"Obviously, neither she nor her paramour were thinking clearly."

They said no more as Timmons rolled in a cart bearing a pot of cocoa, cups, and some fruit and tarts. "Thank you, Timmons. I'll take care of it from here," Trajan said.

"Of course, Your Grace." The butler nodded and quietly left the library, closing the door after himself.

Trajan was about to resume their conversation when a shadow outside the window caught his attention.

It was only a flicker of something. Perhaps a branch blowing across the back lawn. Or a night owl in flight.

Florence noticed his sudden tension. "What is it?"

"I don't know. Something feels off." He rose and crossed to the window but saw nothing in the blackness. He shook his head and sighed. "I must be seeing things."

"We are both on edge," she muttered. "Trajan, I had another thought."

"Yes?"

"Frampton may have more than the packet of letters belonging to Lady Simmons. Would we not be doing a service to the Crown if we stole back any incriminating letters concerning other lords and ladies he may be extorting?"

"By all that is holy," he muttered. "Florence, I did not want you involved in retrieving those belonging to Lady Simmons, and now you want to expand your mission to save every highly placed idiot in government?"

"It was just a thought," she countered. "Obviously, you do not think it is a good idea."

He laughed. "Unbelievable. Frampton is no gentleman blackmailer. First, he took shots at us, although he clearly meant them for you. Then he followed you to the Weymouth Inn. He has shown himself to be a most determined man. What do you not get about this?"

"He is a bit scary, I will admit. But why would he want to hurt me when he cannot be sure what I am after, or if I am after anything?"

"Because he thinks like a cornered animal and will do anything not to be caught. He did not coincidentally appear at the inn on a lark just as I was packing you up. He may not be certain what you are after, but he knows you are after *something* he has, and hell will freeze over before he willingly hands it over to you."

"I know."

"Then why are you persisting?" Trajan sighed and shook his head. "He has to be worried you are digging around and getting too close to whatever illicit business he is conducting."

"I am not happy to be doing this, but I cannot return to London without those letters."

"You will be carried back dead if you do not stop this right now. You pose a threat to his entire operation, and men like that eliminate threats. Enough, Florence. You are a terrible liar and will never be able to talk your way out of danger if he traps you."

She buried her face in her hands and nodded. "I understand. But how does this change anything? I cannot ignore this command from the Princess of Wales herself."

"I'll stand by you upon our return to London and make her see the impossibility of what she has asked you to do."

"And if she doesn't see it? Would you have me destroy your good name, too?"

"Do you think I care? I am not going to abandon you to the wolves." He raked a hand through his hair. "You will have my protection for as long as you need it."

She looked up at him, and he saw the anguish in her expression. "Thank you for being so wonderful to me, Trajan. I mean it sincerely."

"Ah, then you are not trying to soften me up merely because I am useful to you?" he said with light teasing.

She managed a wobbly smile and a gentle laugh. "I would never do such a thing to you. But to be clear, you are proving to be more of an impediment than of use to me," she teased back.

He supposed this was true, which was why he could not retain any anger toward Florence. She was caught up in circumstances beyond her control and doing her best to survive her assignment, while he was doing his best to keep her out of harm's way and just have her survive.

"Please believe I am genuinely grateful to you," she said. "Even if I am giving you a hard time about this."

"Let's figure out how to get you out of this mess. Anything else important for me to know?"

She blushed. "I have no idea what you mean."

He sighed. This was going to take longer than he'd expected.

"Right, first the cocoa." He moved from his chair to sit beside her on the settee because it was easier for him to pour the hot liquid into their cups, as well as fill their plates with the tarts and fruit set out on a small tray on the tea cart.

But that shadow by the window suddenly caught his eye again. He hadn't imagined it.

Someone was lurking outside.

He set down the pot, rose, and had taken a step toward the window when he caught the glint of metal.

"Florence, get down!" He shoved her down and threw himself atop her, knocking over the tea cart and all its contents in the process.

The pot smashed, spilling cocoa all over the two of them, the settee, and the carpet. Then…nothing.

Silence.

Florence lay flat on her stomach, her face buried in the seat cushion while his big body lay atop her.

"That was close. Are you all right, Florence?" He eased up the slightest bit, and grunted as she elbowed him in the gut while turning around to face him. But this left the full length of his front facing the full length of hers for just that moment before he raised himself off her.

However, it was a moment too late, and this was how Timmons and the two footmen who raced in behind him found them…him still atop her.

"Dear heaven," Timmons muttered, the sight of them halting him in his tracks.

Trajan knew there was no extracting himself from his and Florence's betrothal now.

He rolled onto the floor and groaned, landing in more wet cocoa that had seeped into the carpet.

Timmons would not stop gaping at him. "Your Grace…I…I…"

Yes, the butler now believed him to be a maniacal fiend who

could not keep his wicked paws off the innocent beauty. "This is not what it appears. I was protecting Lady Florence."

"Kindly explain how landing atop me with your crushing weight protected me," Florence remarked, now humiliated and probably seething with anger. She would have cracked the pot of cocoa over his head were it not already shattered and leaving a mess all over the floor.

"There was a man pointing a pistol at us just outside the window."

"Really?" Florence sat up sharply, and a trail of cocoa seeped down the front of her gown. She ignored it and shot to her feet. "Then what are we doing just standing here and staring at each other? Let's find him. There had better be fresh footprints by the window, or…"

"Or what?" Trajan asked.

"I shall shoot you myself," she said with determination.

"Isn't that a little harsh, Florence?"

"Maybe," she grumbled in acknowledgment, "but my gown is ruined."

"Which would you have preferred me to protect, the hot cocoa or you?"

CHAPTER FIVE

A S IT TURNED out, not only did Trajan find fresh boot prints, but the window also had scratch marks around the latch to indicate someone had tried to break in. Since Florence, Timmons, and the two footmen had come outside with him, the two footmen holding torches above their heads in order to shed light on the scene amid the darkness, they now deemed him exonerated.

He was relieved not to be thought of as a fiend who accosted innocent maidens for his own lurid ends.

"You are forgiven," Florence muttered once they had all walked back inside.

"Shall we search for the trespasser, Your Grace?" one of the footmen asked.

"No. The man will be long gone by now, and I do not need him shooting any of you if you happen to stumble upon him in the darkness. Leave it until tomorrow and hopefully the hunting dogs will pick up his scent."

Trajan suspected the man's trail would lead them straight to Frampton's home. If so, they were better off approaching in broad daylight. Frampton would not attempt anything when witnesses were around.

"I shall notify Mrs. Albright to wake her maids and have them clean up the mess in the library," Timmons remarked.

"Yes, a good idea." Trajan would have to replace the damaged furniture if the stains set in and could not be washed out. "Advise her to take Lady Florence's gown to be cleaned once she changes out of it."

"And your clothes too, Your Grace."

He nodded absently. "Yes, I'll go up and change now. But first, Edgar and I will search Lady Florence's room to make certain her chamber is safe."

"Is that really necessary?" Florence asked.

"Perhaps not, but why take any chances?" He motioned for one of the footmen, the reliable Edgar, to follow him, and then turned to Florence, casting her a pained glance. "We'll walk you upstairs, but I want you to wait in the hall until we are done checking your room."

"All right." She appeared more worried than angry now. With good reason, for the fact that someone brandishing a pistol had been lurking outside the library window had to be as alarming to her as it was to him.

"Do you want one of the maids to remain in the room with you tonight?" he asked as they walked upstairs.

"No, I'll manage on my own. I doubt the man will dare return tonight."

Trajan nodded. "Edgar, do you think you can stay awake and take night watch? I'll have Timmons assign three of you to the task for the next few nights. Who on the staff would you recommend to join you in patrol duty?"

"Herbert and Alvin, Your Grace. We often go hunting together. They can handle weapons and know how to listen for anything out of the ordinary."

"Fine, let Timmons know I want you three put on night rotation."

He and Edgar quickly searched Florence's bedchamber and found it clear. Of course, Trajan did not think anyone had managed to get into the house and hide in her chamber. But one could not be too careful when dealing with Frampton and his ruffians.

For good measure, he conducted a thorough search of the house, checking it from top to bottom to make certain the doors and windows were secure.

Florence had changed into her nightclothes by the time he returned upstairs. He noticed she had her door open, no doubt hoping to hear him as he marched down the hall. He considered stopping in to bid her a good night, but had just decided against it when she came scurrying out. "Trajan, is all well?"

He cast her a wry smile. "Yes, all secure. You're safe here, other than from me. I'm sorry I squashed you earlier."

She gave a light laugh. "You only meant to protect me. I'm not angry now that I understand the reason. In fact, thank you. It was yet another brave and protective thing you did for me. I'm not used to such chivalrous treatment."

He frowned. Wouldn't her family do the same for her?

Perhaps not, if the hesitation when speaking of her brother or her parents earlier were any indication. But digging deeper into her family relations was something better left for tomorrow. She was tired, he could tell by the slight droop of her usually bright and sparkling eyes.

He was tired, too. He could not imagine what tomorrow would bring for them, but knew he had better be well rested for whatever might transpire. "Good night, Florence."

"Good night, Trajan. I am sorry to be so much trouble for you."

"You're all right. I am not complaining. Get some rest."

She shook her head and walked back into her room, shutting the door behind her.

He went into his own, tossed off his soiled clothes, and placed them in the hall for his valet to collect in the morning before collapsing naked onto his bed.

He'd jokingly said life would never be dull with Florence, but this was perhaps a little too much excitement for one day.

Good grief, had it only been a day? It felt like fifty. What would tomorrow bring?

More chaos, he suspected, because Frampton wanted Florence out of the way, and Florence, being Florence, had no intention of cooperating with that fiend. She wanted those letters.

How was he to keep her safe, especially if she persisted in her assignment?

He fell asleep contemplating the problem.

Sometimes, by sleeping on a matter, one could come up with a solution. Unfortunately, he had a blistering headache and still no answers come morning.

His valet was fussing about his bedchamber and had drawn the drapes aside by the time Trajan roused. He heard the quiet *bong* of the large clock in the hallway as it rang the eight o'clock hour. "Is that right, Reed?" he muttered, rubbing his temples as he sat up, certain he must have counted wrong.

"Yes, eight o'clock, Your Grace."

This was much later than he usually remained abed, so he hastily tossed off his covers, donned the banyan that his valet had placed at the foot of his bed, and marched to the window to peer out onto a gray, dreary day.

A steady rain was falling and began to pour down in buckets as he watched, so he saw nothing of his usually splendid view, only these sheets of water.

"Doesn't look like it will end soon," Reed remarked.

Trajan nodded. This storm would likely last all day. Once the rain slowed to a drizzle, the mix of moisture and heat would leave his grounds blanketed in fog. It would take a strong wind to clear the clouds and dampness from the air any time soon.

This foul weather might rein in Florence's desire to snoop, he realized.

However, it would also interfere with his ability to follow that lurker's trail. No point in putting his dogs on the scent now. The downpour would have soaked into the soil and washed away all trace of that man by now.

"Shall I order your bath brought up, Your Grace?"

"Do you know if Lady Florence or her aunt are awake yet, Reed?"

"Miss Hermia has not stirred yet, Your Grace. But I believe Miss Florence has just gone downstairs."

"Blast. Never mind the bath. No time for it. Set out my shaving gear and my clothes, nothing fashionable. Good work clothes will do." He tossed off the banyan and poured water from his ewer into the basin. Soap and a wet washcloth would serve just as well to scrub his body clean. He slopped water about while hastily washing his hair, but Reed was ever efficient at mopping it up as the droplets fell.

He allowed Reed to shave him because he was already fretting about Florence being left on her own, and was going to carve his chin up if he rushed through the ritual to get himself downstairs faster.

It felt like an eternity but could not have been more than ten or fifteen minutes before he was groomed, dressed, and ready to join Florence at the breakfast table.

He left his valet to his tidying, and tore down the hall.

Perhaps he was worrying too much about Florence. What could she do in this inclement weather?

Still, she was a determined force of nature and he would not put it past her to leave the comfort of his home in order to spy on Frampton again.

He leaped down the stairs and raced past Timmons, who was dutifully at his post by the front door. "Morning," Trajan called to his butler, and hurried into the dining room.

Florence looked up from the cup of tea she was about to put to her lips, and immediately set it down. "Is something wrong?"

"No. Why? Good morning, Florence," he said, his manner casual although he felt as though he'd just run three miles over enemy terrain. "Did you sleep well?"

She smiled at him. "Yes, and you?"

Gad, how did such a little troublemaker manage to look so sweet and pretty in the morning? Vulnerable, too. He wanted to wrap her in his arms and assure her all would work out, that he'd keep her safe.

But he knew better than to think she was in any way frail and in need of his protection.

Well, she *did* need protecting, but mostly from herself because of her stubborn refusal to acknowledge the danger and keep away from Frampton.

She sighed. "Did you stay awake all night thinking up ways to keep me safe?"

"I might have done." He went to the buffet and poured himself a cup of coffee before taking a seat at the table beside her. He noticed her plate was clean and empty. "Were you waiting for me to come down before having your breakfast?"

She nodded. "Yes, I thought it would be rude to start without you. Besides, I wasn't very hungry. Yesterday's adventures were a little upsetting."

He laughed. "Only a little?"

"All right, a lot upsetting. But you needn't worry about me. I—"

He growled softly.

Gad, when had he ever growled at a woman? But Florence was already infuriating him, and she hadn't done anything other than smile at him.

"Trajan," she said with a slight purse of her lips that now had him fixing his gaze on them and wishing to kiss her, "I am not going to go off and climb trees in this downpour. I cannot even pretend to bird-watch, since you tossed my binoculars into the undergrowth and Frampton now has them. Nor will I ask to borrow yours, since you are going to hit the ceiling and put a hole straight through it if I ever dare ask."

He managed a chuckle, realizing he had walked in riled and taken it out on her when she had done nothing to deserve it…yet. "Then what are you going to do?"

"With your permission, I would like to sit with Mrs. Albright and review the menu for tomorrow's tea." She let out a breath. "Your footman delivered Lady Frampton's invitation this morning."

"You sent him out in this miserable weather?"

She stared down into her tea. "Yes, but it wasn't raining hard at the time and he was back here by the time it started pouring. Still, I apologized profusely for sending him out in the rain. I suppose that still does not make it right, but I did not want to give you the chance to countermand the invitation." She now looked up and met his gaze with one of defiance. "I saw no reason to cancel it, and where's the harm in ladies having a friendly chat over tea? Let's see how my afternoon with Lady Frampton goes before we worry about what to do next."

"*We?* I love how I am now dragged into your assignment."

"You don't have to be. You are the one who insists on inserting himself. And before you puff up like a…like a big, puffing bird… Oh, what is that look now? Why are you rolling your eyes?"

"A *puffing* bird? This from the chairwoman of Lower Bramble's notorious ornithological society? You might have said like a grouse or robin, or a thrush. They puff up to keep warm or as a sign of aggression to ward off rivals."

"Oh, good grief. I am trying to make a point here."

He leaned forward so that their noses were almost touching. "So am I. If you are going to take on a disguise, you had better master it, or else you will be found out and shot."

"Well, no one is going to shoot me except Frampton, and I'll do my best to avoid that."

"How? He's already shot at you several times, and last night was meant to send you another message." He sank back in his chair. "Or do those shots he fired at you yesterday not count because you fell out of a tree and they flew over your head? Had he realized you had fallen and landed on me, he would have aimed lower and killed both of us."

"Stop being angry with me. I liked you much better when you were kissing me."

He glanced around, hoping no one on his staff was listening. But they happened to be alone in the dining room. No one but

Timmons was anywhere near, and he was standing at his post by the front door, too far away to hear what they were saying.

Edgar and Alvin were the footmen who usually attended the dining room at mealtimes, but he saw no reason to require their presence when those two had been up all night guarding the house, and he and Florence were competent enough to pour their own tea or coffee from a pot.

He would attend to Hermia if she chose to join them, although he suspected she was like most ladies of a certain age who preferred their breakfast served in bed. Would she even bother to get out of bed at all today?

"Will you ever kiss me again?" Florence asked, her expression turning soft and dreamy.

"I don't know," he grumbled, never mind that he was absolutely going to do this, assuming one of them did not die of gunshot wounds first.

"Well, you have my permission if ever you decide to tolerate me again."

Tolerate her?

He wanted to toss her onto his bed and ravish her, which only proved he was going mad and probably already delusional.

Well, he was hungry and she looked delicious. Really luscious. She wasn't even trying to look tempting, not with that serviceable gown of dark-green muslin that was buttoned to her throat. And her hair. *Dear heaven.* She must have done it up herself, because the pins were not going to hold that lovely mass much longer. The slightest breeze would have those silken curls spilling down her back.

"What would you like for breakfast?" He rose, grabbed her plate, and marched over to the salvers atop the buffet.

Her eyes widened and she cast him another endearing smile. "That is quite gentlemanly of you. Just some eggs and a slice of ham will do."

"What else have you planned for today, besides preparing a menu that will take you all of three minutes to complete?" he asked while piling eggs onto her plate, and knowing he had to stop growling at her before she had even done anything to deserve it.

Well, she had gotten that invitation out to Lady Frampton.

He turned and scowled at her.

"Did I just call you a gentleman?" She sighed. "I take it back. You are being impossibly cantankerous again."

He piled more eggs onto her plate.

"I tend to be a morning person," she said, no doubt trying to engage in polite conversation, which might have worked were he not already worrying about what the day would bring. "I wake up cheerful and smiling. You will find me most pleasant company at the breakfast table."

"I prefer to have my coffee in peace and quiet."

"Well, that is not going to happen with me around, is it? Does your surliness also extend to a ban on any smiles before noon?"

He arched an eyebrow. "That is not a bad idea. I'll add it to the house rules."

She sighed again. "If you have no plans for us, seeing as going on a picnic or taking a hike is out of the question in this rainstorm, I could have Mrs. Albright show me around the house and introduce me to your staff. It would be expected, since I am currently betrothed to you."

That was actually a good idea.

"Then you would be free to attend to Weymouth business matters while I am *safely* occupied elsewhere in the house."

"What about your aunt?"

"She won't rise for hours yet. We can plan an outing if the weather clears, or I could entertain you this afternoon with songs."

"What?"

"I sing," she said with a grin. "And I can also play the pianoforte. I know you have one in your house."

"Oh, dear Lord. You aren't one of those deluded fribbles who will break my eardrums as you screech out a high note, are you?"

She laughed heartily. "No, I can really sing. Although I will not rule out purposely screeching or singing flat if you irritate me. Gad, you are such a bear in the morning."

"And you are as annoyingly chirpy as a chirping bird," he said with a chuckle.

"A chirping bird? Seriously? This from the man who just admonished me for describing birds who puff up as puffing birds? Well, I can tell you what birds chirp in the morning."

"Go ahead, enlighten me."

"A robin or a wren. How's that for two?"

He arched an eyebrow. "So you think this makes you an expert on birds?"

"I merely claimed to be chairwoman, never to actually know what I was talking about," she said with another endearing smile that threatened to put him in good humor.

Florence could be surprisingly lovable when she put her mind to it.

He set her plate before her, then grabbed his and piled eggs, kippers, sausages, and whatever else was to be found under those salvers onto his plate.

Florence watched him as he sat and began to eat.

He glanced up. "What?"

"Nothing. I am enjoying sitting here with you. It feels nice, even though you are remarkably grumpy. But it is in an endearingly bearish way."

"Are you going to stop talking and let me eat in peace?"

She nodded and mimicked buttoning her lip.

He smiled despite not wanting to be coaxed into good humor. It surprised him that she looked happy just seated beside him. In truth, it felt nice to be beside her, too.

As though they felt *right* together.

He would not mind looking at her pretty face each morning. Despite the gray weather, there was a lovely pink blush to her cheeks.

He did not even mind her chirpiness because she was not silly or dithering. Florence had a keen intelligence that he liked very much.

He was just about to agree to hearing her sing later when there was a commotion at the front door.

He quickly rose and was about to reach for the pistol in his boot when the strains of laughter reached his ears. "My cousins have arrived," he said as the tension rushed out of him. "Care to meet them?"

He held out his hand to Florence, only afterward realizing how natural this intimate gesture felt to him. But it must have felt right to Florence as well, for she did not hesitate before entwining her fingers in his.

Well, they were into this betrothal ruse up to their eyeballs. Why not go along with it?

He kept Florence's hand in his as they walked out to greet his cousins, who were soaked to the teeth, but at least their boots were not muddied, although wet leather was never comfortable. He should have ordered them to enter through the kitchen, but their boots were merely wet and not filthy, so they were not going to track mud through the house.

Yes, he was getting to be an old curmudgeon, and he wasn't even nearing forty yet.

But Gull Hall was a magnificent house that his granduncle had left in pristine condition. He hated to be the doltish duke who ruined it.

While Timmons efficiently had his footmen bring in the bags and tote them up to the rooms that had been readied, Trajan introduced Florence to his cousins, who were rudely staring at her. "Lady Florence and I are recently betrothed. Her aunt is with us, too. But yesterday was a bit harrowing for them, and her aunt is still abed."

"Betrothed!" the eldest, Andrew, exclaimed. "I thought you would never..." He swallowed his next words, which were probably going to be a remark about his unrequited love for Eden and how, in a fit of idiocy induced by too much brandy, Trajan had once proclaimed he would never get over his love for her.

He felt rather foolish about it now. Especially since he had met Florence shortly after that drunken jag, and she had been the lady on his mind from then on.

That was last year, and he hadn't thought about Eden all that much since. Which proved he had not *truly* been in love with her.

Not that he loved Florence or had been besotted and swooning over her, either. But she had lingered in his thoughts, constantly popping up like a persistent little gnat.

Perhaps this was why their betrothal did not feel fake, nor did it alarm him that it might have to become real in order to protect Florence's reputation.

"Well, you've chosen the loveliest bride," Sebastian remarked. He bowed over Florence's hand. "A pleasure to meet the woman who has captured Trajan's heart."

"Finally," Nathan muttered, next to bow over her hand. "Are you by any chance the fake bird watcher?"

Florence gasped and turned to Trajan. "This is how you described me to your cousins?"

He arched an eyebrow. "Aren't you surprised I talked about you at all?"

She gave it a moment's thought and her eyes widened. "Oh, you talked about me to your family? What exactly did you tell them, other than convince them I know nothing about birds?"

"Mostly nice things. *Lots* of nice things," he said, managing a grin. "You know I liked you from the first."

Which was true, although she had tried hard to avoid him back then.

"Florence, you've been in my thoughts ever since we met last year."

She cast him a surprisingly vulnerable smile that touched his heart.

For a young woman with family, she seemed incredibly alone in the world. Well, hers must have lost patience with her because she was headstrong and would not bend to their will. But had they made it a habit of withholding affection throughout her life? Even as a little girl?

Perhaps they had. Why else would she be so reluctant to talk about them?

"Now I see why he was so swept away with you," Andrew said, bowing over her hand as his brothers had done once Trajan introduced him.

"I'm delighted to meet you all," Florence responded with genuine warmth. "Are you hungry?"

Andrew laughed. "Always."

Florence offered to have the salvers restocked while Trajan took his cousins up to their rooms so they could change out of their wet clothes.

She tugged gently on his arm as he was about to lead them upstairs. "Would you rather the four of you were left alone to chat? I do not need to be in the dining room with you. I can see to my aunt in the meanwhile."

"No, Florence. You are welcome to join us. We won't be speaking of anything confidential."

"Not even... Er, surely they must be surprised by our be-trothal."

Her expression said it all. He had made an idiot of himself over Eden, and now Florence thought his cousins were going to ask about her and wonder whether he was settling for her as second best because his supposed true love was now married to the Duke of Lynton and out of his reach. "Check on your aunt, if you wish. But come down and join us afterward."

In the meanwhile, this would give his cousins a few minutes to ask their questions.

He hoped Florence would join them, for he liked being with her. However, she was taking his efforts to keep her close the wrong way. She thought he was doing it on purpose in order to keep watch over her.

There *was* a little of that. He needed to guard her from Frampton.

But he enjoyed her company, too.

Florence marched upstairs along with them and then parted from them to look in on her aunt. She went one way while he led his cousins the other way, toward his wing of the house. His cousins were to be placed in the rooms next to his.

Once they had washed and changed into dry clothes, they met him in the dining room. Florence had not come down yet, and Trajan wondered whether she would join them at all. Perhaps she wished to leave them to themselves.

"Lady Florence seems nice," Andrew said, regarding Trajan thoughtfully. "But what is really going on between you?"

Trajan frowned. "What do you mean? You know I have gotten over Eden."

Andrew nodded. "Yes, I suppose. So you've told us. But we weren't quite sure."

"And now?"

"Yes, we believe you," he said. "Florence is beautiful."

His brothers nodded.

"But, Trajan," Andrew continued, his tone suddenly uncertain, "I was referring to the menacing-looking gentleman poised with a hunting rifle we encountered at your front gate."

"What gentleman?" Trajan said, leaping to his feet.

"More like a ruffian off the London docks," Sebastian said, motioning for him to sit back down. "The man is probably long gone by now. But we were immediately wary and asked what he was doing there."

"And?"

"He claimed he was just passing by and asked us to bid Lady Florence a good day. Those were his exact words."

"Blessed saints," Trajan muttered, rubbing the back of his neck.

"He did not give us his name," Nathan said. "Frankly, he does not seem to be anyone she would know or ever acknowledge."

"Did he say anything else to you?"

Andrew nodded. "He mentioned that Lady Florence is accident prone, and cautions her to tread carefully, lest she suffer a serious injury."

"What in blazes did he mean by that?" Sebastian asked. "It sounded like a threat to me."

Trajan frowned. "Because it *was* a threat."

Nathan set down his coffee cup. "What does this ruffian have against your Florence? She seems very nice."

Trajan wasn't certain how much to tell them, but they had come here to help him out, albeit with the expectation of assisting with his Weymouth holdings. But why not enlist them in protecting Florence, too?

There was danger associated with this task, so he resolved to tell them the truth about what was going on and let them decide whether to accept the challenge or not.

Florence would not be happy about his revealing her mission, but this was no game, and he could not leave his cousins ignorant of the peril. If they agreed to help, she would then have four Aubreys to protect her.

He would take on the most burdensome responsibilities, of course. His cousins would remain in the shadows, watching his back while he watched over her.

"Then your betrothal is merely a ruse?" Andrew asked once Trajan had finished relating yesterday's adventures.

"Yes… Well, no. That is…" Trajan sighed. "It feels real."

"It looks real," Nathan said.

Trajan shrugged. "I'm not sure if it will ever lead to anything more. That will be up to Florence to decide."

"Then you really like her?" Sebastian asked.

"That depends on what you mean by *liking her*. She is smart and quite beautiful, but I also want to throttle her most of the time because she is so bloody stubborn."

Andrew shook his head. "Understandable, but I can also see her point. How can she ignore a personal request from the Princess of Wales? And it was awfully brilliant of her to invite Lady Frampton to tea tomorrow. Sounds like she and Lord Frampton were playing a game of chess with each other and she checkmated him. Now Lady Frampton must return the invitation, and this will get Florence into his house."

Sebastian and Nathan grinned, apparently also admiring Florence's quick thinking.

"You seem to be missing the point, Andrew. That invitation is the one thing Frampton did *not* want to have happen," Trajan muttered. "But Florence is going to plow ahead anyway. She's really too clever for her own good."

Andrew eased back in his chair. "We'll all stay close to protect her."

"I don't know how we will manage it while she is inside his home," Trajan grumbled, hoping Hermia's presence there would somehow rein in Frampton. More to the point, he hoped she might be enlisted to rein in Florence. *Someone* had to keep her from running amok.

"Then you are in?" he asked his cousins. "Are you sure? This is a dangerous undertaking."

All three nodded.

Florence walked in just as they put their hands forward and placed them one atop the other. "To protecting Florence," they said as one.

She gasped. "You told them?"

Trajan hurriedly rose. His cousins shot to their feet, as well. "Yes, I had to."

"Why?" Her dismayed gaze flitted from one to the other, taking them all in. "How could you?"

"You mustn't blame Trajan," Andrew said. "We walked in knowing something was amiss."

"Frampton had one of his lackeys standing with a rifle at *my* front gate, and gave *my* cousins a threatening message for you from that miserable cur."

"Frampton did that? The unmitigated gall." She curled her hands into fists. "How dare that lowly coward… I ought to—"

"Gad, Florence!" Did she always have to make his heart shoot into his throat? "You ought to do nothing at all. Do you hear me?"

She cast him a stubborn look.

He threw down his table linen and turned to his cousins. "See what I mean? She is as obstinate as a donkey. Are you sure you don't want to back out?"

"No," Andrew said. "All the more reason we Aubreys must stick together. We are in this with you to the end, Trajan."

"But what is to be the end?" Trajan's gaze bored into Florence. "This is no longer just you and me at risk. This involves my cousins, too. And what of Hermia? Do you think she will be safe if you push Frampton too far?"

He knew his remarks were cruel and had gutted her. She stood in silence for a long moment, then her chin began to wobble and her eyes watered.

Good, let her cry.

It was never in his nature to be cruel, but how else was he to make her see reason? Let the Princess of Wales send an army to upend Frampton's house and grab whatever scandalous letters they could find. Why in blazes did it have to be a one-person clandestine operation? And why was Florence the one person chosen to carry out this task when it was clearly beyond her expertise and would get her killed?

Florence was no fool. In fact, she was extremely intelligent. So why was she refusing to let go of this assignment?

Something else had to be going on, something she had not told him yet. "Florence, you now have four men who have pledged to die for you. I think we have the right to know everything. And do not think to deny that there is more to this story than you have told me. What have you left out?" He glanced at his cousins, realizing Florence may not want to speak in front of them. "Do you prefer for us to speak alone? You and I can discuss this privately in my study. I would suggest the library, but it is being cleaned right now."

He was purposely bringing up last night's incident to serve as a reminder. They were fortunate the man with a pistol at his library window last night had not fired a shot at them. Perhaps he was never meant to fire a shot, merely scare them.

By why aim a weapon at someone if you had no intention of using it? It seemed odd that their lurker would be instructed to do nothing more than stand with his face at the window until they noticed him. And then what? Was he merely to run away?

None of this made any sense.

Well, whatever the man's reason for being there last night, Trajan and Florence were fortunate there was no harm done beyond a smashed cocoa pot, soiled clothes, and a stained carpet and settee.

Florence sniffled, but still held her chin high. "Your cousins may as well join us. You will repeat everything I tell you anyway. They may as well hear it directly from me."

He took her hand, liking how small and soft it felt in his.

This was why Florence was so dangerous to his heart, this softness about her. She was intelligent, quick-witted, and independent. Yet achingly vulnerable. She brought out his protective instincts.

But did he not have the right to behave like a wild ape when she was behaving like a stubborn donkey?

There were four plump leather chairs arranged beside the hearth in his study, and he motioned for his cousins and Florence to sit while he remained standing.

He began to pace. "All right, Florence. Let's have the rest of it."

Her anger fled. She no longer scowled at him or cast him a stubborn look. Instead, she slumped her shoulders and buried her head in her hands. "I am so ashamed."

She burst into sobs before all of them.

Trajan paled.

His cousins stared at him, confusion, remorse, and horror mingled in their expressions.

Oh, gad.

What had he done? What vile secrets was he forcing Florence to tell them?

CHAPTER SIX

FLORENCE FELT AS though her heart had just been flayed bare.

She wanted to cry, wanted to be left alone to weep buckets of tears, because Trajan and his cousins would now know her shame.

She had to tell them, for they deserved to know the truth. But how was she to reveal the facts to them without their losing all respect for her?

She offered no resistance when Trajan drew her out of her chair and placed his arms around her. "Florence, love. Are you sure you do not wish to speak to me in private? I never meant to humiliate you. My cousins can leave the room while you tell me what this is about. But you must tell me. I cannot remain in the dark to whatever is going on."

"I know."

"Oh, love." He caressed her cheek and gently stroked her hair in an attempt to calm her down. But she had kept so much sealed up inside, it was hard to stop the deluge now that her dam had burst.

"They can stay. Just give me a moment." She withdrew her handkerchief and used it to dab her eyes, leaving it well and truly soaked, because she had held back so many tears for so long, and now they were flooding out of her.

After a moment, she eased out of Trajan's arms and sank back in her chair. He knelt beside her, studying her with genuine worry.

"I didn't do anything wrong," she said. "These tears aren't for me."

She felt the soft rush of air as he released a breath. "Then who? Are you protecting someone?"

She nodded. "My brother. The golden child. The firstborn who can do no wrong in the eyes of my parents. But Matthew is about to be brought up on charges of dueling. Fortunately, he merely winged the son of a marquess who had called him out for cheating at cards."

"Bloody blazes," Sebastian muttered. "Did he cheat?"

"Yes. And he has also run up a sizeable debt at the copper hell he frequents. This is the bargain I really struck with the princess. She has agreed to erase his debts and squelch that dueling charge in exchange for the return of those letters. It seemed a good bargain at the time. All those marks against my brother suddenly made to disappear."

"She ought to have warned you about Frampton," Sebastian retorted.

"Assuming she knew how vicious he was."

Trajan rolled his eyes. "Oh, she knew it, all right."

"I really don't think so. But fine," she said in response to his continued disbelieving gaze, "she used me as her dupe. Does this make you feel any better? I was a naïve idiot, but the fact remains, my parents will be devastated if my brother is criminally charged. I don't think they know of his gambling debts, certainly not the extent of the hole he has dug for himself."

"And you mean to coddle your brother and let him get away unscathed for his bad behavior?" Trajan remarked. "Your family never knowing he is a lying weasel?"

"He is still my brother, and they adore him."

"And what about you?" he asked with mounting anger. "What do they think of you? They cannot be happy you are risking your life to protect him."

"You would be wrong," she said, her voice brittle and on the verge of shattering.

He rubbed his hand across the back of his neck. "Florence, what are you saying? That you have no value to them?"

She cast him a pained smile. "I always knew you were clever."

"They would rather risk the worthy child to save the unworthy wretch?" He shook his head, still in disbelief.

"Now *you* are being naïve," she said. "What makes you think they ever considered me worthy?" She wanted to burst into tears again, but did her best to maintain her composure. "Why do you think I am independent and so much on my own? It is of necessity. They have never cared for me. Well, my father did once…perhaps he still does, but he will never stand up for me. My mother…" She felt a physical ache at the thought of this woman who would not blink if Florence fell at her feet and died in front of her. "My mother has never… She wishes I had never been born. My father goes along with whatever she demands because he wants to maintain a tranquil home life, and it is easier to say nothing rather than argue with her."

She felt a tomb-like silence descend upon the room, and knew she must have shocked these Aubreys, who were a close-knit family and could not imagine their parents or siblings hating them.

But she had been raised unwanted.

Florence could not bear the silence. This had been her upbringing, an awful and constant silence. Her presence ignored. Her words falling upon deaf ears. She was merely vapor to her family. A phantom. A wraith.

In truth, being sent off to boarding school at an early age was a welcome relief for her. There, people liked her. She made fast friends and had kept up a friendship with several schoolmates, most notably Jocelyn, who was now Duchess of Camborne.

"Lady Simmons did give me an advance," she said as the silence persisted, "but her obligation is only to pay for my out-of-pocket expenses, since the princess was not *that* generously inclined to help out her foolish friend. My expenses were the responsibility of Lady Simmons to pay, but my actual fee is the release of my brother from his debts and the dueling charge." She let out a ragged breath. "So, you see, there is no possibility of my leaving here without those letters."

"I'm so sorry, Florence," Sebastian said with genuine remorse, and his brothers nodded in sympathy.

"I'm not sorry. I am angry," Trajan said, pushing away from her chair and beginning to pace in front of her. "Let your brother retrieve those blasted letters himself. He got his worthless arse into this mess, so let him deal with getting himself out. He might learn something from it."

"He'll learn nothing, and he isn't competent to handle anything," she replied, wondering how two siblings could have grown up so different. Perhaps being raised unloved had made her stronger, while her brother was showered with affection, his every misstep overlooked, and this had left him pampered and weak. "Besides, he would probably hold on to the letters and blackmail Lady Simmons himself."

Trajan muttered something unintelligible, probably a curse.

"My parents would be devastated if harm befell him. Do you not get it? They care about *him*. They do not care about me. If not for Aunt Hermia, I have no idea what I might have become." Hermia was the only one to ever show her the affection one would expect from a mother to her child.

"Well, that is everything," she finished. "The entire truth. No humiliating stone left unturned. Do you still wish to help me? Because I am not turning back."

Trajan raked a hand through his hair as he stared at her. "Does Hermia know all of what you are doing?"

"No, she thinks we are on a bird-watching holiday."

"Dear heaven." He raked a hand through his hair again. "Did you not give thought to what might happen to your aunt if Frampton killed you?"

"I did not realize until yesterday just how dangerous he was," she said in her own defense. "No one warned me, and I sincerely believe the princess did not know. Besides, Hermia is not witless. She would have made arrangements to have my body shipped home and properly buried."

"Buried? Gad, Florence. Do you hear yourself?"

Oh, she was riling him worse than ever.

"What if I married you? Now. Today. We'll head straight to Weymouth and obtain the license. The vicar at St. Michael's will not deny me. My cousins and your aunt will serve as our witnesses. You are of age to consent."

"Marry me?" Her head began to spin. "How will that help the situation?" Had she heard him right?

"I don't give a fig about the *situation*. I care about keeping you safe. You'll be my duchess and forever under my protection. To blazes with Frampton, Lady Simmons, the Princess of Wales, and your family. Hermia, of course, is welcome to reside with us if she wishes."

"I would never do this to you, Trajan. How can I drag you further into this impossible affair and damage your family name? Nor do I wish to marry because you pity me. So, take back your pity proposal, although I am exceedingly grateful for the offer. You are kinder and more valiant than I deserve."

"You are refusing me?" He seemed surprised, but why ever would she agree to a marriage that would only bring him endless headaches?

"I would not refuse you if you genuinely loved me, but we all know where your heart lies." She shook her head and held back her tears, trying not to think of Eden. She was the fortunate lady who had captured his heart. "You have been incredibly good to me. But I cannot live in a marriage as I have lived with my parents. I want someone who loves me best, who puts me first in his heart, and who cannot be without me. Not in a suffocating, all-consuming way. Just someone who likes to have me around, who might smile if I enter a room, and who would talk to me instead of telling me to keep silent."

"Gad, Florence." His eyes widened. "This morning at breakfast, I—"

"You wanted me to be quiet," she said with a gentle smile. "You have every right to enjoy your peace and quiet. I know you did not mean it unkindly. You are a bear in the morning, that much is obvious. But I have dealt with silence all my life. I cannot endure it with a husband. I simply cannot."

"Nor would I ask you to, especially now that I know what it represents to you. I would let you chatter like a magpie at our breakfast table."

"And give you headaches daily?" She shook her head and laughed lightly. "I appreciate this, and I believe you would sincerely try to put up with me in the mornings. But my reluctance comes from more than that. I cannot marry for the sake of convenience, although how convenient can it be for you, a husband who finds me an imposition and does not really want me around?"

"That is not so. When have I ever wished you gone?"

"Oh, I expect you are wishing it right now. Even if you are not, it is not possible for your feelings to be that strong for me."

"How do you know?" He stared at her in a smoldering way that burned into her soul. But this ability to melt a woman's heart was precisely the reason he had become known as a Silver Duke.

"Are you suggesting that you love me?"

He hesitated.

"I thought as much. Do you understand now why I cannot agree to a loveless marriage, even if we are genial to each other and might get along as friends?"

"And you think I merely want us to be friends?"

She nodded. "I am not dismissing its importance. A happy marriage must have more than, er…encounters in the bedchamber for the purpose of siring heirs."

He groaned. "Cousins, out. I need to talk to Florence in private."

They all scrambled to their feet.

"I hope you reconsider, Florence. You would be happy joining our family," Sebastian said in all earnestness. "Trajan will not ignore you. He'll be a good and devoted husband."

Andrew expressed a similar opinion.

So did Nathan. "Trajan would not have proposed to you unless he believed yours could be a successful marriage. He just wouldn't have done it. We know him. He isn't a soft touch and is not asking out of pity or a sense of noble sacrifice. He sincerely likes you, Florence."

"I like him, too," she admitted. "But is this not more reason for me to worry about him? Should I not care that Frampton might hurt him?"

"No," they all replied at once.

"Out," Trajan said more gently, nudging his cousins to the door. "I'll join you in the parlor shortly. Or let Timmons know if you are still hungry and I'll meet you in the dining room while you have a second breakfast."

"Good idea," Andrew said, grinning as he rubbed his stomach.

Florence wished very much to accept Trajan's offer, for she was already halfway in love with him and had been since meeting him last year. She also found his cousins so kind and welcoming. All these Aubrey men were honorable and brave. Who else would agree to risk their lives for her, a stranger?

She could not allow them to do this for her.

But what a wonderful group they were.

Trajan was the handsomest, of course. His sunburst of golden hair fell in perfect waves even on rainy days when no one's hair looked good—but his did. *The wretched fiend.* He also had gorgeous green eyes that she could stare at for hours on end.

Not to mention he was tall. Handsome. Had divine muscles.

His cousins also had the makings of handsome men, although they needed a few more years to fill out as nicely as Trajan had done. All three had hair darker than his, ranging between tawny and very light brown. Their eyes were a dark blue, much like the deepest blue of the ocean. Sebastian, the youngest, had a sparkle to his eyes and an elfin grin. Nathan, the middle cousin, had ears that stuck out and round eyes reminiscent of an owl's. However, those features fit his face perfectly and did not detract at all from his good looks. Andrew, the eldest, had short, spiky hair that she expected would look devastatingly appealing once his face matured enough to give him a square, rugged jaw to counterbalance his "casually" styled hair that was not really casual at all.

What did they think of her?

Well, no matter. She was not going to marry their cousin and become a part of their family.

"Florence," Trajan said as the door closed behind his cousins, the deep rumble of his voice making her melt a little as it slid over her like a perfectly aged Madeira wine, "I am not proposing to you out of pity."

"Then you are proposing to me out of a misguided sense of valor."

"Nor is it valor."

She took his hands in hers. "You are the most wonderful man I have ever met. But I will not ruin your life by accepting you. However, I shall be more than willing to receive your offer after this mess of an assignment is over, assuming you are not sick of me and never want to come near me again."

"But you won't accept me now?"

"How can I?"

"It is easily done. All it takes is a simple *yes* from you."

She shook her head. "It is not simple at all, as you well know. Can we put off this discussion until after tomorrow's tea with Lady Frampton? Let's see what happens then."

"We already know what proper etiquette requires her to do. She is going to return the invitation and invite you into her home."

Florence nodded. "I hope she does, and Aunt Hermia will come with me. So do not bother to rage at me. I am not going to do anything foolish while we are there."

"Just being there is dangerous and ridiculous."

She ignored his comment. "Hermia and I will have a lovely

chat with Lady Frampton once she invites us to her home. We shall share cakes and buttered bread, and then we shall leave. I am not going to attempt to steal those letters during our visit to Frampton Court."

"Is this supposed to ease my mind when I know you will wait until nightfall and break in then?" he said with a growl. "And Frampton will be waiting for you."

"You think I cannot outsmart him?"

"Dear heaven, Florence. I will have a full head of gray hair because of you before the week is out. I will be the *silverest* among the Silver Dukes."

She cast him a wan smile. "Is this not another reason why you should avoid marrying me? I have my important reasons, too. If we were to marry, you would gain total control over me, and the law will always be on your side whenever you try to stop me from doing what I must do."

"Must do? Yes, how wicked and beastly of me to try to stop you from getting yourself killed," he said, his voice dripping with sarcasm. "Blast it, Florence. I just want to protect you."

"I know, and I am falling in love with you because of it. Truly, no one has ever treated me as wonderfully as you have, and most of the time you are irritated with me. I suppose this does not say much for me. Should this not give you warning?"

He gave a wry laugh. "Oh, warning bells have been going off in my head from the moment I met you. I am fully aware of what I would walk into if I married you."

"Chaos. Disaster."

"No, Florence. I would be binding myself to someone who would be a match for me, someone who could keep up with me, often best me, and always be faithful to me and honor our marriage vows. This is who you are, and I know this in my heart. Do not ask me to explain this *rightness* I feel about us. Let me take you under my wing."

"Under your wing? I am not your little bird to protect."

"Yes, you are," he said with a soft growl. "Am I not an experienced bird watcher?"

She managed a small smile because she was not angry with him at all, certainly not after his impassioned words and wonderfully apish need to keep her safe.

His own smile soon turned earnest. "I like you, Florence. Very much. I doubt I would feel this way about anyone else."

Not even Eden?

She dared not pose the question, for she already knew the answer. He loved Eden most of all.

She let out a ragged breath. "I need to protect my brother in the same way you wish to protect me. My heart compels me to do this, just as your heart seems to be compelling you to guard me. I know he doesn't deserve to be saved, but when has life ever been fair? I cannot ignore his situation."

"Oh, yes. You can. The Princess of Wales can be made to see reason. You are the one choosing to put your life at risk for an undeserving brother. I just don't get it, Florence. What has he done to earn your loyalty?"

"Him? Nothing. I do this for the sake of my family. You should understand this, considering how close you Aubreys are to each other."

"Do you think this will make your parents love you? That it will be the magical cure to make up for their years of neglect?" With a grunt of exasperation, he slipped his hands out of hers and began to pace like a caged beast in front of her. "They will not even thank you. And your brother will repeat his foolish behavior because he suffered no consequences for his actions."

He was going to make her cry again. Everything he said was true.

And still, she needed to do this for herself. Even if her family never showed her the slightest appreciation, she would know that she had saved her brother.

Her father would know it, too. This was all that mattered to her. She would not require her father to ever utter a word of praise, but she would know he understood what she had done and be grateful for it.

Her mother would also know.

Perhaps this was the real reason she felt compelled to risk her life for her brother. Her mother would know, and possibly despise her all the more for it.

But Florence would see the recognition in the woman's eyes each time they met. *I saved your golden child. Love me or hate me, I don't care. Just* feel *something.*

Anything was better than the complete indifference she had endured all her life.

"All right, Florence. Let's see what happens tomorrow," Trajan said. "But I want you to know the offer of marriage was sincere on my part."

She nodded. "And my joy in receiving it was just as sincere."

"Then why hesitate to accept me?"

Her heart gave a little hitch, for she really wanted to shout with glee from the rooftops and consent to marry him. But Eden was first in his heart, and she did not know if she could handle this in their marriage. Could she be happy being merely second best in her husband's affections? Having to look at him every day and know he was wishing for Eden to be the one by his side?

Even if he hid his disappointment well, and even if he was kind to her—which she knew he would be, because he was a very good man—she could not spend the rest of her life as someone's leftovers. This was what she had been all her life. She would rather remain alone than have to endure it to the end of her days, especially from Trajan...this man she loved.

No, she meant...this man she *could* love.

Was it not too soon to admit one was in love? Or to know it for a certainty?

Perhaps she was thinking too much about this.

Could marriage to him work? Was kindness enough to sustain them in a good marriage, even though she would be the only one truly in love?

He studied her for a long while before speaking again. "This is about Eden, isn't it?"

She tipped her chin up. "I have no idea what you mean."

"Oh, Florence. Your heart is an open window and I can see straight through it. I am not in love with Eden. I know this is what you are thinking."

She was, but she merely pinched her lips together rather than acknowledge it.

"I will admit to holding a torch for her when I arrived at the Bromleighs' house party last year. But then I met a fake bird watcher," he said with an endearingly boyish smile, "who caught my attention, and I haven't been able to get her out of my heart ever since."

Her eyes widened. He'd said *out of his heart* and not merely *out of his thoughts*.

"Me?"

He laughed softly. "Yes, you. Imagine my surprise when you tumbled back into my life yesterday. I haven't stopped thinking about you since the day we met. In fact, I was lost in dreams of you when you happened to fall atop me."

She shook her head. "No."

"Yes. I considered returning to London in the hope I might find you there. That's what I was doing while walking in my woods yesterday morning. Thinking of *you*. Suddenly, there you were."

She winced. "Crash landing on you."

"It was a wish come true for me," he said with remarkable sincerity, and held out his arms for her. "Your sudden appearance, that is. Being shot at and threatened by Frampton was not quite in my plans."

"Nor mine." She moved into his embrace and rested her head against his chest, simply breathing him in. She loved the sandalwood-and-citrus scent of him, and the muscled heat of his body.

"Just put my marriage proposal in the back of your mind for now. Let it simmer. You'll give me your answer whenever you are ready."

"All right."

"But Florence, I do not want a fake betrothal between us."

"You are asking me to make this betrothal real?"

He nodded. "Yes, I would like it to be."

She wanted it too. "Just what would it entail?"

"Kisses. Honesty in our feelings."

"And what about the bedchamber? Is this not what happens when couples become betrothed?"

He tipped her chin up so that she faced him. "That is not a requirement. If you wish it, then I am more than willing to oblige. But if you prefer to wait until marriage to give yourself to me, that is all right, too."

"Truly?"

He nodded.

"Very well, I agree. Our betrothal is no longer a lie."

"And we work toward marrying?" he asked, arching an eyebrow when she turned pensive.

She did not answer him. There were too many impediments to work through first.

He sighed. "All right, too big a step for you right now. We'll inch toward it."

She hugged him fiercely. "Thank you for understanding."

In truth, she ached to accept him. But he was already too fiercely protective of her.

What would he risk if their hearts were truly pledged to each other?

Chapter Seven

T RAJAN SPENT THE rest of the rainy day closed in his study with his cousins, reviewing the Weymouth ducal holdings and determining who was to take on what responsibilities. However—and this was perhaps underhanded of him—he had Timmons report to him from time to time what Florence was doing.

He had phrased the request in terms of his wanting to make certain she was not bored while he was preoccupied with his cousins, but he really wanted to keep her under surveillance to make certain she would not sneak out and do something foolish.

To his surprise, Florence had not only stayed put at Gull Hall but seemed to have taken the initiative. She walked through the house with his housekeeper and apparently took notes on the running of it. Afterward, she ventured into the kitchen to compliment Mrs. Palmer for her cooking, and discussed the menus not only for tomorrow's tea with Lady Frampton but for all the family meals for the week, starting with this evening's supper.

Once done, she and her aunt, who was now up and about, had settled in the ladies' parlor and spent their time embroidering.

"Egads," Trajan muttered jovially after Timmons had given him this latest report and returned to his post. "Who knew she could actually behave like a duchess?"

His cousins laughed.

"Seems she has no end of talents," Andrew remarked. "Now, all you have to do is make certain she does not come to harm retrieving those letters."

"She is not entering that lion's den for those letters," Trajan said with a growl.

"How are you going to stop her? She seems determined." Sebastian stretched his legs before him and tossed an arm casually atop the back of his chair. "I think she'll do it. I would not wager against Florence."

"Nor would I," Nathan agreed.

Trajan shook his head. "Do not take the matter lightly. Frampton knows she is after something that he is not willing to turn over. How is she going to retrieve those letters without his knowing it and coming after her?"

"I don't know," Nathan admitted. "But I have every faith she will find a way. Do you think this will be her last assignment? Or is she going to accept more after you are married?"

"It would have to be her last if she married Trajan," Sebastian mused.

"This assumes she will agree to marry me." Trajan rubbed his neck in dismay. "I don't know what she will do."

"How can she not? Clearly, she is in love with you," Andrew said, seeming surprised by his comment. "She lights up like a fireworks display whenever she is near you. And surely she would stop her investigative work if you asked. Why would she take on more once she is a duchess? Would you even allow it?"

Trajan set aside the papers he was holding, leaned back in his chair, and folded his hands across the back of his head. "What makes you think Florence will ever listen to me?"

Nathan leaned forward. "But she'll be your wife and must obey you."

"Gad, how can you be so naïve? You did graduate from university, did you not? So you must have learned something in all those years."

"Apparently not enough about women," Nathan grumbled. "Is it not in the marriage vows? Would she not promise to love, honor, and obey you?"

"I can guarantee you that *obey* will be stricken from her vow," Trajan said with a wry smile. "Florence, to my endless frustration, is not the sort to bend a knee to anyone. If she cooperates, it is because she has a mind to do so, not because she is commanded to do so."

Andrew frowned. "But that sounds awful. Should she not be a dutiful wife?"

"I just hope she is a *sensible* wife. I want her to think for herself, which Florence will do. Would any of you truly want a wife who will mindlessly do whatever you command? We are speaking of marriage here, not military duty."

Andrew tossed him a wicked grin. "Well, it could be fun having an obedient wife in the bedroom."

"Discussion of Florence and bedroom matters is off limits." Trajan rolled his eyes. "I want an intelligent wife, one who will also take my feelings into consideration. In truth, I think Florence will…most of the time."

"And if she does not?"

"Like now? Then I'll protect her because it is my duty to keep her safe."

"Are you sure you are not in love with her yet?" Nathan asked. "Because it sounds an awful lot like you are."

Trajan did not bother to answer, but perhaps Nathan was right. Was it not too soon to fall in love with Florence? Considering how headstrong and determined to rush into danger she was, should this not give him pause? Cast doubts? But he understood this need to prove herself to her family, even if he disagreed with the perils she was willing to face in order to accomplish it.

He also liked the fact that she needed *him*. He had saved her yesterday, actually saved a living soul, and he felt rather good about it, especially since the one he had rescued was Florence.

Trajan put a halt to further discussion of Florence, since his cousins seemed to have taken to her like frogs to a lily pad and were quite fascinated by her. He did not want them encouraging her to pursue Frampton.

When Sebastian suggested they place wagers on whether or not she would succeed in retrieving the letters, Trajan threatened to toss them out of Gull Hall if they persisted.

"Sorry," Sebastian muttered.

"No more talk of Florence. And no wagers. There's already a betting book on me, and that is quite enough." Trajan waited for them all to nod before he renewed their discussion of family business affairs. "Andrew, you seem to have a knack for management."

Trajan assigned him to run the port of Weymouth warehouses that stored spirits, lace, and tea brought in from France, although the tea originated from China and traveled through Holland before reaching English shores.

"Sebastian will help you until he must return to university," Trajan said. "It will be no easy task. There'll be pilfering by the haulers and carters, not to mention the revenue officers cannot be trusted. They'll have their hands out, and we'll have to give them something if we want our cargo kept safe."

"What's my task?" Nathan asked.

"You'll be in charge of the Dorset farms and dairy. The old duke," Trajan said, referring to their granduncle, "hired a good manager to run the farms, but the man is getting on in years and I don't think he will be up to the task much longer. He'll train you."

"What will you handle, Trajan?" Sebastian asked.

"The Lothmere properties that will now be absorbed into the ducal holdings. The banking and investments, the contracts for products we'll import for resale in England, the pottery works, the brewery. Basically everything else in addition to attending Parliament when it is in session."

His cousins were to share in the profits, for he wanted them to have a vested interest in the business enterprises. They would become wealthy men if the Weymouth holdings remained profitable.

He had assigned Sebastian to help out Andrew, but meant to use him as a roving manager, someone reliable to help him out or Nathan whenever there was a need. Right now, the most urgent need was those warehouses.

The rain stopped by suppertime and the sun came out for the few hours remaining before nightfall. He and his cousins had done a solid day's work and would resume tomorrow, for there remained the stud farm, the financial investments, and the London properties to discuss.

He made clear all final decisions would be his, and his cousins voiced no objections. After all, not only was he the eldest among them, but he had run the Lothmere properties for several years before his father passed, and these ducal properties for several months, even though he had only inherited the title a short while ago.

None of the cousins had his experience.

Still, Trajan wanted their opinions regarding these holdings. Even if he did not always take their advice, it was good practice for them to learn how to analyze what new businesses to acquire, if any, which of the less profitable assets to sell off, and how to respond to unexpected setbacks with efficiency.

"Lord, I'm stiff," Andrew muttered, arching his back and groaning.

The others agreed and similarly stretched their muscles. So did Trajan, no doubt having a few more aching joints than his younger cousins.

Sitting at a desk for long hours was something he would have to get used to, because he would be inundated with reports and other matters that needed his attention on a daily basis.

Perhaps it was a good thing Florence had not leaped at the chance to marry him. Nor had she rejected him, so that was something. He knew she held him in deep affection, for she would have refused his proposal outright if she felt there was no chance for them.

But he had also noticed the way she looked at him and never hesitated to place her hand in his, as though craving his touch.

Also, she respected his advice, even if she had no intention of following it.

Perhaps she was falling in love with him.

He had to admit, it warmed his heart.

However, he would have little time for Florence over these next few months while he mastered his role as the new duke. For someone who had spent a lifetime ignored by her family, this could be a difficult thing for her.

Did she not deserve an attentive husband? This was what he wanted to be for her.

More important, he *needed* to be this for her, because he did not want her feeling their marriage had been a mistake…assuming there would ever be a marriage.

He still did not understand why he felt so comfortable with the notion of Florence as his wife. But both his mind and his heart were telling him this was right, so who was he to disagree?

"I'm famished," Sebastian remarked.

Nathan nodded. "Me too. What's for supper? Any idea, Trajan?"

Trajan shrugged. "No, but Mrs. Palmer is a good cook. Whatever it is will be delicious. I think Florence planned the menu."

"Uh oh," Andrew teased. "Is that good or bad?"

Trajan chuckled. "I guess we'll find out soon enough."

They marched out of the study and joined the ladies, who were now in the formal parlor. Hermia was at the small writing desk with quill pen in hand, having just finished a letter. He wondered whether she was reporting to Florence's parents or merely writing to a friend.

Florence was seated on the settee reading a book, but she set it aside and rose with a smile to greet him as he strode in.

"I'm sorry we took so long," he said. "There's still a lot for me to learn in managing the Weymouth properties, in addition to bringing my cousins into their roles. How did you spend your day?"

"Aunt Hermia and I managed to keep busy," she assured him. She was still smiling, which meant she was not at all put out by having to manage on her own on this rather foul day. "While my aunt worked on her embroidery, I asked Mrs. Albright to take me on a tour of the house, ending with the kitchen. I offered some suggestions for tonight's meal. I hope you don't mind."

He grinned and gave her cheek a light caress, for he was pleased she had taken an interest in the running of Gull Hall. "As long as it is edible, we'll have no complaints."

She blushed. "I think you will like it."

"Are you set for tomorrow's tea?" he asked.

Perhaps it was a good thing Florence would be hosting Lady Frampton tomorrow. This was a sensible way of gathering information, assuming Frampton's wife had any to give. But it also kept Florence occupied within the house while he was working with his cousins. The last thing he needed was for her to be running off while he was meeting with them and distracted.

He intended to greet Lady Frampton upon her arrival, of course. It would be rude not to introduce her to his family, as well. But then he meant to keep out of Florence's way and let her wheedle whatever information she could from the lady. He would figure out what to do about protecting Florence once she told him what she had learned.

Trajan walked into the dining room with the others and immediately noticed a subtle change. First of all, Florence had chosen to remove the extension leaves from the dining table that had been set up to easily seat forty. With the leaves out, it would hold no more than twelve comfortably. This was still more than they needed, but far cozier than before. Also, the Aubrey men were broad shouldered and could use the extra space.

He noticed the room was brighter, and it was not merely due to the presence of the ladies. He was not so besotted to attribute shining lights to Florence's mere presence.

But she had done *something*. More candles, perhaps? Wherever had she found the silver epergne now placed in the center of the table? That was it, the source of the additional illumination. The epergne was not merely decorative but also practical, since it had candlesticks at each end, where Florence had inserted tapered candles to brighten the table.

She had also cut scented herbs, along with some greenery and a few flowers from the conservatory garden, to give the table settings that extra touch of refinement and delicacy.

Who knew his fake bird watcher, this little sprite who had almost felled him when tumbling out of the tree, was so talented domestically?

"I like what you've done, Florence," he said, and smiled to show his appreciation.

She let out a breath. "Thank you. I hope you do not find it too much."

"Not at all. It's lovely, and far better than anything I could have done or ever would have thought to do. It is a touch of warmth. Perfect, in fact. I like it very much."

He seated Florence beside him while Andrew escorted Hermia to her chair.

"I have also made a small change to the menu that I hope you won't mind," Florence said, still smiling over his prior compliment.

"I'm sure none of us will mind at all." Trajan laughed. "I assure you, we Aubreys will eat anything that does not eat us first. What have you changed?"

"Well, I noticed that you particularly liked the mutton Cherish served at her house party last year, and—"

His eyes rounded in surprise. "You noticed that?"

She nodded. "You and I even spoke of it later that evening. In fact, you were raving about it. I liked it too. Cherish gave me the recipe, which I then gave to my family's cook, but..."

His heart sank when he saw the lovely glow on her face suddenly fade. "Your family did not like it."

He stated it as fact rather than as a question, because he was growing to understand how shamefully her family had treated her. If she were excited about something, they would go out of their way to squash the life out of it.

"We are all going to love it," Hermia said, giving her niece an encouraging nod.

Trajan silently vowed to lick his plate clean even if he despised the meal, which he knew would not happen. Florence had planned their menu with love, and this was what he was determined to give back to her by the bucketful.

The mutton was served after the soup course, along with roasted potatoes and leeks.

His cousins did not fail him, either. All three of them devoured their servings like starving wolves, as did he. No one spoke other than to toss compliments at Florence between mouthfuls.

"This is even better than I remembered it," Trajan declared, and motioned Edgar over to serve him more. "This is really, really good, Florence."

"I refined the recipe a little."

"Well done," he said, pausing a moment between bites.

"I hope you don't mind, but I had your staff test the recipe."

Trajan laughed. "You had it served for their supper? Good gracious, you will have my entire household staff in your thrall. No wonder Edgar is struggling to hold back a smile. How did you like it, Edgar?"

His capable footman let out a breath and broke into a satisfied grin. "Best meal I have ever tasted, Your Grace."

"And you, Alvin?" Trajan asked the other footman standing in attendance.

"Delicious, Your Grace. The staff is in raptures."

Andrew raised his glass of wine. "Three cheers for Florence!"

Everyone raised a glass and repeated the toast.

Florence's eyes turned watery, but she quickly dabbed them

with her table linen and smiled at all of them. "I'm glad you liked it."

"Liked it?" Sebastian said. "I am going to dream of sheep tonight instead of the buxom maid at Crawley's Tavern."

"I know the one you mean," Nathan replied, casting his brother a wicked grin.

"Gentlemen, there are ladies present," Trajan reminded them, although he did not think Florence or her aunt were in the least offended.

It truly hurt his heart to watch Florence absorb their dinner conversation like a little sponge. A joyful sponge. He had always thought her pretty, but she seemed radiant now. Approval and compliments were all new to her.

His cousins had eaten so many servings, they needed to be rolled away from the table.

Night had fallen by the time they all moved to the parlor for after-dinner drinks. Trajan took a moment to speak to Edgar and Alvin, who had slept most of the day and come on duty for their usual attendance at supper. But now they would take night watch again, and Trajan wanted to make certain they had everything they needed.

"Aye, Your Grace. We're set. Alvin and I will be guarding the house while Herbert patrols the grounds with Dodger," Edgar said, referring to his best bloodhound. "He and Dodger are already on the task. Figured he'd start as soon as the shadows began to creep across the garden."

"Wake me if you notice anything at all, even the smallest sense that anything is amiss."

"Aye, Your Grace," Edgar said, and left with Alvin to take up their guard posts.

Trajan joined the others in the parlor, still tense as he drank his port. But he knew his staff was up to the task of protecting Florence should Frampton decide to menace her again.

In all likelihood, Frampton only meant to have his ruffians show their faces from time to time as a reminder not to mess with him. After all, the man at Trajan's study window last night could have gotten off a shot and lost no more than one or two seconds in fleeing.

But he had just fled. No shot fired. So, either the pistol had jammed and he could not fire, or Frampton had given orders to scare them and nothing more.

Those orders might change after tomorrow, especially if Florence learned something of interest from Lady Frampton during her afternoon tea.

Since his mind had been on Frampton's next move and not the casual conversation going on between the ladies and his cousins, Trajan was surprised when everyone suddenly rose. "Where are you going?"

"Haven't you been paying attention? We're going to the music room," Andrew said. "Your lovely bride-to-be is about to give us a piano recital."

"And sing for us," Nathan cheerfully added.

Trajan groaned inwardly. This evening had gone smoothly, and he did not want it ruined by Florence's bad singing or playing. Not that he would ever insult her, nor would his cousins. But they were already marveling over her mealtime triumph, so why not leave it at that?

His cousins already approved of her joining the Aubrey family in marriage. There was nothing more she needed to do to win them over.

Florence poked him lightly in the ribs. "You are frowning, Trajan. Do you have no faith in my musical talent?"

He grimaced. "I am sure I am going to love your recital."

"Liar," she said with a soft laugh. "You have convinced yourself that someone as independent and obstinate as myself would never bother to learn the feminine arts."

Frankly, he did not care if she sang like a crow instead of a nightingale. He would be well satisfied so long as they were good together in bed, which they would be, because Florence had passion.

The only feminine art that concerned a man was the art of the bedroom. If a woman could please a man there, she would have him in the palm of her hand forever.

Florence, to his great relief, did not start her recital with one of those overly complicated and endlessly boring compositions that alternated between soft passages that had everyone straining their ears to hear, and loud, banging chords that had them stuffing handkerchiefs into their ears with all due haste. Instead, she led off with a lively country air that he and his cousins knew well because the song was popular in the taverns they frequented.

Not that he frequented such places all that often. But he and his cousins liked an entertaining night out whenever they got together. His cousins sang along with vigor.

Florence arched an eyebrow at him, an indication that he ought to join in.

Yes, he needed to get into the spirit of the evening. His voice wasn't so bad, either.

He saw the surprise on Florence's face when she heard him sing.

When the country lilt ended, he strode to the piano. "Play another one."

She chose a Scottish ballad, one of those plaintive tunes where everyone dies because the Scots never backed down from a fight no matter the hopeless odds, and they were always fighting because their irreverent nature always got them into trouble.

A hush fell over the room, and Trajan did not think anyone breathed while those dulcet notes sprang from Florence's lips.

She had not been jesting when she said she could sing. No high-pitched, operatic singing, either—her voice had a simple purity and clarity. The voice of an angel.

The cousins cheered her with shouts of "brava" as they shot to their feet and clapped.

Trajan was already on his feet, but it took him a moment to join in because he was that impressed by her talent.

Florence took everyone's compliments with humility.

"You were incredible," he whispered, and then kissed her on the cheek.

But he was still unsettled. Florence had behaved herself all day, shown herself to be thoughtful in presenting them with a meal they would remember, and then regaled them with an excellent concert that proved she was remarkably talented.

And yet her parents ignored her. They had never shown her any love or approval.

The brief conversations he'd had with Hermia revealed there was nothing in Florence's past that would have explained this.

If that were so, then the only explanation was the existence of an explosive family secret.

A girl with a heart so full of love should not have been shunned as Florence had been throughout her life.

What dark secret were her parents hiding from Florence?

CHAPTER EIGHT

Yesterday's rain was a thing of the past, and the sun shone brightly on Florence's face as Mrs. Albright came in to draw aside the drapes. "Ah, are you just waking up, lamb?"

"This bed is most comfortable," Florence said, stretching as she smiled. "I hardly did anything yesterday, and yet I slept as soundly as a log."

The hour was eight o'clock, and she had asked to be awakened no later, since she wanted to join Trajan for breakfast—and perhaps they might take a walk together before he disappeared into the study with his cousins.

"Is His Grace up yet?"

"Oh my, yes. Several hours already. He likes to go for a ride in the morning before it gets too hot. He's just back now and gone up to properly wash and dress. I'm sure he'll be down to breakfast within the half-hour."

"I'll join him there." She tossed off her covers and walked to the window to open it and peer out onto the day. "Oh, I love the scent of the sea," she said, inhaling. "And there's a lovely breeze today. Open the other windows, Mrs. Albright. I can smell the roses, too. Light and lemony to mix with the salt of the sea. It's simply wonderful."

The housekeeper smiled at her. "I think you are meant to be duchess here. His Grace must have sensed it, too. He's a clever fellow. I did not think anyone could be smarter than the old duke, his granduncle. But I think His Grace will be a match for him. And you will be a perfect match for our new duke."

"Oh, I think I have quite a way to go before I prove myself worthy."

"No, Lady Florence. You have already proven yourself to him and shown your fine qualities. This is why His Grace wishes to marry you. It is a love match and will bring much joy to this household."

"That is very kind of you to say, Mrs. Albright. I would hate to disappoint His Grace."

"You won't, lamb."

"Well, I will give him a fright if I come downstairs with my hair looking this wild. I may need help with it this morning."

"I'll send Jenny up to you. In fact, I'll assign her to be your lady's maid. She has a good sense of fashion."

"Unlike myself," Florence said with a light laugh. "I am truly hopeless when it comes to keeping up with the styles of the day."

"That is because you have more than frivolities on your mind. Clothes may be important when making a first impression, but they will not mask a meanness of spirit. It is what one wears in one's heart that matters."

"Very well said, Mrs. Albright." She liked this sensible woman who made the running of this house look easy, when Florence knew the task would have been too daunting for almost everyone else. The housekeeper was organized, efficient, and, perhaps most important, very good at anticipating whatever might be needed.

Mrs. Albright soon left, and it was not long before a young maid with a cheerful countenance popped in. "Good morning, Lady Florence. I'm Jenny."

"Good morning, Jenny. Your arrival is timely. I've just donned my gown and now I need my mop of hair done up properly."

"I'll do you up proper, never you worry," she said with a merry smile.

The pleasant girl grabbed Florence's hairbrush and began to

comb out her hair. Florence sat patiently, eager to see how the hairstyle would turn out, for the girl seemed to know what she was doing.

"Here, have a look in the mirror," Jenny said, turning her around.

Florence loved the elegant yet simple way Jenny had braided, twisted, and pinned back her hair, leaving a few soft curls to frame her face. "It is perfect. Thank you."

Jenny beamed. "My pleasure. His Grace won't be able to take his eyes off you at all today."

Florence laughed. "Oh, I think he'll manage. He still has a lot of work to get through with his cousins. I expect they will settle in the study again to slog through all the reports."

Jenny nodded. "Yes, it will have to be his study, since the library will need another day or two of sunlight to dry everything out before being usable again. It still has a musty smell. Not very pleasant."

Unfortunately, this meant Florence could not settle herself in one of the cozy library chairs and curl up there with a good book.

"Miss Florence, which gown should I set out for you for this afternoon's tea?"

In truth, Florence had not given it much thought. This was foolish of her, since she would need to dress elegantly to receive Lady Frampton. Unfortunately, she had brought only a few suitable gowns for such an occasion, since she had mostly planned to hike, climb trees, and sneak into Lord Frampton's home.

"This lavender silk will be perfect," Jenny suggested, drawing it out of her wardrobe. "But it is slightly wrinkled. Let me take it downstairs for you and freshen it up."

Florence thanked her and then made her way down to breakfast, suddenly wishing she had donned a prettier morning gown than this serviceable forest-green muslin that would blend in perfectly with the local foliage and make Trajan think she was going to climb trees again.

She had no intention of wandering far from the house today.

Why would she risk another dangerous encounter when Lady Frampton was coming to her?

She was pleased to find only Trajan at the dining table when she arrived. He was nursing his coffee while he read the morning paper, but set it down with a smile and rose to greet her. "Good morning, Florence. Did you sleep well?"

Oh, he looked so handsome in his casual attire, buff breeches, a shirt of whitest lawn, and a waistcoat of meadow green, a shade darker than his eyes. He wore no cravat or jacket, since the day would be hot and he would be sequestered for hours in the study with his cousins.

She smiled back at him. "Yes, I slept quite comfortably. It looks to be a perfect day."

He nodded. "There was a cool, dry breeze while I was out riding earlier. I didn't think to ask if you wished to join me. Will you forgive me? I just assumed you would decline, since you never joined us on our morning rides during the Bromleigh house party."

"Nothing to forgive. I'm not a very good rider," she admitted. "I could never have kept up with you."

"I wouldn't require you to do so. I could have slowed down for you. It's just a ride. I don't need to tear across the countryside. I'd enjoy your company tomorrow, if you are of a mind to join me."

She settled her in the chair beside his. "I would love to, but it will have to wait until my next visit. I haven't brought along my riding attire."

He cast her a wicked grin. "You could ride on my lap."

She laughed. "Are you serious? That would certainly raise eyebrows."

"Do you care?" His expression turned more sober. "I meant it when I said I was willing to marry you, Florence."

Since the footmen usually assigned to attend them at break-fast had been on guard duty throughout the night, they were not around to pour coffee or tea. Florence delayed having to respond to his remark by pretending her throat was as dry as the Sahara sands.

She rose hurriedly to pour a cup of tea for herself. As she stood by the buffet, she realized Trajan had purposely neglected to assign footmen to replace Edgar and Alvin on breakfast duty. And she, so eager to see him again this morning, had fallen right into his trap.

They were alone.

This now gave him the golden opportunity to ask her more of the difficult questions she did not wish to answer.

The salvers atop the buffet were filled with ham, eggs, kippers, and other items she could only guess at by the pleasant aromas that wafted toward her. She delayed responding to him by pretending to peruse the salvers and beginning to pile a little of everything onto her plate.

Where were his cousins? Why had they not come down to breakfast yet?

When she sat down again, she dug into her food with voracious zeal as another means to delay responding.

He sat with arms folded across his chest while watching her. "What are you afraid of, Florence? Besides choking on your food if you do not stop shoveling it into your mouth as though demons are going to catch you if you do not swallow it down fast enough?"

"It is delicious, and I am famished."

"You are avoiding having to talk to me. Never mind. Forget it."

She was grateful that he did not press her for an answer, although he hadn't really asked her anything in the form of a question. All he had done was make clear he was ready to marry her.

Was it not obvious she ached to marry him?

But how could she agree to it yet?

"Last night's supper was incredibly good," he said, folding up his paper and tossing it onto the empty chair beside his. "I wondered whether you would alter this morning's breakfast menu."

"I thought it better to take small steps and see if you liked the supper changes first, but I could mention it to Mrs. Palmer if there is something in particular you would like added to the morning fare."

"No, I'm satisfied with what there is. You really did a wonderful job with supper last night."

Warmth spread through her body, for she had not expected the sincerity of his compliment or ever expected any compliment at all. "Mrs. Palmer deserves the credit. I merely supervised the recipe."

"I liked all the little touches you added to the dining table, too."

"Truly? I did not think you had noticed."

"You ought to know by now that I notice everything. However, I would not have complained if you had left things as they were. It meant a lot to me that you did make these small changes. It showed that you were thinking of me and you cared. Your improvements are turning this house into a home."

She did care about him. Very much so, she realized.

And was it not an awful thing to care so deeply for him? How could she give her heart to him while she was in the midst of dealing with her most difficult assignment yet?

"Men are fairly simple creatures, Florence. When we have what we want, we do not stray. Give us good food, a bed, and a sweet, warm body beside us, a smiling face to greet us as we wake up to each new day, and we'll be content."

She pursed her lips in thought. "But so many men do stray. What makes you think you won't?"

"Because it is not in the Aubrey nature. No mistresses or affairs for us. We do not marry to turn our wives into housekeepers and go seek our comforts elsewhere. Being an Aubrey means coming home to our wives every night. I know this is not what most *ton* marriages are like. Most in the Upper Crust believe wealth and power are more important than a happy home life."

"I would bring very little wealth and no power whatsoever to our marriage," she said.

"Do you think I care? I want a love marriage such as my parents had. I think you and I can have this. After all, you are the one who made those subtle changes to our supper last night and reminded me just how important a good home life is to one's happiness. This is how I was raised and want my children to be raised."

"I like the stories you've told me about your father and mother."

His expression turned doting. "My father was a character, certainly not like the typical nobleman."

"Starting with the naming of his children—Trajan and Persephone. Your father was one to carve his own path and did not bend to *ton* rules or expectations. I admire that very much."

He nodded. "So do I, although I have no intention of saddling my children with such names."

Florence laughed. She was sorry never to have met the man before he passed. However, much of him was reflected in his son. The intelligence, the thoughtfulness, and the love of family.

Trajan's parents may not have started out as a love match, but his father obviously sensed it could turn into that and had done all in his power to make his wife fall in love with him. Florence thought this was wonderful.

She did not know if she could ever describe what her own parents had together as love. Her father did not stray. At least, not that she was ever aware. But neither did her parents ever show each other great affection.

And yet they were a cohesive unit when it came to elevating her brother and casting her aside.

Trajan put his hand over hers to regain her attention. "You turned sad, Florence."

She shook her head. "I got lost in my thoughts for a moment. You are awfully attentive to me this morning. I did not mean to interfere with your reading the newspaper."

"I'll read it later. You are not interfering. I like having you beside me."

"I like being here," she admitted.

"I am sometimes a growling bear in the morning, but I don't mind a bit of chatter most days. You caught me on a bad day yesterday, but that was because I was still overset about what had happened the day before."

"Any remaining soreness or bruises?"

"From your landing atop me?" He grinned. "No, I'm fine. You?"

"Not a scratch, and I will do my best to keep it that way," she added before he could chide her. "All is in readiness for Lady Frampton's arrival. Is there anything you would like me to ask her?"

"Something you have not already thought of? No." He took a sip of his coffee and then set down his cup. "I expect you have been doing nothing but thinking of questions for her."

"Yes, but mostly how to ask them within the flow of a conversation so that she does not grow suspicious of my true intentions."

He shook his head. "Florence, do you not think her husband will have warned her?"

"Well, yes, I'm sure he will have, but that cannot stop me from asking my questions. And I have considered something else."

"What is that?"

"What if she is not happy with what he is doing?"

His eyes widened. "Are you thinking to have her betray her husband?"

"It was just a thought, something to keep in the back of my mind. Of course, it will not work if she is just as ruthless as he is. But what if she is softhearted and cannot bear the way he is destroying other people?"

"Being softhearted is one thing. She would also have to be

exceptionally brave to ever dare defy him. It could be a death sentence for her. Have you thought of that?"

"Yes, but there are some risks that are worth taking."

"And some that are not. His downfall would also lead to her downfall. You are not only asking her to be brave but willing to destroy her own reputation and comfortable life, and for what? Your brother, who deserves the punishment he is about to get? Or some nameless man who was stupid enough to put his torrid extramarital thoughts in writing? Are either of these fellows worth the risk?"

Her heart sank, for he was right. Her mind was so clouded by her own need to save her brother, who was not worth saving in the first place, that she was not properly considering the danger to Lady Frampton. Of course, this assumed the lady would consider helping her get those letters back.

Nor were Florence's motives pious. She wanted to save her brother in order to shove her good deed in the faces of her parents. In her heart, she knew her mother would never love her. Nor would her brother ever show the least appreciation.

"Oh, Florence," Trajan said with an ache to his voice. "Are you going to cry?"

She nodded. "Everything you said is right. I have been so obsessed with my own desire to be appreciated by my family that I was blinded to everyone else I might hurt."

He placed his hand over hers. "Wanting to save your brother is a noble sacrifice."

"But my heart is not noble. I agreed to retrieving the letters because I wanted to show my family that I was the better person," she said with a shake of head, struggling to hold back her tears. "My foolish brother was the perfect foil, the perfect means to a selfish end. My motives were not honorable. He is a cruel and wretched person. I would be happy never to see him again."

She took out her handkerchief, as her tears now fell. "And what does this say about me? I am just as horrible as he is, not even thinking of the harm I might do to Lady Frampton if she were ever so kind as to help me."

"Come here, sweetheart." He drew her out of her chair and onto his lap, wrapping his arms around her. "See, I was going to get you onto my lap one way or another."

"Smartly done," she said, laughing between her tears.

She hugged him fiercely. He was proving to be her anchor upon the uncertain sea of her life.

"It is too late to rescind Lady Frampton's invitation to tea. But that's all it will be. I will not steer the conversation to those letters or tempt her in any way to betray her husband. If you plan to return to London shortly, then may I impose on you to allow my aunt and me to stay with you at Gull Hall and return to London with you?"

"It is no imposition. Stay as long as you wish. You know my feelings on the matter."

"I do." She nodded. "I thought you were a man I could love from the moment I met you. Now, I know it for certain. All the more reason to get the Frampton matter behind me before I dare move forward. Once back in London, I'll let the princess know the task was beyond my abilities and deal with the repercussions."

"I'll stand by you."

"No. Please don't. Let the brunt of her wrath fall upon me and only me. How angry can she be when I did not cause any of these problems? And what harm can she do to me when I have nothing to lose? No wealth of significance. No estates. Not even a parent or sibling who would ever stand up for me."

"She might confiscate your father's assets."

"I doubt she would ever go that far and risk word getting out about what she was doing—and why. It is the *why* of it that she doesn't dare reveal. Then everyone she was trying to save would be exposed. This might lead to Lord Frampton's downfall, but it would also blemish her reputation, and wouldn't this thrill the prince regent who already detests her? Imagine disliking your own wife to that extent."

"Unfortunately, these royals have no choice in whom they

marry. Perhaps we would all be better off if they did."

"Or worse off, perhaps. People in love do foolish things. Look at the damage those love letters might do to Lady Simmons and her unknown admirer."

Trajan took the handkerchief from her hands and gently dabbed at her tears. "Whatever happens, just know that I will be ready to catch you should you fall."

She kissed him on the cheek, inhaling the scent of lather on his freshly shaved skin. "I hope never to put you through another crash landing," she said with mirth.

She gave him another kiss on the cheek and rose to walk over to the window to peer out of it when she heard his cousins pounding down the stairs. After hastily drying her tears and hoping her eyes did not appear too watery, she turned to greet them.

They were a jovial threesome, and thankfully too hungry to do more than bid her and Trajan a good morning before grabbing their plates and noisily making their way from salver to salver, piling everything they saw onto them.

"Hey, leave a sausage for me," Sebastian griped when his brothers determined they should serve themselves in age order and shunted him to the back of the line.

When Trajan's cousins sat down and began to dig into their breakfasts, Florence returned to her seat and managed to eat a little more of her own. But the moment she set her fork down, Sebastian placed his over the remains on her plate. "You going to eat that sausage?"

She laughed. "No. Help yourself."

The three of them ate like wolves and exercised no table manners whatsoever. This delighted Florence, for it meant they considered her a part of their family.

She smiled at Trajan. He winked back at her.

This would be her life if she accepted his proposal.

She adored it.

After breakfast, Trajan delayed his meeting with his cousins for thirty minutes in order to spend a little time with her. They merely took a stroll through the garden, but he took her hand in his as they walked along, the gesture more intimate than walking arm in arm, and more proprietary.

It was a quiet but unmistakable statement that she was meant to be his.

But he wasn't demanding any decisions from her, merely showing her what they might have as husband and wife if she were to accept his proposal.

She would, in time.

Florence spent the rest of the morning in the ladies' parlor with her aunt, who was now dressed and had come downstairs to continue her embroidery while Florence read a book.

After a light midday meal, they retired to their bedchambers to prepare for tea with Lady Frampton.

Jenny came in to assist Florence in donning the lavender gown and freshening her hairstyle. Looking at her reflection in the mirror afterward, she thought she looked very much as a new duchess ought to look.

Was this how Trajan saw her?

When she returned to the parlor, she saw that Mrs. Albright had set out their tea service beautifully. The best china and silverware were used for this occasion, and the table had a lovely lace tablecloth with matching lace table linens. Tarts, cakes, and buttered breads, some with cucumbers and some without, were just being brought in on tiered dishes that were also of the finest porcelain.

"Thank you, Mrs. Albright. It is a lovely display."

The housekeeper smiled and nodded. "One of the footmen will serve the tea once Lady Frampton arrives."

Trajan and his cousins stepped out of his study when Timmons informed them that a carriage was approaching. Florence happened to step out of the ladies' parlor at the same time, eager for what this afternoon visit would reveal.

Sebastian whistled at her. The others grinned.

Trajan bowed over her hand. "You look lovely, Florence. These lighter colors become you."

"The bees would attack me if I ever dared go bird watching in these softer colors," she said, blushing as she glanced at her lavender gown. "They would mistake me for a flower and…" She meant to add "and pollinate me," but that sounded too lewd, so she said, "and sting me."

Lady Frampton descended her carriage followed by her maid, who looked quite a surly thing, while her mistress was all smiles.

Florence was not certain what she had expected Frampton's wife to look like, but it certainly was not this delicate woman who appeared to be in her mid-thirties and had the kindest eyes and warmest smile for her.

Her maid was completely the opposite in character—cold, hard, and seeming to be in charge even as she took a position in the corner of the room as any subservient companion would. Some maids had the ability to blend into the furniture and be forgotten, but not this one. There was such a disquieting hardness about her that immediately caught Florence's attention and held it throughout.

She had no doubt Lady Frampton's companion was more of a guard rather than a servant or companion, which meant every word spoken would be reported to Lord Frampton.

For this reason, Florence was glad when Aunt Hermia took the lead in their conversation, which resulted in a twenty-minute discussion of embroidery patterns and which shops sold the best threads and yarns that left Florence numbingly bored and probably did the same to the maid watchdog.

That boring conversation was followed by another one, a yawn-inducing discussion on the various teas available in England, which London shops carried the best ones, and which were their favorite blends.

Only after the topic of tea varieties had been wrung dry did they move on to discussing the latest *ton* scandals.

The maid's ears instantly perked.

Having been made to see sense by Trajan, Florence was going to give up this love-letters quest. She meant to steer the conversation away from any mention of Lady Simmons or government leaders, but her aunt inadvertently brought up the very thing she had hoped to avoid.

"I hear Lady Simmons has taken on a new lover," Aunt Hermia said with gossiping glee. "Poor Lord Simmons. I wonder whether her antics will cost him politically."

Lady Frampton paled. "Oh? I hadn't heard. In truth, I pay little attention to political intrigues. It seems such a dirty business."

"I agree, quite low and dirty. Nor do I care for it," Florence said. "But I am curious to learn more about the upcoming crop of debutantes. I hear the Earl of Mowbry's daughter is quite the beauty."

Lady Frampton let out a breath and smiled. "Oh, yes. She is quite pretty, and kindhearted, too. Those traits rarely go together in one of her station. Beauty often seems to walk hand in hand with vanity, don't you think?"

Florence nodded. "Yes. Too often these girls are taught that their good looks will grant them all the entitlements one can offer. There is never any stress on independent thinking or consideration of the feelings of others."

Lady Frampton set down her teacup and took Florence's hands in hers. "I think we are of one mind, Lady Florence. I am so looking forward to your marrying the Duke of Weymouth and settling here permanently. We shall become fast friends, I think. Would you and your aunt be available this Thursday? I would love to have you over for tea at my home."

Florence ought to have refused, for after this morning's conversation with Trajan about the dangers of involving Lady Frampton in her intrigue, she had decided to drop the matter of retrieving those letters.

But this was about a desperately lonely woman reaching out for friendship, and she understood this feeling quite well. Having been raised unloved, she could not leave Lady Frampton stranded. "We would love it. Is that not so, Aunt Hermia?"

They spent the remaining time with Florence taking Lady Frampton on a tour of Gull Hall's main rooms, ending with a brief sojourn into Trajan's study, where he and his cousins were hard at work. The men set their papers aside to engage them for several minutes before resuming their tasks.

Next, it was on to the garden for a quick turn about the flower beds. It turned out Lady Frampton was an avid gardener and had cultivated some prize roses. "I hope to enter my cinnabar rose in next year's flower competition at the Weymouth Fair. Most fairgoers are drawn to the pie competitions, and the local farmers love the hog competitions, but we have a small circle of horticultural enthusiasts in Weymouth, and it would be quite an honor to win the garden award for the best rose."

"Does your husband share your love of flowers?" Florence asked.

"Him?" Lady Frampton gave a curt laugh. "He would sooner tread on them."

"Oh, I see. But do tell me more about your rose cuttings. I would love to have some for Gull Hall's garden."

The afternoon turned out to be surprisingly enjoyable. Florence sincerely liked Lady Frampton.

They addressed each other by their given names when it came time to say farewell. "The afternoon was delightful," Lady Frampton said before climbing into her waiting carriage. "I'll set aside some of those flower cuttings we spoke about and give them to you when I see you on Thursday, Florence. Thank you again for a lovely afternoon."

"My pleasure, Sylvia. I look forward to seeing you and learning more about your prize flowers."

As Florence bussed Lady Frampton's cheek, the lady whispered, "And there'll be a little something extra for you within the carton of cuttings. I dare not say more."

Florence smiled and moved away as though nothing had

been said, but her heart was beating frantically.

Was Frampton's wife referring to those love letters taken from Lady Simmons?

There were hugs and cheeks bussed all around, for Hermia was not to be excluded. The icy maid took it all in without the glimmer of a smile.

Florence and Hermia stood on the front steps waving good-bye until the Frampton carriage was out of sight. Hermia tucked her arm in Florence's as they made their way back into the house. "That is one sad and lonely woman."

Florence nodded. "I wonder if she has any family close by. I ought to have asked."

Hermia nodded. "Nor did I think to ask, but we can pursue that conversation on Thursday. Perhaps once we are settled here, we can form an embroidery circle. Invite ladies from local leading families to join us once a week for tea and stitches."

Florence's heart warmed. "Yes, that is a wonderful idea. Does this mean you would stay on with me if I married the Duke of Weymouth?"

"If?" Hermia frowned. "Is there a possibility you *wouldn't* marry that gorgeous man?"

"Well, we've made no firm plans yet. No wedding date set. He may decide he does not want to marry *me*."

"Nonsense, child." Hermia paused as they were about to enter the house. "I have never seen two people look at each other with so much love in their eyes."

"Oh, Aunt Hermia. No, that cannot be right."

"Why?"

"We hardly know each other."

"Have you not known him an entire year?"

Florence nodded. "Yes, but..." She could not reveal the extent of their farce. "How can anyone know for certain how suitable one is for another until they live together day in and day out for an extended period of time? Weather all seasons? Stand together through hardships and joys?"

"Florence, sometimes you think too much about things," Hermia said with a shake of her head that made the fat curls about her ears bob and sway. "All I am saying is that you and Weymouth are off to a very strong start. You each have moonlight in your eyes when you look at each other."

"All right, I will accept that."

Florence walked in smiling and eager to talk to Trajan about Lady Frampton's visit.

When Hermia went up to her bedchamber, Florence decided to knock at the study door. She only meant to ask him when might be a good time for them to chat, but he surprised her by setting aside his work and dismissing his cousins. "We've done enough. Go off and enjoy what remains of the day."

His cousins cheered and immediately decided to ride to Weymouth.

"Don't wait up for us," Nathan said, tossing Trajan a wicked grin.

"Stay out of trouble," he shot back as they thundered off with all the grace of a herd of rampaging elephants.

Florence laughed.

Trajan shrugged his shoulders. "Looks like it is just you and me now."

"Do you mind?"

"No. I've been looking forward to it all day." He came around to her side. "Care for a lemonade on the terrace?"

"I'd love it. A lemonade and a chat?"

He nodded. "Yes, I am eager to hear how your tea with Lady Frampton went. You look as though you are leaping out of your skin to tell me."

Florence nodded. "I am."

"Oh, hell. She told you something, didn't she?"

"Yes."

"And you are going to do something about it, aren't you?"

Florence nodded again.

How could she not when Lady Frampton was taking this big risk upon herself?

CHAPTER NINE

"I NEED YOUR opinion. I'm not sure what to do."

Trajan pursed his lips as he sat beside Florence in a shaded arbor on the terrace, both of them sipping lemonade while she related in detail all that was said during her tea with Lady Frampton.

He was pleased she trusted him enough to confide in him, and this gave him reason to quietly cheer and put him in good humor, since the hot day and weight of his work had dampened his spirit.

It did not help that he had also worried about Florence the entire time.

He eased back in his chair and stretched his legs before him as a light breeze blew off the water, offering some relief from the sweltering heat. But it was not nearly enough to cool him down after all those hours spent confined in the study with his cousins, his sleeves rolled up and his shirt collar unbuttoned. He ought to have made himself more presentable.

But Florence did not seem to mind his informality, so he remained as he was and simply sat back in comfort. "So far, you've told me about embroidery and tea blends. What is the real heart of concern that has you seeking my opinion about Lady Frampton's visit?"

She leaned forward, her voice softening to a whisper. "She said that she was going to give me some rose cuttings for your gardener."

"So?"

"Then she whispered that she will have something else for me within the carton of cuttings. I think she was referring to those letters she stole from Lady Simmons. Oh, Trajan, now that I have met her, I am truly worried for her. I had not expected Lady Frampton to be as nice as she was. Well, I had no idea what to expect. It was awful of me not to give this any consideration at all until today. My mind was so fixed on my task, I did not regard her as a person with a heart or feelings, just someone to manipulate into giving me back those letters."

"And now you think she is going to turn them over to you because of what she said?"

"It was more in the way she looked around furtively before she whispered in my ear, making certain that ogre of a watchdog did not overhear. Why take that precaution if it were not about those letters? Which leads to another problem."

"What is this new concern?" he asked, although he was fairly certain he understood where this was going.

"If I am right and she does turn them over to me, then her husband is going to notice them missing and might blame her. What if he hurts her? How can I let this happen?"

"You cannot control every potential situation. It is quite possible he will never suspect her. After all, she did his bidding when stealing those letters. I only spent a few minutes greeting her, but she did not appear to be the sort ever to defy him."

Florence let out a breath. "She seemed awfully sweet and kind in my opinion, too. But there must be a measure of spine in her, because that so-called maid watches her like a hawk. Why would he assign that humorless woman to his wife if he weren't concerned about her loyalty?"

Trajan would have grinned at the remark if it weren't for the seriousness of the situation. "Oh, I expect his concern was more about you. He had to be wary of the young lady he knows was spying on him from the shelter of the woods. He realizes you are too independent and likely to do something reckless, such as stealing back those letters."

"How could he think I would when he does not know me at all?"

"His nature is to be distrustful, especially of pretty, green-eyed strangers who climb trees to peek into his home with their binoculars."

"He cannot be sure it was me," she grumbled. "But that watchdog had her eyes on Lady Frampton as much as she had them on me. She was there mostly to keep tight control on his wife. I'm certain of it." Florence sighed. "I would suffocate if forced to live like that. Perhaps this is why she wants to help me. She would gain a measure of freedom for herself if he were brought to justice."

"Florence, tread carefully. We have no idea what goes on between the Framptons. Do not read too much into her words."

"How can I not? It is the whispers and furtive glances, you see. She must have heard her husband talking about those letters and knows he will try to stop me from getting them."

He frowned. "So, now you are back on this mad quest to steal the letters?"

"I would be reclaiming them. It isn't the same as stealing. But I don't know what I should do. This is why I am trying to talk it through with you. I trust your judgment."

He was pleased she thought highly enough of him to ask his opinion, even though he was not happy about this situation.

"I tried my best to avoid any mention of Lord Simmons or his wife, or politics, during the tea, but Hermia unwittingly brought up the latest affair Lady Simmons is having. You should have seen the look on that maid when their names were brought up. She is such a mean-looking thing."

"Well, it is obvious she was not here as an amiable companion."

"I'm sure she was listening in on everything we said and will report our conversations *verbatim* to Lord Frampton."

"But you kept the conversations innocent, so what harm will be done when she does report to him?"

"None, I suppose." She took a sip of her lemonade, staring into the glass a moment before she looked at him again. "But the fact remains, Lady Frampton might give me those letters, and now I must do something to protect her."

Trajan's tension had been increasing throughout their conversation because Florence was once again proposing to leap into danger, and this meant he would be dragged in, too. "You cannot save everyone."

She cast him a big-eyed, defiant look. "Why not?"

This was what he loved about Florence—and why she also infuriated him. She felt a passionate need to do good. He expected that passion would also translate into enjoyment in the bedchamber, but right now it was going to lead her straight into danger.

How was he to protect her when she was determined to be everyone's hero? Could she not simply choose one, her brother or Lady Frampton, to save? Let the other fend for himself or herself. Saving Lady Frampton would be simplest, for all Florence would need to do was whisper a warning in her ear to do nothing about those letters. There. Done. Nothing taken from Lord Frampton. No suspicion on Lady Frampton.

However, that would not save her brother.

Trajan knew Florence was not going to take that route because she so desperately wanted her family to take notice of her.

"Frampton's wife is no thief," she continued, and he could see the thoughts continuing to whirl in her agile brain. "That her husband forced her to steal the letters does not sit well with her at all. I will ask her to tell me where he hid those letters, then I can create some sort of diversion to make it look as though I stole them while she had us over for tea."

Trajan groaned. "So he can hunt you down and shoot you? Think again. I wish you hadn't accepted her invitation. You could have held her off and then come up with an excuse to decline."

"But I wanted to see her again, and she wanted the same, obviously. She's so lonely and afraid. How can I abandon her? Help me out here, Trajan. She's going to have the Frampton gardener prepare those rose cuttings and give them over to me when I see her on Thursday. I am certain those letters will be hidden in there."

"Bloody blazes," he muttered, knowing this could not possibly end well.

"Frampton has to be made to believe the letters she is going to hide in those cuttings were stolen by someone other than her."

"Namely you?" He leaned forward, their faces closer. "No."

She studied his expression, now confused. "What do you mean by 'no'?"

"How is 'no' not clear enough for you? Her husband is already itching to shoot you, and I am not going to let you give him a reason. Besides, you are going about this all wrong."

She perked. "How am I wrong? Oh, Trajan. Wait…have you come up with a brilliant idea? You have! I can see it in your eyes."

"I don't know how brilliant a plan it is, but I think it is better than anything else proposed."

She inched forward to the edge of her chair. "All right, out with it. I am listening."

"It isn't a question of who to blame for the theft."

She stared at him. "It isn't?"

"No. What will keep you and Lady Frampton safe is his believing those letters have not been stolen at all."

Her eyes widened. "A crime no one knows has been committed?"

"Precisely."

"Trajan, that is genius! But how are we to pull it off?"

"I'm not sure yet. This is what you and I must work out."

"Us? Together?" She nodded enthusiastically. "Truly, you are the smartest man I have ever met. It is such a delight talking things over with you."

He groaned. "We haven't worked out any details yet."

"It doesn't matter. I'm sure we will, and it will be perfect and excellent because you are perfect and excellent. I think you are not only the smartest man in all of England but the handsomest, too."

He shook his head and laughed. "Save your flattery for after we pull off this idiotic scheme. Gad, I cannot believe you are sucking me into this."

She cast him a doe-eyed look of innocence. "I want you to know right now how grateful I am to you. And it is not an idiotic scheme. It is *brilliant*. I happened to read a book like that once. The perfect murder. Everyone believed the victim had died of natural causes and the villain got away with the crime. He wound up with the money and the love interest, and they lived happily ever after. Utterly immoral, but fascinating reading. So, how do we get away with the theft?"

"Our first step is to duplicate that packet of letters."

"Duplicate them?" Her eyes lit up. "Oh, you are so very clever! I should have thought of this. What an idiot I am! But you are so logical and sensible."

"Stop with the flattery, Florence. I'm helping you, aren't I? I do not need more coaxing."

"It isn't coaxing. May I not be honest with you and express my complete and utter admiration of your abilities?"

Were the choice left to him, he would appreciate her enthusiasm more in the bedchamber. Remarks in awe of his powers of seduction would be welcomed.

Ooh, Trajan. My big, strong stallion.

He cleared his throat, for this was neither the time nor place for those wayward thoughts. "Lady Simmons gave you a good description of those letters, did she not? I don't mean what was in them, but what the packet looked like. Size, color of parchment, how they were bound."

"Yes!" she said with obvious pride. "I insisted she provide me detailed specifications. After all, it would be disastrous if I retrieved the wrong packet. For this reason, I insisted on actual samples of the parchment used and the silk ribbon with which she tied the letters."

"You have those?"

She nodded.

Gad, she was an efficient little thing. Quite organized and resourceful.

"Well done. Now we'll know exactly what we must look for. It was clever of you to demand those samples."

"Thank you." Her smile was beaming. "Despite what you think, I am good at what I do. But you have taken this a brilliant step further."

He gave her pert nose a light tweak. "Do not get too excited about this plan. It won't be easy to pull it off. However, first thing tomorrow, we are going to take a trip into Weymouth."

"To find a match for the parchment and ribbon?"

He nodded. "As the new duke, it is expected that I should have my own stationery made up. Calling cards, too."

She smiled at him. "Absolutely."

He leaned forward and took her hand. "Since you are to be my wife, we'll need to order some for you, as well. And perhaps acquire some for Hermia. Then this besotted duke is going to purchase some pretty ribbons for his soon-to-be wife and her aunt."

"And no suspicions raised because every new duke requires his own letter paper." Florence cast him another smile that was bright as a beacon. "Trajan, I shall say it again—you are the cleverest man I have ever met. Oh, I wish I had thought of this first. But no matter, it is a most promising plan, and you deserve all the credit for it."

"These are just the first small steps," he cautioned her.

"We should be able to find the exact parchment and ribbon we need. I think this will be the easiest part of the plan."

"I hope we can, or we are finished before ever having started."

"We will find the perfect match. I'll bring along my samples," she said with confidence. "In truth, we only need to find close enough matches to fool Lord Frampton's eye. But finding the exact match is best."

"Assuming we do find what we need, the next step is to duplicate the look of those purloined letters. Do you have any idea how many letters that lovelorn idiot sent?"

"Eight letters in all. I questioned Lady Simmons on this because even one letter left behind would be damaging and entirely defeat the purpose of my work."

"You'll have to write something in each fake letter before we bundle them up. Frampton might notice if they were left entirely blank," he suggested.

"Hermia and I can attend to this."

"Good, but the hardest part comes next. Lady Frampton must somehow switch these fakes with the originals."

"Or I can do it, assuming she will tell me where he kept them hidden."

"Oh, gad. Florence, that is out of the question. No."

"But her surly maid will be watching her too closely."

"And you think that woman will not notice you suddenly disappearing for twenty minutes? Or others on his staff won't notice you popping your head into every room? Do you think he is just going to leave those letters sitting atop his desk?"

"No, I know he has them securely hidden."

"Bloody right," Trajan muttered. "He'll have them under lock and key, or in a guarded safe. Even if the safe is unguarded, you wouldn't be able to open it without the combination. Do you think he will leave those numbers conveniently written down for you to find?"

"Of course not. But if I cannot do it, then who will make the switch?"

"Lady Frampton is the one who must take the risk."

"While I create a distraction?"

"I am certain you are quite proficient in that," he teased. "You are the most distracting young lady I have ever met."

"Is that a compliment or an insult?"

He shook his head. "Frankly, I don't know. But the point is, no one must ever realize the switch has taken place. I think Lady Frampton must know the combination to the safe, assuming the letters are hidden there. Or she will have the key to any locked drawer or strong box. How else would she be confident enough to get them to you in that carton of cuttings?"

"True."

"So, she has to be the one to switch those letters. She will be safe enough because no one will think twice if they see her in any particular room of her own house."

She nodded.

"And one more thing, Florence."

"Yes?"

"Before you undertake anything, you must be sure that gift she has hidden within the rose cuttings is that packet of letters and not some damn tin of biscuits."

Her eyes rounded in surprise. She looked so pretty while listening to him with rapt attention. While he hated her involvement in this affair, he very much liked this rapport they had with each other.

"*Ugh*. It won't be a tin of biscuits. The greater concern is keeping Lord Frampton from opening any of the fake letters, or he will know at once they have been switched."

"I don't think this is in his nature. He'll see the letters wrapped in pink ribbon and leave it at that. He may not realize he has been duped for days, weeks. Even months from now. Perhaps never."

"Because we have pulled off the perfect crime," she said in a reverent whisper.

Bloody blazes.

Could this possibly work?

He hated this entire business, but Florence was going to do this with or without him. Better that she do it with him.

"I shall howl at the moon with joy if we can pull it off," she said, now smirking. "And won't he be surprised when the Princess of Wales and her allies slam him to the ground and threaten *him* for all his misdeeds? Hah! I'm sure he will not like that turnabout at all."

Trajan lolled his head back and sighed. "Do not get ahead of yourself. There are so many variables to be considered."

"Such as?"

"Will Lady Frampton have taken the original packet and hidden it in the cuttings *before* the tea starts? Or is she thinking to do it *while* the tea is in progress?"

"Does it really matter? We just have to figure out how to plant the fake packet in her husband's hiding spot before he notices they were ever gone."

"He will have his guards on high alert and watching for anything suspicious. If he has even an inkling that something is going on, all hell will break loose. If he searches you, then you had better not have the originals or the fakes on you."

"He would not dare search my person."

Trajan raked a hand through his hair. "Are you serious? That man has no scruples. He will use physical force on you if he thinks you have thwarted him."

"Are you sure about this? After all, I am betrothed to a duke and will not be shy about reminding him of it. That ought to give him pause."

How could she be so clever and naïve at the same time?

"Let me be clear about this," he said with a soft growl. "At *no* time are you ever to have those letters in your possession."

"Not even the fake packet? But that is impossible. How am I to plant them, or give them to Lady Frampton to plant, if I don't have them?"

"You are *not* the one to do it. You'll have to rely on Hermia."

"My aunt?" She stared at him in surprise. "But how? She is not nimble. She might not even remember what to do. What if she panics? Or simply forgets and says something she shouldn't."

Trajan did not think Hermia would falter. That dithering,

dotty-aunt routine was just a façade, or so he hoped. But he was rarely wrong about the nature of people. Hermia may be slower in the gait, but she was as clever as Florence.

Gad.

Why did he have to be worrying about any of it? Florence had been ready to give up her mission until Lady Frampton and her whispered words put her right back on the scent.

"I mean it. You do it my way or I do not allow you to do anything at all."

"But this is my investigation," she said, sounding indignant.

"But you are my beloved."

Oh, bloody hell. He had meant to say *betrothed,* that she was his *betrothed.*

She stared at him open-mouthed. "Beloved?"

Why had he spilled his thoughts when it was the worst thing he could do to her at this moment? This was what Florence had always dreamed to be, someone adored and cherished. Loved and accepted. Appreciated instead of dismissed.

Beloved.

"Aren't we supposed to be a love match?" He gave a shrug, trying not to make too much of his slip, since he was not ready to spout any love declarations yet.

She would run roughshod over his heart if she knew. And he needed to maintain tight control over this Frampton situation, rein her in for her own protection. She was too adventurous and fearless for her own good.

"And have I not already suggested we marry?" he muttered.

"Yes, because you insisted it was the only way to protect me."

"That's right, and we have stayed in character, you and I. We've done a good job of convincing everyone the betrothal is real. Is this not how you wished to keep things between us? Pretense. No commitments."

"But you wanted more."

"Because I thought we could turn this betrothal into something more. But you obviously are not ready. You needed time. You wanted time. I am giving it to you."

He saw the light dim from her eyes as she said, "Yes, we agreed upon this." She turned away a moment, let out a heavy breath, and then turned back to him after swallowing her disappointment. "We ought to have two identical fake packets."

Ah, she was back to the task. Obviously still hurt, but she was the one not ready to commit to marriage.

She could change it all with a word. He wasn't going to do it for her. She had to take this first step on her own.

This was cruel of him, perhaps. He could have just told her that he loved her. It might have changed things for her.

Or just bogged down matters without solving anything.

"Two packets? Why?" he asked.

"It is always good form to have a spare. But if you think I am going to involve Hermia without being certain she can handle the responsibility, then you can forget your idea."

"She can handle it. I think she is a master at distraction and creating illusions. She even has you fooled, hasn't she?"

"What do you mean?"

"You'll see. It is time we let Hermia in on all that has been going on."

Florence cast him a worried look. "Must we tell her everything?"

"Yes. What you are doing is dangerous. She cannot walk into the lion's den and not know the lion is watching you both and waiting to pounce. But I'll do my best to protect you."

"How? You cannot join us for tea."

"I can peer into the parlor, can I not? Weren't you doing just that when I found you stuck in the tree? Although you had your binoculars trained on his bedchamber. Did you think the letters were in there?"

"It was a possibility, but I believe he has them in a safe in his study."

"Perhaps Lady Frampton can confirm this."

She nodded. "I'll try to get as much information out of her as I can."

"Be careful when you do. Her ogress maid will be listening in.

Take no risks."

"So you've told me at least three times during this conversation."

"Because what you are doing is risky, and I honestly hate this, Florence. How can I make you stop?"

"You cannot, so do not bother to try. But can you imagine if after all our plots and contortions, all Lady Frampton ever thought to give me in those rose cuttings was a tin of biscuits?"

"Hilarious," he said with obvious sarcasm.

"Perhaps I'll have Mrs. Palmer bake some biscuits and bring a tin of them to Lady Frampton."

"Now you are just riling me."

"Sorry. I couldn't resist. All right. No more teasing you. Just business. Do you know that you look irresistibly attractive when you are serious, and even more so when you are irate and frowning?"

"Florence…"

She sighed. "The duplicate packets. An ingenious switch. And Aunt Hermia to create a distraction if one proves necessary. Satisfied?"

He glanced up at the heavens. "Let's pray this plan works."

She had leaned forward again and was now practically tipping out of her chair. "You are so very clever, Trajan. I cannot thank you enough for all you are doing for me."

Blessed saints. "Enough with the compliments. I will not be happy about this, no matter how much you think to soften me up."

She would not think he was so smart if he got her killed.

He pointed to her empty glass. "Care for another lemonade?"

"Yes, I would love one," she said, smiling at him. "Shall we toast to our success?"

Gad, she was going to be the death of him.

He poured another for each of them, and then drained his lemonade in two gulps and set the glass down on the table. "Florence…"

"This will work," she insisted. "Frampton will never suspect the letters have been taken."

"Let's hope, because he will come after you with a vengeance if this plan goes awry."

"That's a risk I am willing to take," she said with resolve.

"But one I am not. I'll see him burn in hell if he ever tries to harm you." He drew her onto his lap and placed his arms around her because he needed to hold on to her and inhale the light lavender scent of her skin.

He ached to protect her.

"Why did you pull me onto your lap?" But she did not seem to mind, and wrapped her arms around his neck.

"Don't mind me. I'm just behaving like a protective arse."

She leaned her head against his shoulder. "I like those protective instincts of yours. Even if I am not your beloved."

Ah, his remark still hurt.

"You could be in time," he said, sincerely wishing to repair the damage. "But you are a lot to handle at the moment."

"I know. I'm sorry."

"Not your fault. It's just these rotten circumstances."

"Yes, they are quite awful. I do not mean to be so difficult, but my heart really is in pieces, and I need to heal it as best as I can."

"By saving your brother?"

Her eyes began to tear.

"Don't, love. Don't cry." Because his heart was defenseless against her vulnerability, and she was incredibly vulnerable right now.

"I can't help it." She pressed against him.

He felt a shiver run through her, so he wrapped her more securely in his arms. "Florence, love. Look at me."

"Why?" But she did look up and gaze into his eyes.

"This might help," he whispered, and crushed his mouth down on her pert lips, for who knew what tomorrow would bring?

CHAPTER TEN

T RAJAN KNEW FLORENCE had been aching for this kiss, too.

She melted into him, her arms flung around his neck and holding on to him as though she might drown if she ever let go.

He was her steadying anchor. "Trajan…"

"I know, love." He pressed his lips to hers with greater urgency, parting them to delve deeper into the minty velvet of her mouth.

She moaned at the first touch of his tongue to hers, and invited more.

Fire tore through him as she urged him to expand his exploration.

And he did so.

There was something glorious about her body. The way she felt in his arms.

He wanted to ravage her. He wanted to protect her.

He wanted *her*.

In this moment, in this kiss, everything felt perfect.

A gentle breeze surrounded them and lightly tossed her dark curls. A shaded arbor protected them from the heat of the sun and the sight of those indoors. He breathed in the lavender scent of her skin.

He could kiss her and inhale her forever.

Yes, she was perfect.

Even her breasts were just the right plumpness against his chest. Her bottom was just the right amount of pertness. He felt her every wriggle as she squirmed against his thighs.

Yes, they would be good together in bed.

He needed to marry Florence.

By the heat of her response, he knew she would give herself to him this very night if he asked. She was so hungry for love and to be loved.

So was he. For her.

Only for her.

It saddened him that she had never been properly courted. His loveable, fake bird watcher deserved better than a stolen kiss or two in an arbor, did she not?

He could court her after their marriage, perhaps. It might be perceived as unusual. But everything about Florence was unusual, so why not? He meant to marry her as soon as this Frampton affair was over and done.

Mine, Florence. You are mine.

She was the first to ease away from their blistering kiss, laughing lightly while catching her breath. "Oh my. That was…"

He arched an eyebrow. "Unexpected?"

"Yes." Her expression softened and her eyes held the loveliest glow. "And wonderful. I could kiss you forever."

He gave her cheek a gentle caress. "Mutual, Florence."

"But I think we chased poor Timmons away. He was about to step onto the terrace with a tray in hand when you suddenly swept me up in your arms and kissed me into eternity. He sprang away like a mountain goat being chased by a leopard."

Trajan laughed. "He knows I am going to marry you. No harm done, unless you still think marrying me is a bad idea."

"No, it was always an excellent idea. There was never a doubt in my mind." She placed her hand over his heart. "Any reluctance on my part has to do with fear of *you* coming to harm. I am so sorry you were dragged into my problems."

He kissed her again, this one deep and gentle, but packing

more heat as his mouth moved over hers in a slow and sensual grind.

"Trajan, *dear heaven*," she whispered.

Her breathy moans undid him. He shuddered and drew his lips off hers before things went any further.

"That was nice. It felt awfully naughty, but very nice," she admitted, casting him a soft smile.

"Ah, Florence. You have no idea what *really naughty* feels like."

"Will you show me?"

"Yes," he said with a wicked arch of his eyebrow. "But not here and not now, or Timmons will have a seizure."

She grinned. "Oh dear. We must not have every vital organ in his body falling into spasms. Look, he's peering out the parlor window to see if we are still locking lips."

"Ah, and he's started toward us."

She darted off his lap. "Do not kiss me again or he'll run away."

"So what?"

"I am thirsty again."

So was he, but his thirst was for Florence.

The poor butler's face was a fiery red as he approached with a fresh pitcher of lemonade, set it down on the table, and then sprinted back into the house with a lively spring in his step to resume his post by the front door.

Trajan laughed. "Well, we made quite an impression on him."

Florence buried her head in her hands. "Oh, this is awful. Now he thinks I am a shameful wanton."

"No, love." He took her hands in his and had her look up at him. "Florence, this might scare you. It surely scares me. But it is very possible we have already fallen in love with each other. Not just on the way to it, but there."

"Do you think so? Is this why you mistakenly called me your beloved earlier?"

He nodded. "But it was no mistake."

"It felt nice, as though you really meant it. Why did you pretend it wasn't real? Oh, never mind. I know why. Because of this horrid Frampton affair. I cannot wait until it is over and done."

"Nor can I."

"About that…I will need to leave for London as soon as I get my hands on those letters."

"Agreed, but *we* will go together. There's no negotiation on this. You are not taking that trip alone."

"All right. In truth, I prefer to have you with me, since a woman alone would be an easy mark for every highwayman and cutpurse from here to London. We ought to travel on horseback, even though I am not a very good rider and will likely slow us down. But horses are still faster than taking a carriage, are they not?"

"Mail coaches are even faster."

"Oh, you've given our getaway plan some thought?"

He nodded. "If you manage to grab those letters, then we'll ride to Bournemouth and take the first mail coach to London from the coaching inn there."

"What of the horses?"

"I know a reliable stable owner. He'll hold them until one of my cousins rides over to pick them up."

"We have to worry about Frampton following us."

"Yes," he said. "I've thought of that, too."

"What's your plan?"

"Nothing complicated, but it will require the cooperation of Hermia, my cousins, and some of the Gull Hall staff. Most have been in service here for years under my granduncle and can be trusted to follow my instructions to the letter."

"Are you sure it isn't complicated?"

"Yes, I'm sure. We may need a decoy."

She cast him a questioning look. "What sort of decoy?"

"It ought to be simple enough for Timmons to make a show

of piling our trunks onto my ducal carriage. Perhaps have Andrew and one of the maids with similar height and hair coloring to you climb into the carriage with him."

"To what purpose?"

"Their destination will be Bath, where Lady Simmons is presently staying. She and her husband like to take the waters and mingle with others in the Upper Crust spending their summer there."

"How do you know this?"

"I believe I told you she was after me for a while, so I learned a few details about her husband's routine."

She frowned. "You mean you learned his schedule so you would know when he was not present and could conduct your assignations."

"She pursued me, not the other way around. But there were no assignations, I promise you. Besides, their current whereabouts were reported in one of the London rags."

"So, your carriage heads to Bath while we ride for London?"

"That's right. We'll be on horseback," he reminded her. "So we won't be able to bring much, only what can fit in our travel pouches. And once we have those infernal letters, we had better plan to leave before first light on the chance Frampton decides to put his men to watching Gull Hall."

"Sneaking out while it is still dark?"

He nodded.

"Frampton might not be on his guard if the fake letters switch works."

"That man is always on his guard," Trajan insisted. "But I don't think he realizes it is the Princess of Wales who put you onto this task. He'll think you are reporting to Lady Simmons, and this confusion will work to our advantage. If he sends men after us, hopefully they will ride for Bath and not realize we are making for London."

"And what if he is not fooled?"

Trajan laughed. "Then we will be in a heap of trouble, won't we?"

In truth, Frampton was not Trajan's only concern. The Princess of Wales might also cause problems, for these royals could be fickle or forgetful whenever it suited their purpose. He was going to stand beside Florence and make certain the princess lived up to her agreement.

He would not let anyone cheat Florence. For this reason, he needed to be with her at all times. If she fell, he had to be there to catch her.

But she could be thickheaded at times.

"If questioned by Frampton," she rattled on, "your cousins could—"

"Stop, Florence. I think you are giving me a blistering headache. Let me make this simple for you." He pointed to her. "You." And then pointed to himself. "Me."

"Yes?"

"Together. Always. *I* travel with you. *I* protect you. Whatever the ultimate plan, we stay together."

"Gad, you are such an ape." But she was smiling and casting him a moon-eyed look, so he took the remark as a compliment.

Another thought crossed Trajan's mind, one he knew she would resist. "We have not given enough consideration to the fact you may be walking into a trap and that Lady Frampton has fooled you into believing she is innocent and harmless."

Florence stared at him, miffed. "She is innocent. I saw it in her eyes."

He leaned forward and caressed her cheek. "And if you are wrong?"

"Then there will be nothing but rose cuttings in what she gives me, and that will be that."

"You had better be sure of this before you hand over the fake packet of letters."

"I know. I will do my best to be sure before I give her anything or ever say anything to her." She leaned back in her chair and closed her eyes a moment.

"What are you thinking now, Florence?"

She looked so pretty in the soft lavender gown and her hair drawn back to show off the delicate features of her face.

"I am thinking that I love this," she said with her eyes still closed. "Us. Sitting out here together and talking over problems."

Despite his concerns, he smiled. "Me too. We've tossed out a lot of possibilities. Let's set them aside for now, sleep on them, and let them sink into our heads. We can discuss the best ones while on tomorrow's ride to Weymouth."

She readily agreed. Yes, this matter of switching letters had both of them very much on edge.

"Hermia ought to join us tomorrow," he added.

"Oh, I don't think she will. It is too long a day out for her."

But when they mentioned Weymouth later that evening at the dinner table—just the three of them present because his cousins were still off doing whatever stupid things all young men did to slake their thirst for drink and women—Hermia clapped her hands. "I would love to join you! What fun!"

Trajan grinned at the shocked look on Florence's face. She was an incredibly pretty thing.

"Really, Aunt Hermia?"

"Yes, dear. I do still have a little life in me. Although I will admit that some of the spring has gone out of my step. Kindly do not place me in my burial tomb just yet."

"Aunt Hermia! I would never—"

"There, there, dear," she said, patting Florence's hand. "Do not get all worked up. I shall come with you, and that is that...and then you will tell me what nefarious deed you have been plotting. Oh, do not dare deny it, Florence. You are working on something that obviously involves the Framptons. I can be useful, you know. People think I am old and doddering, so they do not pay attention to what I am doing."

Florence stared at Trajan. He arched an eyebrow and calmly sipped his wine.

"Trajan," she prompted him, obviously looking for assistance.

He turned to her aunt. "Are you saying you play up your

feebleness? That you have been doing so all along and fooling even Florence?"

"Yes, dear boy." Hermia raised her glass of wine to him. "But you saw through my subterfuge, did you not? Very little escapes your notice."

He nodded.

"My mind happens to be as sharp as ever. But I find that I have grown quite impatient with age and easily tire of people. Have you noticed how dull so many of them are? Well, old age does have its advantages. Nobody questions you when you claim fatigue or start to dither. I have gotten out of many intensely boring family dinners and unwanted invitations that way."

Florence gasped. "What a consummate actress you are! You had me completely fooled."

"I know, and I am rather proud of it because you are quite a clever thing, too. But it seems even the sharpest of us are prone to seeing what we want to see." Hermia cast Florence a chiding look. "Is that not so?"

"What do you mean?"

"You tried to do the same to me, Florence. Wanting to trick me by pretending this dear boy had been courting you all year long when you probably met him just that morning. Shame on you, child."

Florence had the good grace to look remorseful. "I am truly sorry, Aunt Hermia. I did not mean to deceive you. But it wasn't a complete lie. Trajan and I did know each other. We met last year at the Bromleigh house party. I hadn't seen him until the other day when he brought me back to the Weymouth Inn."

Hermia smiled at Trajan. "Have you been in love with Florence since last year?"

He laughed. "I would describe my feelings at the time more as aggravation. Your niece can be quite infuriating. However, our being in love might prove to be real in time. It is too soon to tell."

"Oh, dear boy. Forgive me, but you are wrong. It is obvious to me that the two of you have that spark of magic, and this is a very rare thing."

"Why do you say that?" Florence asked, obviously surprised. "Trajan is right. He and I mostly found each other irritating. But I did think he was quite handsome and wondered whether we might meet again. I did not think I had made any impression on him at the time."

"But you had," Trajan assured her. "You were constantly in my thoughts."

She nodded. "I am finding this out now. I had no idea back then."

Hermia cleared her throat. "Then it is a good thing you two have met again. Now, let's get to the juicy bits. Why are we going to Weymouth? And what has this trip to do with the Framptons?"

Once again, Florence turned to Trajan. He caught her aunt up on all that had happened.

"Fascinating," Hermia said when he'd finished his report. They lingered at the dining table, finishing a lemon syllabub that had warmed and melted over the course of their conversation. "So, you think Lady Frampton is innocent in all this?"

"Well, she stole those papers from Lady Simmons," Florence remarked. "I'm sure her husband scared her into doing it. Did she look like a thief to you?"

Hermia pursed her lips. "No, but you are about to steal them back, and you do not look like a thief either."

"That is different," Florence grumbled.

"How so? Because you are doing it for a good cause? Lady Frampton may believe that advancing her husband's stature is also a good cause. I mean, Florence, you are not saving orphans here. You are reclaiming lurid love letters between a married lady and her lover, who is probably also married."

"I am doing it for the Princess of Wales...and Lady Simmons."

Hermia rolled her eyes. "You are doing it to save your worthless brother and hoping your parents will love you for it. He won't be saved and your parents won't love you."

Trajan knew he liked Hermia for a reason. Florence's aunt, now that she had set aside her dithering façade, was sharp as a tack and had a way of getting to the very heart of the matter.

But the matter of Florence's parents was a raw and gaping wound for her. He wished Hermia had shown a little more mercy toward her niece.

He reached over and took Florence's hand.

She cast him a wobbly smile. "I'm all right. Everything my aunt has said is true."

Yes, Hermia had said a mouthful about Florence's family situation. More important, she had been around long enough to know the true story behind her family's resentment of their own daughter.

While Hermia probed further into their plans for Frampton and those purloined letters, Trajan resolved to take her aside and ask her what she knew about Florence's history with her parents. Because there was something definitely off about their treatment of Florence.

She was bright and beautiful. And a girl like that should have her father's pride and her mother's warmth.

So, why did Florence's mother hate her?

CHAPTER ELEVEN

T RAJAN SPENT THE hour-long ride to Weymouth sitting across from Florence and wishing they were alone so he could kiss her.

But that was never going to happen while Hermia rode with them.

Florence did not even wish to sit beside him.

This was understandable, because he had broad shoulders and would take up most of the seat bench, while her aunt was the size of a pea and took up no space at all.

However, having to sit across from Florence and look upon her was not helping matters. She grew prettier by the day.

Her expressions were endlessly fascinating, which made his thoughts revert to the bedchamber, because there was just something about her that aroused him and left him appallingly distracted.

"Weymouth. Stationery," he muttered, determined to get his mind off Florence and the wicked things he intended to do with her when he finally got her into his bed.

"I've brought the parchment sample and a measure of the silk ribbon," she said, the amber flecks of her eyes sparkling as they were caught in sunlight.

"Let's hope the stationer has the matching paper," Hermia remarked, ever practical because their plan relied entirely on this. "I'm sure the ribbon will be less of a problem. Any haberdasher or ladies' shop will have ribbons in all colors and widths."

"They had better, or we'll have to come up with another plan," Florence said.

Hermia arched an eyebrow. "Or scrap the plan altogether, especially if the surprise Lady Frampton has hidden for you in the rose cuttings turns out to be something other than those letters."

"We have come this far," Florence insisted. "We are not scrapping any plans."

Hermia sighed. "Stop being so stubborn, child. Nor do we need to argue about it when we have no idea if there will be a problem with the stationery. We are getting ahead of ourselves."

They engaged in trivial conversation for the remainder of the journey and made it to Weymouth by late morning. There were several stationery shops in Weymouth, but they started with the one the old duke had used for his personal letterhead.

"Your Grace, it is an honor," the owner said, rushing out to greet Trajan. "How may I be of service?"

Trajan and the Newton ladies kept the shopkeeper on his toes for the next hour, poring over samples and surreptitiously comparing Florence's sample to those brought out until they found the exact match.

Trajan then ordered personal letterheads for Florence and her aunt, as well as calling cards for the three of them.

He was pleased when Florence made no fuss about it, for he thought it meant she would accept to marry him and assume the role of his duchess.

She had not outright confirmed this to him yet, but Florence was also thrifty by nature, and he could not see her agreeing to the extravagance of stationery she would never use.

She cast him an endearing smile as the shopkeeper totaled their purchases. It saddened him a little that this had started as a fake courtship between them.

There had been no romantic moments for Florence. He had swept her in his arms and kissed her thoroughly that first time to prevent Frampton from killing her. Kissing her in the arbor yesterday also had to do with plots against Frampton.

There had been no instant in time when his kisses had been for *her* alone. They had merely slipped into a betrothal in furtherance of the plots and intrigues swirling around them.

It would have to do. They would create memorable moments after they married, hopefully none that would end with one or both of them shot dead or seriously bloodied.

"I'll take some of this parchment stock to tide me over until the embossed letterhead arrives," Trajan said, glad to have this part of the plan successfully concluded.

The ladies walked next door to the haberdasher's establishment and had found the ribbon's exact match by the time Trajan finished settling accounts for the stationery and joined them. With the ribbon purchase also successfully concluded, it left them free to enjoy the rest of the day and the surprisingly pleasant weather.

Since Hermia was tiring, they decided to stop for lunch at the Weymouth Inn and dine *al fresco*, because there was a soft breeze off the water and the day was sunny and dry.

Florence seemed to blossom as the day passed.

Perhaps it was merely his falling deeper in love with her. She could be quite captivating when being her natural self, and sparkled whenever she laughed.

He was pleased to see her happiness shine through, even if only for the span of their afternoon sojourn.

He did not think she had been happy in a very long time.

He also learned she could be quite charming when she put her mind to it. In truth, she had it in her to be an impressive duchess.

"Hermia, do you mind if I take Florence for a short walk along the harbor?"

"Not at all, dear boy. I shall be quite content to linger over my cup of tea. I—" Hermia suddenly tensed.

He frowned. "What is it?"

"Lady Frampton's prison guard is here."

Trajan let out a breath. "Yes, I know. She has been following us since we left the haberdasher's and stopped for lunch here at the Weymouth Inn."

Florence pursed her lips. "Do you think she saw us at the stationery shop?"

"No, I had my eye out. No one followed us there."

She let out a breath. "You really are remarkable, you know."

He chuckled. "I like to think so. Come on, walk with me. You will excuse us, won't you, Hermia?"

"Yes, dear boy. I am perfectly comfortable here."

He and Florence left the inn.

"Nothing slips by you," she said in obvious admiration as they strolled along the harbor walk.

"That's part of my training, especially now that I am a duke. One needs to be alert to those hanging about on the edges."

He paused to give her a soft kiss on the cheek.

"Part of the pretense," she said with a nod. "That ought to throw Attila the Hun in skirts off and have her believe we are a couple in love, out enjoying a pleasant day in the company of my aunt."

"I kissed you because your cheek is soft and I wanted to kiss you. No ulterior motive. She can think whatever she likes."

Florence blushed. "I have no idea why you like me, but thank goodness you do. Would you care to kiss me again?"

"Yes, desperately." He cast her a smoldering look. "But not here and now. Attila is not the only one watching us. I'll give you a proper kiss tonight before you retire to bed."

"Who else is watching us?"

"Oh, anyone looking to make a few shillings and eager to sell a story to the gossip rags about the Duke of Weymouth and the beautiful bit of fluff he was seen kissing by the harbor." He gave her chin a light tweak. "I wrote to my mother and sister yesterday about us, just letting them know we were betrothed. No wedding date set yet, and I would let them know more when I saw them in London later this month. I won't press you to write to your parents, but it is something you ought to do."

He realized bringing them up had been a mistake when he saw the immediate shift in Florence's expression.

Blast.

That was stupid of him. He ought to have left the matter alone.

Florence did not need to have anything to do with them. He would ask Hermia to attend to the task of notifying them. After all, anyone could inform them. It did not have to fall upon Florence. But they *did* have to be told. Would it not be worse for Florence if her own parents were the last to know of her betrothal?

"They won't care that I am marrying, other than feeling relief I will no longer be a burden to them."

"They will care." Trajan cleared his throat. "Duke here. They'll care about my status."

"Only for the advantages they can wrest from a connection to you. They won't care about me, nor care if we are happy or in love. They'll just wonder whether you are in your right mind to choose me and praise the heavens and their good fortune that you did."

The wind picked up a little and the clouds began to thicken.

Trajan glanced up at the sky that was a deep blue earlier but was now fading to gray. "Time to return home before we are caught in a downpour."

She glanced up as well. "Do you think it will rain?"

"I don't know, perhaps a passing shower."

"It would freshen the air and clear out the heat and dampness."

He took her by the arm. "We ought to get back, in any event. We have those fake packets of purloined letters to prepare."

They made their way back to the inn, collected Hermia, and were about to climb into their carriage when Trajan spied his cousins walking to the stable to retrieve their horses. He called out to them.

The three of them smiled and started toward him.

"What are you doing here?" Sebastian asked.

"Nothing important. Just a day at leisure." Trajan laughed. "You look like a trio of alley cats on the losing end of a fight."

Florence coughed as they got too close, because they reeked of cheap perfume and stale beer.

"See you at home," Trajan said. "I recommend baths for the three of you. And burn those clothes, they reek. What in blazes did you get into?"

Sebastian winced. "I have no idea. Can't remember a thing."

Nathan groaned. "Nor I."

Trajan sighed. "No after-dinner drinks for you tonight, either. I need you sober for tomorrow."

"What's happening tomorrow?" Andrew asked, squinting as he looked at Trajan. "Gad, the sun's so bright."

Trajan rolled his eyes. The sun had disappeared behind a fat cloud, but *everything* hurt one's head when one had a bad hangover. "I'll tell you once we're home."

He helped the ladies into the ducal carriage and climbed in after them, settling in the seat opposite theirs. But as the carriage rolled away, Florence shifted places and settled beside him, resting her head on his shoulder.

He glanced at her, somewhat surprised.

"Thank you for a lovely day."

He gave her cheek a light caress. "Productive and lovely."

She nodded.

Hermia said nothing, for she was tired and soon drifted off to sleep.

Trajan did not know whether she was faking, but he did not mind riding in silence with Florence curled up beside him.

He took her hand in his and kept hold of it as they rode back to Gull Hall, the gentle sway of the carriage lulling even him to close his eyes.

But the gentle rocking did not put him to sleep because his mind was too much awhirl. Too many concerns still occupied his thoughts.

But yes, it had been a lovely day. And it felt quite nice that the woman he was growing to love was nestled by his side. He put his arm around her to hold her close as she seemed to drift off.

This was too perfect.

Something had to go wrong, didn't it?

CHAPTER TWELVE

FLORENCE'S HEART WAS in her throat as the Weymouth carriage, led by a team of matched bays, wound its way over the two hills separating Gull Hall from Frampton Court the following afternoon. Of course, one could cut that time in half by walking through the woods between the two properties, as she had done when encountering Trajan the other day. But she and Hermia were dressed for afternoon tea. Their silk gowns and dainty slippers were completely impractical if one had to make a run for it.

Never mind that Hermia was not able to run anywhere, since her sprinting gazelle days were long past. For several years now, it had been a task to get her down a flight of stairs.

Or had this been a charade on her part too?

Trajan rode in the carriage with them, having insisted on personally delivering them to the Frampton residence on this rather gray day. The rain had held off, so the roads were conveniently dry.

"You really did not have to accompany us," Florence muttered. "It might put Lord Frampton even more on edge."

"More on edge?" he grumbled, for this plan did not sit well with him at all. "I doubt that is possible. The man is so tightly wound, he's about to pop a spring."

"As are you," Florence observed.

"Can you blame me? I must be losing my mind to allow you

to do this dangerous thing, not to mention actually *abetting* you."

"Because you are caring and wonderful," she said.

He cast her a stern look. "Gad, Florence. Do not compliment me, for it will only rile me."

"All right."

He sighed. "It cannot hurt to remind him I am a duke."

"You like being *the* duke, don't you?" she remarked, noting the way his chest puffed up at the mere mention of his rank.

He shook his head. "It isn't the title I enjoy but the power one can wield with it. I find it most convenient, especially in this situation. I want Frampton to know that I will kill him if he dares touch a hair on your head."

Florence smiled. "I love when you make these marvelously apish comments."

"Because you are mine to protect. By extension, so is your aunt."

Hermia was seated opposite them in the carriage. Florence was seated beside Trajan, finding she needed the comfort of his touch to maintain her resolve. She also simply loved snuggling against him, for his shoulders were broad and muscled, and his scent was divine. Lather, citrus and sandalwood, and male heat. "You needn't worry about us. Aunt Hermia and I are all set in our plan. Right, Auntie?"

Her aunt snuffled and opened her eyes, for she appeared to have nodded off despite their having just undertaken the journey.

Oh dear. This did not inspire confidence. The entire ride would take no more than ten minutes, and they could not have been in the carriage more than two of those minutes.

"What, dear?"

"This is what worries me," Trajan mumbled. "I wish I could be there with you."

"You are the one who wanted to give Aunt Hermia a larger role," Florence said with exasperation. "I fear she was so excited about participating, she did not sleep a wink last night. I should have handled this on my own."

"Nonsense, child," her aunt intoned, proving she was not hard of hearing. Yet another thing she feigned from time to time, especially when asked a question she did not wish to answer, or engage in a conversation with a dullard she wished to escape.

Truly, Hermia had honed her dithering and doddering to a fine art.

"I'll be fine," she insisted. "You just worry about yourself."

Trajan took Florence's hand and gave it an affectionate squeeze. "My cousins and I will remain as close as possible. I'll be watching you through my binoculars from a vantage point in the woods."

"The tree that I fell out of?"

His lips twitched. "No, but close to it. Let's hope Frampton leaves the parlor drapes open."

"Aunt Hermia or I will insist on having them drawn open if they are not. Oh, we're almost there. Wish us luck."

He was back to frowning at her again. "I'm wishing for your safe return, Florence. Do not do anything foolish."

"I won't."

"I wish I could believe you."

"I promise." She kissed him on the cheek, to which he responded with a soft growl to warn her that he wasn't happy, and no amount of cajoling on her part would make this undertaking right.

"Just remember to save yourself and Hermia if things go awry. Lady Frampton will have to manage for herself."

But what if that ogre of a maid tried to hurt her mistress?

Well, Florence would do what she could to save all three of them—and grab the letters, too. Of course, the entire point was to get out of there alive. She would keep her plan flexible and adjust it as necessary.

Lady Frampton was standing on the front steps of the imposing manor house, smiling and waving to them as their carriage drew up under the portico. Her husband was standing beside her, looking quite grim.

Trajan hopped out as soon as the carriage drew to a halt. A Frampton footman hurried forward to assist him in helping Hermia down, because she gave a masterful performance of an old lady struggling to maintain her footing.

Trajan insisted on attending to Florence himself. "Be careful," he whispered, as though she required yet another warning.

"I love you," she answered back, surprising him and herself.

"Gad, what a time to tell me this."

"I know, but I do. Truly and sincerely. With all my heart."

She wanted him to know her feelings on the chance that things went horribly wrong and she would never see him again. Perhaps this was not the best time to dump this confession on him, but was it not worse to say nothing at all and leave him uncertain?

Not that he ought to have any doubt when she gushed and turned moon-eyed whenever she was with him.

"Weymouth!" Frampton strode forward, putting an end to their whispered conversation, which was untimely anyway.

She probably should not have said anything, because Trajan now looked even more riled.

"Frampton," he replied with curt politeness.

"I did not expect to see you with the ladies."

Goodness, Frampton sounded so *oily*.

"I rode along to assist Florence with her Aunt Hermia," Trajan smoothly explained. "She is old and rather frail, as you may have noticed. Make certain she does not walk unattended, because she is not all that steady on her feet. Yet she is stubborn and refuses to use a pushchair. But I see your wife has offered her arm and is being most careful with her."

Frampton glanced at Hermia and his wife, his expression turning even more dour.

"If you do not mind, I shall push off now and leave the ladies to their party." Trajan turned to Florence and gave her a kiss on the cheek. "I will see you shortly."

"And I shall count the minutes," she said, slightly breathless.

He arched an eyebrow, warning her not to overdo it.

Florence wanted to linger nearby to hear more of Trajan's conversation with Frampton, but she dared not be too obvious. "I'll hurry along and catch up to the ladies." She batted her eyelashes at Trajan for good measure.

He shot her another warning look.

She started up the stairs, but paused just inside the front door. Since the head butler and several footmen were close by, she pretended to dig through her reticule as though searching for something. "Did I leave it in the carriage?" she muttered to herself as Frampton's footmen and butler looked on. This allowed her to linger by the door and hear the brief exchange between Trajan and Frampton.

"As soon as our marriage plans are settled," Trajan said, surprisingly cordial, "Florence and I will host a dinner party for our friends and neighbors. We hope you and your lovely wife will attend."

"We shall try, of course. You've caught me at a very busy time."

"Government matters, Frampton? Rumor has it you are in line for an important Home Office post—or is it the Foreign Office?"

"Among other possibilities," Frampton said, being purposely evasive. "But my wife is one for parties. She will be pleased to receive the invitation. By the way, have you and Lady Florence set a wedding date?"

"Tentatively," Trajan said, equally evasive. "Waiting on confirmation, family schedules and all that. But I am quite keen on marrying her soon. It is my hope that Florence will be my duchess before the end of the month."

Having given Frampton the not-so-subtle reminder that he was dealing with a duke, Trajan climbed back in his carriage and rapped on the roof, commanding his driver to take him home.

"Ah, yes. I do have it," Florence now said, and hurried along before Frampton walked back inside the house and found her lurking.

She had noticed the malice in his expression in an unguarded moment before he entered the house. The man was indeed a coiled spring ready to unwind at the slightest provocation.

She scampered into the parlor and joined the ladies. Sylvia was wringing her hands as she stood beside the sofa where Hermia was now seated. She smiled as Florence approached. "It is so nice to see you again."

She took both of Florence's hands in hers and gave them a light squeeze.

Florence thought for a moment she meant to slip a key or a note into her hand, but it seemed Sylvia simply wished to give her a warm greeting.

"Same here, Sylvia." She leaned forward and bussed her cheek, hoping Frampton's wife might have something to whisper in her ear.

But she said nothing. Perhaps her husband was too close. He had walked in immediately after her and now stood frowning in the doorway.

"Well, I see that you are eager for your hen party. I shall not get in your way." He walked out.

Sylvia let out a breath. "Come sit next to me. We have much to catch up on since the last time we met."

The ogrish maid, whose name was Rutledge, was also present, perched like a predatory night owl on her stool in the corner.

Sylvia joined Hermia on the sofa while Florence sank into one of a pair of embroidered chairs beside them. The embroidery was particularly intricate, a lovely, pastoral scene that included lambs and a shepherdess under a tree in a meadow. "Did you embroider these, Sylvia?"

"Why, yes."

"They are beautiful," Florence said with genuine admiration.

The three of them went on to chatter about the embroidery circle they simply had to form, which then led to discussion of other trivial matters.

Not that Sylvia's talent was trivial, but the conversations were designed to be harmless and boring. They spoke of their neighbors, Sylvia doing most of the talking about them, since she had lived here for years and knew most of the Upper Crust residing in Weymouth.

"I cannot wait until Weymouth and I are married," Florence said, purposely referring to Trajan by his title. "We shall host a lavish party to introduce ourselves to all our neighbors. You shall be the first one invited, of course. I do wish we were married already. He is quite eager for it. So am I."

"You will be husband and wife very soon," Hermia intoned. "Your betrothed has many fine qualities, but patience isn't one of them. He knows what he wants and goes for it. Woe to those who seek to get in his way."

Florence nodded. "Yes, but he is a dear and so indulgent of me. We will marry imminently. It is just a question of getting our families here. It is all unsettled still. Now, do tell me more about your embroidery. What is your next piece to be? More chairs?"

Hermia had brought her own sewing basket and the embroidery panel she had been working on. Florence had liked the idea the moment Sebastian, of all people, suggested it during discussions around the breakfast table. "Much easier to switch the packets using the sewing basket while Frampton's attention is fixed on the carton of rose cuttings," he'd said.

Everyone had liked this plan, earning Sebastian a pat on the back from Trajan.

"Oh, I think you will be quite excited by my next piece," Sylvia remarked, regaining Florence's attention when she set down her teacup and got to her feet. "Let me bring it here and you can tell me what you think." She scurried out of the parlor.

The maid rose, uncertain whether to remain with them or follow Sylvia. She stood there eyeing them nervously.

Dear heaven. Did Frampton have his wife watched inside her own home, too? How did she manage to keep her sanity?

"Do help me up, Florence," Hermia said, regaining her attention. "I need to stretch my legs." She made a show of attempting to rise, and then fell back on the settee with a groan. "Oh, dear me. Never mind. Perhaps I ought to just sit here for a moment."

Florence went to her immediately. "Aunt Hermia, are you all right?"

"Yes, dear. Just a little stiffness in my legs. It is this damp weather, always brings on my inflammations." She winked at Florence.

Oh, she was setting the scene for the intended distraction to come later.

"Yes, it is awful weather lately. Forgive me, I did not think to bring along the balm for your knees. Well, I'm sure Lord Frampton will not mind assisting you to our carriage once the visit is over."

"Here it is!" Sylvia exclaimed, rushing back in with her basket in hand.

The three of them now huddled over the baskets, Florence purposely drawing her chair closer to block the maid's view, because it was entirely possible Sylvia intended to hand over the packet of letters here and now. This would allow them to hand Sylvia the fake packet, too.

But how was she to advise Sylvia of this plan? If only they could communicate in silence. Or better yet, get rid of the maid for a few minutes.

One of the packets of fake letters was planted in Hermia's sewing basket. Did Florence dare show Sylvia now?

She studied the woman and noted the desperation in her eyes.

Yes.

It was now or never.

But how to make the switch?

Florence lifted the embroidery panel Hermia had been working on to reveal the letters.

Sylvia's eyes widened, then she glanced at Florence in confusion.

Fake, Florence mouthed, and tried to discreetly motion for Frampton's wife to take them.

Sylvia gave an almost imperceptible nod and slid them out of Hermia's basket into her own.

They had their tea and cakes, and then Sylvia invited her and Hermia on a tour of the house. "And we also have a marvelous conservatory. I think you'll love it, Florence. I did not notice, does Gull Hall have one?"

"It does, but I did not bother showing it to you because it has fallen into disuse. However, I would love to revive it. I have a little knowledge of medicinal plants that I would love to grow over the winter. Not to mention herbs, medieval roses, and citrus trees. I will have my work cut out for me."

"Then you must come with me now and see what I have done with our conservatory. Let me put my embroidery basket away and I'll give you a tour."

Hermia gave a light wave of her hand. "You go on without me. I'll stay here with your maid. I'm feeling rather poorly and would appreciate her preparing me a tisane while you are in the conservatory."

"All right," Sylvia said. "Rutledge, attend to Miss Newton."

"We shan't be gone long," Florence assured her aunt.

Sylvia, with her sewing basket in hand, practically sprinted toward the conservatory. "Goodness, slight change of plans. Let me dig the letters out from the rose cuttings. But you'll have to hide them on your person."

"And you'll have to slip the fake packet of letters back where your husband hid the originals," Florence said. "Can you do this now? Before he grows suspicious and checks on where he has hidden them. I'm sorry about this last-minute change in plans, but I doubt your husband would have let the cuttings go without searching the carton."

"I know. I was hoping I could distract him just long enough to let you escape with them. Yours is a much better plan. Here they are." Sylvia dug into the rose carton and withdrew the letters that had been wrapped in a protective cloth.

"Is this how he stored them? Bound in this cloth?"

"No, I just did that to safeguard them."

"All right." Florence checked the bundle to make certain these were in fact the letters and not a trick.

"They're real," Sylvia remarked.

"Forgive me for checking. I do not doubt you," Florence said. Although she had to be wary, especially now that they had gotten this far. "But your husband is highly suspicious and might have done something in preparation for my visit to Frampton Court." She quickly slipped the packet into the hidden pocket of her gown.

"Yes, that was always a risk with him. There are days when one must walk on eggshells around him. But you seem to be two steps ahead of him. What a brilliant idea to have your aunt bring her basket. And this duplicate packet. It's perfect. I would never know they weren't the originals."

"How will you get them back in their hiding place? Where does he hide the letters?"

"He has a safe in his study."

"Typical," Florence said, thinking it was not very clever of him to place it somewhere she would have looked first. "And you must know the combination."

Sylvia nodded. "But he doesn't know that I do. This is why I thought my plan might work. It was such a low thing to steal them from Lady Simmons. I have been hating myself for it ever since. But my husband gave me no choice. I had to do it or face his wrath."

Florence placed a comforting hand on her shoulder. "Sylvia, come with us if you are worried about—"

"No, I'm safest remaining here and playing innocent. Look, the gardeners are returning. We have to plan a distraction quickly. They are my husband's men and cannot be trusted."

"Leave it to Hermia."

"Really? Is she up to the task? My husband and his guards have embedded themselves in the study, and it will take nothing short of an explosion to pry them out."

"We'll do our best," Florence said with a smile, patting the secret pocket sewn into her gown to make certain the originals were secure. She had also placed a second fake set of letters in her garter just as a precaution. It was a simple trick, really. If Frampton were ever to have her searched, the fake letters in the garter were the first ones the searcher would find. The searcher's brain would logically assume they had found what they were looking for and stop patting her down.

If they by chance realized these were fake, she could admit her intention to steal the originals but claim she had never gotten the opportunity.

Yes, it was dangerous. But it would be just enough to put off Frampton. Most important, he might not harm her if he thought she had failed.

Sylvia pretended not to notice they were being watched by Frampton's gardeners and continued with her tour of the conservatory. When they were done, they returned to the parlor. Sylvia had no sooner entered than she realized she was still holding on to her own embroidery basket. "We had such a lovely chat in the conservatory, I completely forgot to run upstairs. Oh, give me a moment to drop this basket in my bedchamber."

The maid rose from her chair and marched toward Sylvia. "Let me take it for you."

"Would you?" Sylvia cast the dour maid a pleasant smile. "Here. Be careful with it."

Florence signaled to Hermia, who gave an imperceptible nod and rose. "Florence, thank goodness you are back. My dear, I am feeling not at all well."

Having said that, she managed to fall atop the tea cart, knocking it over onto the maid, who had yet to take hold of Sylvia's basket.

While Hermia lay flailing atop the tea cart, which remained

atop the maid, pinning her down and probably crushing a rib or two, Sylvia screamed for her husband. "Frampton! Frampton! Come quickly! Lady Hermia is hurt."

Never mind that the ogrish maid was the one who was injured and barely able to breathe, because dear Aunt Hermia was ruthlessly keeping her pinned down.

Well done, Hermia.

Lord Frampton and two of his so-called guards had been cloistered in the study and now burst into the parlor at a run. Florence began to scream as well, gleefully adding to the pandemonium. "Hermia! Oh, no! I think she has collapsed! Someone fetch a doctor right away!"

"I'll go, my lord," one of the guards said, and hurried off.

As soon as he was gone, Florence shouted for smelling salts. "I cannot find hers! She always carries them in her reticule. Where are they?"

Frampton rang for his housekeeper, who tore in with a maid in tow. Sylvia sent the girl up to her bedchamber for smelling salts, putting an arm around her and guiding her into the hallway while rattling off instructions. "At once, my lady," Florence heard the young maid say.

Florence was kneeling beside her aunt, trying her best to also block the ogre from getting up. She had to give it to her aunt— that was one of the best tackles she had ever seen done.

"Where is your wife? Where is she?" the ogre wheezed, pointing frantically at Frampton and then the doorway. His eyes widened.

"Honestly, Rutledge! You are too much," Sylvia exclaimed. "I am right here. I've been standing behind my husband all along. What was I supposed to do? Block his way? Frankly, I've had enough of you. You saw that Lady Hermia was ailing, and what did you do? Nothing at all to help her, and I distinctly recall asking you to look out for her."

"She still has her sewing basket, my lord! Take it from her!" the maid cried out.

Lord Frampton turned to his wife. "Give it to me, Sylvia."

She held tight to it. "Whatever for? I'll take it upstairs myself."

"No, I shall take it," he said, his voice low and menacing.

"Well, all right. Leave it beside my wardrobe. But you really needn't trouble yourself."

"No trouble, my dear." He took it from her hands and marched out of the room—with every intention to search it, no doubt.

Of course, he would not find anything but Sylvia's embroidery, since she had taken the moment of distraction to place the fake letters in her husband's safe.

The Frampton head butler rushed in a moment later. "His Grace has arrived to take Lady Florence and Miss Newton home."

Sylvia, looking believably frazzled, nodded. "Good, do tell him to hurry in. Although I ought to put Hermia in one of our spare bedrooms. Shall I—"

"No," Florence said kindly. "Let me take her to Gull Hall. The ride isn't far, and she will be in familiar surroundings when she revives. Please have the doctor ride over to us. I do apologize for this mess."

"Not at all. We can all do with a little excitement once in a while," Sylvia said mirthfully.

Trajan strode in with his cousins.

Good heavens, he wasn't taking any chances. But Florence liked this show of force.

"Blessed saints! What happened here?" he said, looking believably aghast.

So did his cousins. Well, they probably were genuinely appalled and not acting.

"It is Aunt Hermia. You were right to be worried about her. She is not well," Florence said, faking tears.

"Oh, sweetheart. I am so sorry. Let me take you straight home." He then commanded Andrew and one of Framptons' footmen to carry a limp Hermia to his carriage, and asked Sebastian and Nathan to right the tea cart and assist the ogrish maid to her feet.

"Check the study, my lord!" the wretched maid cried the moment Frampton reappeared. She was wincing and moaning because she had likely broken a rib in the tumult and had to be in pain. But it did not stop her from sifting through Hermia's embroidery basket, her anger mounting as she found nothing but the sample and threads.

"Give me that," Florence said, wrenching it out of her hands after making certain the sour ogre had time enough to give it a thorough search and find nothing.

She ought to have felt sorry for the woman's injuries. Was it awful of her that she felt not an ounce of remorse?

"Rutledge, what are you going on about?" Sylvia remarked. "Rudely grabbing Miss Newton's basket and now *ordering* my husband to check the study. Why should he when he was in there all the while with his men? What in heaven's name are you raving about?" She turned to Florence. "Forgive this mad woman."

"Of course," Florence said with a dose of overdone sympathy. "But I understand why your husband must be careful. He has been very concerned about trespassers. He told me and Weymouth himself when encountering us on the beach. And someone even tried to break into Gull Hall the other night. Both he and Weymouth have to be on edge."

She turned to Trajan. "Perhaps you ought to put on extra guards at Gull Hall. Is it a band of thieves terrorizing the neighborhood, do you think?"

Sylvia shook her head. "No, it's—"

"Quiet, Sylvia," Frampton said, now hurrying back after checking the study and no doubt peering into his safe. "How you do go on. No need to alarm our new neighbors. It is nothing. Rutledge, you are too overwrought," he chided the ogre. "Seeing phantoms where there are none."

"But—"

"You are dismissed," Frampton said, glowering at the woman, who bowed her head and limped out.

Frampton remained agitated but not alarmed, which meant Sylvia had successfully placed the fake letters in his safe only minutes before he ran to his study to assure himself nothing had been taken.

However, he still shot Florence a malevolent gaze, for he knew she had attempted to take his precious extortion letters.

Attempted was the magic word, wasn't it? He thought she had failed.

She tried her best to look frustrated and defeated.

"Take care of yourself, Lady Florence," he said with a sneer.

"Oh, I shall, Lord Frampton. I hope to see you and your lovely wife again soon."

"Yes, I look forward to it. But I am sure you have much to keep you busy now that your wedding is so close. Do take care of yourself, Florence," Sylvia said with much sincerity. "You will soon be the Duchess of Weymouth, and nothing must get in the way of that."

Florence cast Trajan a doting smile.

He looked like he wanted to strangle her. "Frampton, I do apologize for this mess. Let me take on the costs of the damage to your rug. I wasn't certain Florence's aunt should have joined the ladies today, but she and Florence are inseparable. Well, send over the bill for it and I will have my man of affairs attend to it at once."

Florence allowed him to steer her out. Frampton and his wife followed them to the front steps.

"Please let me know how dear Hermia is feeling," Sylvia called out, looking just the right amount of genuinely concerned.

"I will," Florence assured her. "Thank you so much for a lovely afternoon. I'm so sorry it ended this way. But we'll be in touch soon, for Hermia is very eager to establish our embroidery circle."

Frampton still wore his triumphant sneer as he bade them

farewell.

Ha! He would soon get his comeuppance.

She wished she could be there when he learned her *failed* attempt had been successful after all.

Well, perhaps not. The man was a most unpleasant fellow. There would be quite the volcanic explosion when he realized he had been duped.

Trajan practically shoved her into his carriage. Hermia was already in there, sprawled across one of the seats and softly moaning. She was so believable, Florence was convinced her aunt would have been a great actress had she ever taken to the stage.

Trajan climbed in after her and immediately rapped on the roof. "Home, Tucker."

"Aye, Your Grace."

His cousins had come on horseback and followed behind them.

Florence let out a breath the moment the carriage rolled out of the Frampton courtyard. "Trajan, I—"

"Not a word, Florence." He looked mad enough to create his own volcanic eruption. "I do not want to hear what you and your minion have done until we are home and I've had a stiff drink."

"My *minion?*"

Hermia miraculously recovered from her fainting spell and sat up now that they were out of sight of Frampton's house. "He means me."

Florence smiled at her. "You were brilliant, Aunt Hermia."

"I know, child. But I think we have rather upset His Grace. Let's ride in silence, shall we? I think he needs time to recover from what we just did."

Florence nodded.

"But that was rather exciting, wasn't it? Quite more fun than I've had in years," Hermia admitted, smiling at Florence.

Trajan said nothing, merely glowered.

Not even a word of admonishment. Certainly no congratulations. Only silence now.

This was what she had lived with all of her life.
This was the very thing she hated.
She glanced at Trajan again and saw that he was still fuming.
A shiver ran through her.
Was he reconsidering their betrothal?

Chapter Thirteen

T RAJAN'S HANDS WERE shaking because he was so rattled by Florence's sojourn into the Frampton home. He had been watching through his binoculars and seen Hermia take that dive onto the tea cart, which had conveniently landed atop Rutledge the Ogre, and seen Florence's aunt flailing atop that pile like an overturned turtle.

He'd almost fallen out of his perch in the tree in his rush to climb down, for that had been his cue to get the pair of Newtons out of there fast.

Gad, this was such an ugly business. He hated Florence being involved in any of it. He did not know which was worse, that she was involved in it or that she was *not* afraid to be involved.

"May we talk? Are you still seething?" she asked once they reached Gull Hall.

He ignored the question, helped both ladies out of the carriage, and ordered them into his study. His cousins, too. He must have sounded harsher than he realized barking out orders, because they all rushed in without a word of protest.

Could they blame him for being livid? He was still overset and his head felt as though it was about to explode.

He must have looked like a savage beast, for Florence's eyes were wide and her chin began to wobble. "Have you decided you do not wish to marry me?"

He turned to her, startled.

The idea of ending their betrothal had not even occurred to him. Perhaps she thought she had given him reason because what she had done had been reckless and foolish.

But it was also very brave. He loved her all the more for it. She was never going to be a timid mouse of a wife.

He was overset because *he* was the one who should have taken on the risk for *her*. He should have figured out a way to grab those letters and be the one placed in danger.

Instead, he had allowed her to march into the lion's den armed with nothing but a maiden aunt and an embroidery basket. He had done nothing to protect her.

He had yet to ask if she had succeeded in reclaiming those letters.

Had she?

Yes, she must have.

Florence was incredible, and she had now saved her brother.

For all the good it would do her, he thought morosely.

"I haven't changed my mind, Florence. We are betrothed, if you still wish it. We will marry, if you accept to have me as your husband."

She nodded, her expression showing her relief.

And now it would be up to him to accompany her to London and make certain her royal benefactor did not renege on the bargain.

Angry as he was about this entire affair, he would never allow anyone, not even the Princess of Wales, to cheat Florence. She had poured her heart into this assignment and risked her life for her worthless brother and a pair of cheating lovers.

Was this worth placing her life in danger? He doubted anything would change within her family and how they treated her. Nor would Lady Simmons reform her ways and stop taking on lovers.

Florence withdrew her handkerchief to dab at her tears. "Thank you. I do wish to marry you and gratefully accept you with all my heart. Are you positively sure you want me?"

"Yes, love," he said, his voice achingly gentle because he knew how fragile Florence was at the moment. "I'm sure. Never a doubt."

"Then this is finally real?" Andrew asked, smiling.

Florence glanced at Trajan uncertainly.

"Yes," he said, taking hold of her hand and leaning in to give her a soft kiss on the lips, "it's real."

The tears now streamed openly down Florence's face, but she was smiling, too.

His cousins cheered.

Trajan asked her the question she was most eager to answer. "Did you get the letters?"

"Yes! Hermia *and* Sylvia were brilliant. They played their roles to the hilt."

"You were bravest, my dear," Hermia said, casting Florence a doting smile.

"I could not have succeeded without the two of you. But I'm so worried about Sylvia. There is no telling what Frampton will do to her if he suspects her complicity in any way."

"He won't," Hermia assured her niece. "He does not even realize anything has been stolen. We have just pulled off the perfect crime, to which we owe our undying gratitude to you, Weymouth, for coming up with the brilliant idea."

"Yes, *undying*," Florence repeated, casting him a doting smile. "Your plan has kept us all alive, including Sylvia. She is safe for the moment, and hopefully for always."

She turned to his cousins, also smiling at them. "Sebastian, your embroidery basket idea was very clever, too."

The cousins burst into grins and laughter. Nathan and Andrew patted their younger brother on the back and ruffled his hair. "You are not so dumb after all," Andrew teased.

"But you ladies were the ones who carried it off brilliantly," Nathan remarked.

By their wide, hyena-like smiles, Trajan expected the lads were half in love with Florence themselves, and quite in awe of both Newton ladies.

Florence moved over to sit beside her aunt. "Hermia! Your gown is soaking wet. I did not realize so much of the tea had spilled onto you in the tumble, and—"

"Gad, Hermia! Why did you not mention it?" Trajan silently berated himself for being too busy behaving like an angry beast to notice her discomfort. He had not even given a thought to her gown being wet.

But of course it was. She had purposely knocked over that tea cart and spilled tea everywhere. Her gown happened to be a tea color, so he hadn't even thought… Blast, where was his mind?

Hermia remained quite calm and did not appear at all put out. "No, dear boy. It is nothing. This discussion is far more important."

He raked a hand through his hair. "It can wait. I'll ring for a maid to—"

"No, Weymouth. Let's finish this first," Hermia insisted. "Florence needs to unload those letters as soon as possible."

"What's the plan?" Andrew asked.

"Do you have one?" Nathan added.

"Of course he does," Sebastian said. "He is always thinking two steps ahead."

"Not always," Trajan muttered, but he *had* given this eventuality considerable thought. "Andrew, I am leaving you in charge of Gull Hall in my absence. Florence and I will leave for London just before dawn tomorrow."

"What of my aunt?" Florence asked.

"Hermia stays here," he said, turning back to the aunt in question. "We have to move fast. As brilliant as you were today, I don't think you will be able to keep up. My cousins will look after you. Is that all right?"

"Of course, dear boy. I never expected to travel with you to London. I am in no fit condition. I shall be fine right here."

"Not fit?" He grinned. "You are an acrobatic marvel, Hermia."

She winked at him. "I was rather limber in my younger days."

The saucy comment went completely over Florence's head, but this further warmed Trajan's heart toward her. She was so innocent when it came to men.

Her mind was already lost in thoughts of their escape. "Oh, then you and I will be traveling alone."

"Yes, it cannot be helped. You need to get those letters to London and in the hands of the Princess of Wales as fast as possible. We cannot travel with an entourage. Where are the letters?"

"I have them hidden in the secret pocket of my gown."

Trajan arched an eyebrow in surprise. "There's a secret pocket even in that pretty gown? Well done. I never would have guessed."

"And he's been looking closely," Sebastian said with a snicker that earned him a frown from Trajan and a knock on the head from Andrew.

"Dolt," Andrew muttered.

Florence clasped her hands together. "Um, I would need a moment of privacy to withdraw them."

Nathan cast her a leering grin. "I would offer to assist, but I think Trajan would bite my head off if I dared."

"Bloody right, I would. Andrew, give Nathan a knock on the head, too."

"Gladly. Dolt," Andrew muttered again, this time aimed at Nathan.

Trajan crossed to the window to peer out of it. "Florence, leave it hidden in your gown for now. Do you have secret pockets in any of the other gowns you plan to bring along?"

"All of them," she admitted. "They are quite useful."

"Of course," he mumbled, but the notion amused him. This was such a typical Florence thing to do. But this was her, eccentric and also very clever.

However, he did not dwell on all the things he liked about her. He was still on edge, and could not shake off the feeling that something bad was about to happen. Perhaps because their plan had gone off so smoothly.

He continued to stare out the window.

"What has you so engrossed?" Florence asked. "Surely Frampton is at home gloating over what he believes is my failed attempt. He has no idea I have the letters."

Trajan turned back to her and frowned. "Do you not understand the nature of this beast? He isn't finished with you. He's a bloody bastard—pardon the profanity."

Nathan frowned. "Do you think he will do something out of sheer malice? Even though he believes those letters are still in his possession? Shouldn't he be satisfied that he won? Well, *thinks* he won."

Sebastian was also frowning. "Perhaps he will simply gloat and open a bottle of champagne to celebrate."

"He may do that, but it will not be the only thing he does. He is vindictive by nature," Trajan said.

"Would he be so foolish? He knows I will soon be your duchess," Florence remarked. "He wouldn't dare."

Trajan arched an eyebrow. "Wouldn't he?"

She sighed. "I hope you are wrong. I *pray* you are wrong, for the sake of all who are involved. Especially Lady Frampton."

"Did she ask for your help in escaping her husband?"

"No."

"Then do not meddle. It will only put her in greater danger." Perhaps he was being rough on Florence, but he wanted an end to this nasty business, not have it extended. "Lady Frampton understood the risk when stealing the letters. She understood the risk when giving them back to you. She chose to help you, even knowing the consequences to herself if she were caught. You both accepted the danger. What is done is done. You both went into this with your eyes wide open."

Her chin was wobbling again.

He sighed, for Florence was obviously as overset as he was about this business.

"I'm sure she has contrived an escape plan for herself," he said more gently. Florence was too softhearted for this line of work.

"Do you think so?" She regarded him hopefully.

"Yes, I am certain of it." In truth, he did believe Lady Frampton had prepared for this eventuality. "Being married to Frampton cannot be easy for her. She may have devised a plan to leave him long before the letters became an issue. And do not forget, she was clever enough to steal them in the first place. And clever enough to pass them back to you."

This heartened Florence. "That's true."

He grunted in agreement. "So, let's worry about you. I want those letters out of your hands as fast as possible."

"We could leave for London tonight. Within the hour, if you prefer," Florence suggested.

"No, just be ready tomorrow morning. Traveling at night is never safe with all the highwaymen lying in wait to rob the unsuspecting citizenry." He strode to Hermia's side. "The doctor will be here shortly and expects to find an elderly woman recovering from a fit of vapors. I do not want him reporting back to Frampton that you are right as rain and he came upon you dancing a jig."

Hermia nodded. "You make a valid point, dear boy. Let me scoot upstairs and change into my nightclothes. Have a posset brought up to me, and some tea and biscuits. Also, one of the maids should be sitting by my side looking worried. Do you have someone who can be trusted to lie convincingly to the doctor?"

"Right," he muttered. "This is what my household has descended to, liars and frauds."

Hermia took herself off to prepare for the doctor's visit. After a brief discussion of the next steps to be taken, particularly in the running of the Weymouth holdings in Trajan's absence, the rest of them disbanded.

Florence returned to her bedchamber to pack her essentials for tomorrow's journey.

He and his cousins retired to his study to review impending

matters and decide which cousin was to take over whatever tasks that normally would have fallen upon Trajan were he still here. "Plan on these added duties for about ten days, perhaps a fortnight," he told Andrew. "Delegate to your brothers as needed. I don't think it will take us very long to hand over the letters and return to Gull Hall."

Andrew nodded. "Will you marry Florence in London? Or wait until you return here?"

Trajan winced, for he had been giving thought to the matter and wanted Florence to have the protection of his name as soon as possible. "I don't know that she would consider marrying me in London, since Hermia would not be there with her. Nor would I like to wed without you or my mother and sister present. But I don't know that we have the luxury of waiting."

"Do what you must," Andrew said, "and that means getting her to the altar immediately. We can always have a family celebration afterward. After all, a party is a party, and we'll happily overindulge no matter the reason."

Trajan laughed. "Then we are all squared away?"

His cousins nodded.

Trajan was about to go upstairs to look in on Florence when Dr. Pritchard arrived. He escorted the earnest-looking man to Hermia's bedchamber, not surprised when Florence darted out of her quarters with her worried mask in place and sat beside her aunt while the doctor examined her.

Knowing he was not needed, Trajan returned downstairs and strode into his library, no longer musty from being cleaned after the hot cocoa spillage. The carpet was still out for drying, but the rest of the room was basically restored.

He searched for a book to read while this latest charade was playing out upstairs. After choosing one, he settled in a soft leather chair and opened to the first chapter.

Well, he *attempted* to read. It was impossible while his head was filled with thoughts of Florence and what had transpired today. Not to mention all the lies they had been spouting.

He was a fighter, and had done his military service without rancor or complaint. In battle, you knew your enemy, and the object was to shoot him before he shot you. He was not cut out for clandestine operations and the lies and subterfuge that went along with these assignments.

It rankled him to lie to the doctor. He knew it was necessary, because Frampton would be quizzing the man about Hermia's condition, and his answers had to be genuine.

Trajan gave up on the first book he had grabbed and tried to read another, this time settling in with a brandy in hand.

It still did not work. He hardly read a word because he remained too riled to concentrate.

Finally, he gave up, set aside his drink that he had not touched, and walked out of the library just as the doctor came downstairs.

Since it was time for supper, Trajan invited him to join them. "You are welcome to stay, Dr. Pritchard."

"It is most generous of you, Your Grace. But I am a family man and my wife will expect me home. Besides, I prefer not to travel at night if I can help it."

Trajan did not press him, for he understood the man's concerns. He walked the doctor out. "Thank you. Will Hermia be all right?"

"Yes, I think it was nothing more serious than too many strawberry scones."

Trajan managed a smile. "Good to know that's all it was. We were afraid it was something more serious. I am relieved."

Hermia, as a precaution, continued the charade and took her supper in bed.

With the doctor now gone, Florence and his cousins joined him in the dining room. However, none of them were particularly hungry or in any humor to chatter. They ate mostly in silence, something he knew Florence hated.

But it could not be helped. How were they to discuss the letters while servants were bustling in and out to serve them the courses that Florence barely touched?

He and his cousins ate, but not nearly as heartily as they would have done under normal circumstances.

Nor did he wish to talk about their London trip. He thought it safest to make no announcement of their departure until tomorrow morning, just before they were on their way. Servants chatted, especially between neighboring estates, and he did not want word getting back to Frampton tonight and him realizing the letters had been switched.

After supper, his cousins decided to play billiards. Their granduncle had enjoyed the game and installed a magnificent table in Gull Hall.

"Will you join us, Trajan?" Andrew asked.

"Later," Trajan said. "I need a moment with Florence."

He knew he ought to have taken it easier on her, but he was still mad with worry about what she had done. Not so much what she had done, but to whom she had done it…Frampton.

She had gone up to her bedchamber immediately after supper, so he went up there now.

"If all you wish to do is stare at me in silence, frowning for the next half-hour, then let us skip our quiet *moment*," Florence said, noticing him standing in the doorway. "I am exhausted and could do with a good night's sleep."

"We need to talk." But Mrs. Albright was with her, neatly folding the few gowns and other garments and necessities into Florence's travel pouch for tomorrow's journey. "Come downstairs with me, Florence. Just for a moment."

"All right."

He ordered Timmons to bring hot cocoa for them in the library.

"We'll try this again, hopefully without mishap," he said, leading her in. "We need to clear the air."

"Between us? Oh, so you do intend to end our betrothal." She looked utterly stricken, as though he had just stabbed her through the heart.

"I am *not* ending our betrothal. Why do you think I would?"

"Are you not sick of me yet? You certainly seem to be. You have hardly spoken to me other than to admonish me. And you could not look at me at supper. Do not bother to deny it. I am quite familiar with that look of disgust."

His heart twisted in a knot. She was referring to the looks her mother had given her throughout her life.

"I warned you this would happen," she said, her words tight and pained.

"Florence, stop. It isn't you with whom I am angry."

"Then who?"

"Me. Have I not made that clear? I am still unsettled and cannot seem to shake off this feeling of danger. It isn't you. This is why I wanted us to speak. You are the best thing to come out of all this."

"Oh."

"I don't regret a moment of being with you. But the little hairs on the back of my neck feel like knife points, and I do not know why."

Her expression softened. "You are a worrier. That's why you are always two steps ahead of the rest of us. But we got the letters back and no one was hurt. We completely fooled Frampton. Is this not cause for celebration?"

"Yes, it should be. Perhaps I will breathe easier once you turn them over to the princess. But you still have them in your hands, so this is not over yet."

"I know. I suppose this is why you still have your footmen on night patrol." They would come on duty soon, although there were several more hours of daylight remaining.

Timmons brought in the pot of hot cocoa and then left him and Florence to their privacy in the library.

Florence had been perusing the shelves of books and now walked over to sit beside Trajan on the settee while he poured cups for each of them.

"Last time we were in here, you pounced on me and spilled

the cocoa all over us and the furniture."

He grunted. "You Newtons seem to attract this sort of thing. Oversetting tea carts. Hermia was brilliant today, wasn't she?"

Florence smiled as she nodded. "She's little and frail, but she took Rutledge down with the skill of a Roman gladiator."

"My staff has just put this place to rights. Hopefully, we can keep it pristine for more than a day."

She smiled again. "I'll try my best."

"Florence, you needn't ever worry about my feelings for you." He took her hand, surprised to find it cold. "I want you to know that I desired this betrothal and wanted it to be real from the start. My desire has not changed. Whatever happens, we are in this together. Start to finish."

"But you had such a look in your eyes throughout supper. And why the silence?" She let out a breath. "I know you are a man of honor and will keep to your word. But you are struggling with your feelings. More to the point, you struggle with your feelings toward me. I rile you and upset you. Did I not warn you this betrothal would not last? Why should you be any different from my family?"

He handed her a cup. She warmed her hands around it, although the weather was mild and her hands should not have been so cold.

"I am not your parents. Nor am I your worthless brother. It is *my* cowardice in all of this that infuriates and frustrates me."

The remark genuinely surprised her. "You are no coward! Far from it!"

"I let you take all the risk while I sat up in a damn tree and watched from a distance with my binoculars."

"But this was our plan all along. It was the only way it could have worked."

"I know—doesn't mean I liked it. What if Frampton had shot you? I would have been helpless to prevent it. Do you see now why I have yet to calm down?"

"No, I still cannot understand why you are flagellating yourself. I was the only one who could have pulled off the switch. I was the one Sylvia trusted. You could not have marched in and pretended a fascination with embroidery."

He grunted in acknowledgment, for that much was true.

"Nor could you have stopped me from going into Frampton's home. I am very stubborn when I have a mind to be."

"I know," he said with a mirthless grin, and suddenly wondered whether the glint of metal that flickered across the window just now was his mind playing tricks on him again.

Where were his footmen? Was it one of them who had passed by the window while on patrol?

"The hardest part is over and we are safely back home," Florence continued, but he listened with half an ear. "It isn't as though—Ack!"

He shoved Florence down and covered her with his body just as a shot rang out and shattered the pot of cocoa before tearing through his arm.

He cursed as a stinging burn coursed through him.

"Bloody bastard," he muttered, wincing as he reached for the weapon kept in the lip of his boot while at the same time holding Florence down.

And bloody blazes! Cocoa had spilled all over them and the settee yet again. His granduncle must be rolling in his grave.

"Are you all right?" Trajan asked.

"Never mind about me! Are you all right?" She tried to struggle to her feet, but he would not allow her up yet.

"Stay down," he growled.

"I will not! Trajan! You're hurt!"

He attempted to deny it.

"Then whose blood is that dripping onto me?"

Chapter Fourteen

"You must let me up!" Florence cried, trying to wriggle out of his grasp and examine his arm that he insisted was not bleeding. "There's a crimson streak running down the length of your jacket sleeve. Let me up, Trajan! The cur must have run off by now."

"No, give it another moment."

Had the assailant run off? Or was he waiting to take another shot?

"I hear shouts and dogs barking," she said. "Your footmen must be after him by now. How did he get past them? Herbert was patrolling with one of your bloodhounds."

"I know." This was what worried him most. Trajan ignored his arm and nudged Florence down again. "Blast it, Florence. That shot was aimed at you."

A gift from Frampton. That vindictive lord's retribution because of those infernal letters.

"Let me have a look at your arm."

"No, it is only a flesh wound." He was more worried about Florence and the safety of his footmen. Had the assailant slain any of his men?

He heard more shouts from outside the window, and footsteps now resounded through the hall. His cousins had set aside their billiards cues and were running to him.

He finally allowed Florence to sit up, for his dogs were howling right outside the window.

Edgar peered in. "Your Grace! You are hurt!"

"Nothing serious. Get the dogs onto his scent."

"Herbert's got Dodger on him right now. Alvin's gone for the other dogs. I'll help him."

The cousins burst in just as Edgar disappeared.

Andrew rushed to Trajan's side. "You're bleeding! And Florence! There's blood on you, too!"

"It's *his*. Not mine. He's the one that who was shot."

"He grazed my arm," Trajan said. "That's all. Sebastian, take Florence upstairs to Hermia and keep them both safe while—"

Florence grabbed hold of him. "Don't you dare go after him. Oh, Lord. You are a bloody mess! He might have killed you! Trajan…oh, Trajan… I told you I am nothing but trouble."

Timmons rushed in next, followed by several more footmen. Trajan's entire jacket sleeve was now a dark-red splotch of blood.

"Your Grace!" Timmons gasped, and his eyes rounded in alarm.

"I'm fine. Take weapons," Trajan commanded, knowing he was going to punch a wall in frustration if one more person told him that his arm was bleeding. "We'll search the grounds in pairs."

Ignoring Florence's protests and Sebastian's gripes about having to stay behind with the women, he strode to the gun cupboard, unlocked it, and handed out weapons.

"Give me one, too," Florence demanded, following after him and staring at his injured arm with an abundance of concern.

"You have never fired a weapon before."

She cast him a stubborn look. "True, but how difficult—"

"Gad, no!" He shook his head with vehemence. "I want you up in Hermia's room right *now*, and stay there until I tell you it is safe to come down. Why are you giving me a hard time about this? That shot was aimed at *you*, and would have hit *you* if I had not pushed you down."

"But it struck *you*, and we need to take care of *you* at once."

She turned to his butler. "Send a man for the doctor right away. And His Grace should not be joining in the search while he is spurting blood like water out of a whale's spout."

"I'll be fine. You exaggerate. Go upstairs and stop fretting. Timmons, I want two armed footmen posted at the top of the main stairs and two at the top of the servants' stairs to guard the ladies."

"Very good, Your Grace."

He next turned to Sebastian and handed him a rifle. "I want you inside the room with Hermia and Florence. Do not let either of them near the windows."

"Very good, Your Grace," Sebastian said, still grumbling in frustration.

The housekeeper now rushed in to join them.

Trajan turned to her. "My apologies, Mrs. Albright. We've made a fresh mess in the library. It needs to be cleaned up, but not now. It isn't safe yet."

"All right, Your Grace," she said. "I'll gather the maids and keep them in the kitchen until you instruct otherwise."

"I'm so sorry, Mrs. Albright." Florence began to wring her hands because she blamed herself for the chaos created and was obviously distraught over his injury.

"No apology necessary, Lady Florence." Mrs. Albright placed a kindly arm around Florence to lead her upstairs. Florence allowed the woman to steer her out of the room, but cast Trajan a pleading glance on the way out.

His heart skipped several beats, for those were real tears she was shedding.

For him.

He gave the matter no more thought and hurriedly finished handing out the weapons. They took off after the assailant. "Keep a lookout for any accomplices," he warned, although he was fairly certain Frampton had sent only this one man.

Had he meant to kill Florence? Or merely scare her?

Well, that had been a killing shot.

Timmons remained behind to send a messenger for the doctor and assist Mrs. Albright in calming the staff. Trajan organized his footmen in pairs, relieved when all men were accounted for and none of them hurt. He delegated a portion of the grounds to each pair, although he doubted their search would yield any other assailants in hiding. Assassins usually worked alone, did they not?

But there might be clues to be found.

"Edgar, come with me," he said to the most capable of his men.

"Aye, Your Grace. What is this world coming to? Who would want to harm you or Lady Florence?"

"We'll question the culprit once we catch him."

But he knew the answer already—the shooter had come for Florence and not him.

It was not long before Herbert gave a shout. "He's there! I see him."

He released Trajan's prize bloodhound, who tore off after the man, his barks leading them all toward the beach stairs, where Frampton had first caught sight of Trajan and Florence in a torrid embrace several days ago.

The man, obviously in a panic and knowing he would be caught before he ever made it to the shelter of the woods that separated this property from Frampton's, stupidly thought to run down to the beach instead. Perhaps he meant to swim to Frampton's side of the cove, or merely was not thinking at all, for those cove waters were already dark and the wave swells were rough as the tide came in. Even a strong swimmer could be swallowed up by the unforgiving sea.

But the man never made it near the water or even onto the beach. He had barely started down the steps before tripping over his feet and tumbling headfirst along the length of the stairs.

He was dead by the time his body hit the sand.

Since night had now fallen, two of the footmen lit torches to illuminate their way down the stairs, for Trajan did not need anyone else taking a tumble.

All hope of questioning the villain had now faded.

Trajan took a moment to search through his clothing for any identification, but he had none on him. There was nothing left to do but carry the broken body back to Gull Hall.

None of the footmen recognized the man, but perhaps someone else on staff would. Trajan hated to ask the maids, but ladies were often sharper about these things than men, and one of them might have seen him or had a friend in a neighboring estate who knew him.

Trajan suspected he was one of Frampton's crew of ruffians, although he was not among the four who routinely followed Frampton wherever he went. Yet this man had to be in Frampton's pay.

He glanced up at the moon that was tinged red at its edges. A blood moon.

How prophetic.

"Your Grace, let me help you," Edgar said, coming to his side to give him a hand when he began to reel as they climbed the stairs that seemed infernally endless.

"I'll be all right." However, he did allow Edgar to assist him, since he was beginning to feel lightheaded and it would not do to tumble down those stairs and end up as dead as his assailant.

When they finally reached the top of the stairs, he called off the search and ordered everyone back to the house. "I doubt he had accomplices. The dogs would have picked up other scents."

"But what if there *were* others?" Edgar asked. "Should we not alert the neighbors?"

"No, this man had a specific target in mind and is no danger to anyone else. I'll not have my men scouring neighboring properties and be mistaken for villains in the dark. Everyone is to return to Gull Hall."

Trajan would have loved to barge into Frampton Court and haul that malevolent little toad Frampton out on his arse, but what good would it do? Much as he wished to confront the man, he was in no fit condition to do it.

And why give that toad the satisfaction of seeing him wounded?

"Will you allow us to search for clues come morning?" Edgar asked, trying not to sound as frustrated as he was.

"Yes," Trajan said, now worried he was about to cast up his accounts. Fortunately, he managed to quell his roiling stomach.

He returned to the house and marched straight upstairs, ignoring his stomach, which was once more in revolt, and his spinning head that felt as though Thor's hammer was pounding on it.

Florence and her aunt were sequestered in Hermia's bedchamber under Sebastian's watch. He walked in quietly and watched Florence as she paced across the carpeted floor like a caged tigress.

She flew into his arms the moment she realized he was back. "You clot!" she cried, and hugged him fiercely. "You look green! Sit down before you faint."

Hermia uttered a short prayer of thanks that he had returned safely.

Florence nudged him onto the lounge chair by the hearth. He offered no resistance, for his body had reached its limit of endurance. She sat beside him, remaining pressed to him, as though he needed her warmth.

Or perhaps she needed his.

"You fool," she said with trembling voice. "You gloriously wonderful fool. Why did you save me?" She was sobbing now. His return had burst the dam of control she had been holding back. "This is all my fault. How can I ever forgive myself? How can *you* ever forgive me?"

"It isn't your fault." He stroked her hair and kissed the top of her head, for she was more torn up about his injury than he was. "We all know Frampton is to blame."

"But can you prove it?" Sebastian asked, raking a hand through his hair, obviously distressed.

"No, unfortunately. At least, not yet. The assailant is dead.

He had no identification on him. Someone might recognize him, but will they be brave enough to come forward and link him to Frampton? I doubt it. Anyway, Andrew and Nathan have gone off to summon the magistrate."

"And Timmons sent one of the grooms to fetch the doctor," Sebastian said. "The lad tore off on horseback as soon as you marched off to search the grounds."

"I'm sure the doctor will be thrilled to have to return here," Trajan said dryly. "After he takes care of stitching my wound, I'll have him examine the dead man. The magistrate will ask him to do it anyway, since he'll demand a full report." He winced as his head began to reel. "Will you help me, Florence?"

"Yes, of course. What do you need me to do?"

"Help me to my quarters. You too, Sebastian." He needed more than a simple lie-down, for his wound needed to be cleansed immediately. The doctor would do a professional job of it once he arrived, but that could be another hour yet. Or longer if he was off on another call.

Trajan had an excellent bottle of brandy in stock that he had been intending to share with his cousins, but he would now apply that fine blend to the area of the wound. It was merely a flesh wound, so proper application of the brandy and a temporary binding of a clean cloth around his arm to stem the bleeding would go a long way to treating the injury and preventing infection. The doctor would no doubt clean the area of the nasty gash again and make certain no bits of lead remained buried under his skin before he stitched his arm.

If anything good could be said of this night, it was that the shot had torn clear through his arm, and no surgery beyond a few stitches would be necessary.

But that limb was a rather nasty mess at the moment.

Florence was undone by it. She cried as they left Hermia's bedchamber and yelped in dismay each time he wobbled on the way to his quarters, which he did a time or two because his strength was fading fast.

"Florence, perhaps you had better remain with Hermia while Sebastian—"

"No! I am staying with you. Don't you dare make me leave your side. I have to be with you. I *must*."

She cried even harder. Because she was dying inside to see him hurt.

"Hush," he said gently, and kissed the top of her head again. "This isn't your fault."

"It is *all* my fault."

"Stop, love. Not even I thought Frampton was venal enough to send a man to kill you."

"And he almost killed *you* instead. I don't want to lose you, Trajan. I cannot. My heart will never recover. Don't you see that you are the best thing that's ever happened to me?"

"Mutual, Florence."

She shook her head vehemently. "How can you possibly think I am any good for you? All I've brought you is havoc and pain. But you are my dream man."

He laughed.

"You are," she insisted. "All my life, I was made to feel worthless by those who should have loved me. Then you came along and opened *your* heart to me. You cared for me and protected me. I love you so much. I knew it from the first moment I set eyes on you."

He laughed. "Our very first meeting on the Bromleigh property? You were up a tree even then."

She nodded. "And so scared of my feelings that I tried to avoid you as much as possible. Please tell me you will survive this."

He had never seen Florence, this strong, stubborn woman, so vulnerable. Knowing how guarded she had been all of her life, he understood what it took for her to open up and reveal how deeply she cared for him.

He groaned and kissed the top of her head once again because she had kept her eyes downcast all the while, too ashamed of herself to look up at him. "It is merely a flesh wound, love. I will survive it."

"Promise me you will."

"Not only will I promise you, but we are going to leave for London at first light tomorrow, just as planned."

"No!" She stared at him in disbelief. "How can you risk it? You need to recover."

"A night's rest is all I need."

"We'll ask the doctor what he thinks," she said, mistakenly believing the doctor's decision would resolve this disagreement.

It wouldn't. If he was still breathing come sunrise, Trajan was going to ride off with her to London. Nothing mattered more to him than getting rid of those infernal letters.

It was just after midnight by the time the doctor arrived to tend to his injury, which Trajan estimated would require over a dozen stitches to fix.

"That many?" Florence asked, paling.

"A bit more than that, I'm afraid. It could have been worse," Dr. Pritchard replied. "His Grace is fortunate it is merely a flesh wound. There are no fragments of lead lodged in the muscle or bone, just a nasty tear that stitches will repair. However, it will leave a scar."

Florence groaned.

Trajan caught her as she teetered. "You shouldn't be in here while the doctor stitches me up." Besides, his shirt was off, and that left him naked from the waist up. Not a proper sight for an unmarried lady.

Although there was nothing proper about anything Florence had done leading up to now.

"We are betrothed. Where else should I be but by your side?" Florence insisted, looking a little green.

Her voice sounded thin and wobbly, and this concerned him. "Will you listen to yourself, Florence? You are making too much of a mere flesh wound. You really ought to leave. Not only because you cannot handle the sight of my blood. Need I remind you we are not married yet? It isn't appropriate for you to be in here."

"Was it appropriate that you were shot?" Her eyes began to tear again. "How can I think about propriety when your life is at stake?"

He sighed. "Sebastian, bring over that chair. Florence, sit down before you faint and the doctor has another patient on his hands."

"I am not going to faint." She kissed him on the cheek and sank into the chair as soon as Sebastian brought it over.

The doctor voiced no opinion about her presence. He must have dealt with this often enough whenever a patient's loved ones were present.

Yes, Florence surely counted as a loved one. But Trajan had not expected her to be so overset.

And yet he ought to have realized she hid a lovely softness beneath her brash and confident exterior. She'd needed that hard shell to protect her from an unloving family.

But *gad*. She was so soft inside. So filled with love that she was aching to give.

However, she was also racked with guilt and completely torn apart because she continued to blame herself for his injury.

"Florence," he said, giving her hand a squeeze, "I want you to stay with me, but you must stop crying. I am not going to die."

She sniffled and nodded. Then cried a little more.

In truth, it felt good to be needed. And so good to be loved.

Especially good because Florence was the one who needed him and loved him. That she trusted him enough to discard her mask and show her true self was a major step for her.

In truth, it was monumental, for she had worked so hard to prove she could stand on her own, be independent and fierce.

She dried her tears on the sleeve of her gown and cast him an achingly sweet smile that almost broke him.

He liked this gentler side of Florence very much.

Not that he ever wanted her to be tearful or helplessly trembling. This was not really in her nature. Even when scared, she would find the courage to fight with all her heart. But he wanted to fight alongside her, not be held at arm's length because she was afraid to let anyone close.

Well, she was letting him close now. There was something deep and wonderful developing between them.

Was this what people meant when they spoke of true love?

CHAPTER FIFTEEN

T RAJAN HELD FLORENCE'S hand while the doctor stitched his wound.

In truth, he did not know which one of them was offering comfort, because they both seemed to need each other and took heart in holding on to each other. But he thought perhaps Florence needed him more.

He brought her hand to his lips and kissed it lightly. "Be strong for me, love. All right?"

She nodded.

He liked this feeling of caring for someone more than he cared for himself. They were betrothed, and although it had come about for the purpose of protecting Florence from Frampton, it had felt right and good from the start.

"I am going to rub a cleansing astringent on the area of the wound, Your Grace. This might sting a little."

"I'm ready." Trajan was inclined to like this doctor, who seemed a practical fellow and not prone to judging others. Apparently, he was the one who had treated his granduncle, and the staff thought very highly of him.

"So am I," Florence said, tipping her chin up with determination. "What do you need me to do?"

"Just hold His Grace's hand and offer him comfort," the doctor said, arching an eyebrow and grinning at Trajan. "As you are already doing."

"All right." She cast Trajan another achingly vulnerable smile.

If this adoration was merely an act on her part, then she was a very good actress. But he knew there was no guile or artifice in Florence. She was earnest and honest almost to a fault.

And if he were being honest with himself, he had to admit his feelings for her were beyond anything he had ever imagined possible between two people.

He loved Florence.

There was also quite a bit of soul binding going on, too. That nonsense poets spouted about two hearts becoming one, or two souls recognizing each other through time, might not have been so nonsensical after all.

Blessed saints. The loss of blood had left him a bit lightheaded and not thinking straight.

Also, he was in a lot of pain. The stitches hurt, each one feeling like a pin going through his arm as the doctor sewed him up. Which was exactly what the doctor was doing, repairing the ugly gash with needle and thread.

He kept his mind on Florence. He was going to sweep her into his arms and kiss her breathless as soon as the doctor was finished.

He wanted to do more than merely kiss her. His clothes were mostly off anyway. And his bed was big and comfortable.

He shook his head and sighed. Nothing was going to happen between them while they had a houseful of relatives and a worried staff watching their every move.

Botheration.

Lord, he really wanted her.

"Your Grace," the doctor said, taking hold of his shoulder as he was about to insert the final stitches into the gash.

"I'm ready." Trajan turned to Florence, just wanting to look at her and make certain she would stay strong.

The breath caught in his lungs at the look of love she cast him.

The doctor finished stitching him up. He hardly felt a thing now. Was this because he was concentrating on Florence and staring into her eyes of love?

What was *happening* to him?

"Your Grace, I am going to…"

The doctor was saying something to him, but he was only half listening. "Right, fine." His thoughts remained on Florence and her beautiful face.

He was going to kiss away her tears as soon as the doctor was finished with him. Yes, kiss her and see what else might come of it. Tonight, and every other night thereafter.

Why should he care what anyone said or thought?

And if not tonight, then they would be alone together in London soon enough.

Was it not a good time to bind their love? Drop the letters with the princess. Obtain the marriage license. Marry Florence. Make her his.

Not necessarily in that order.

That the two of them—

Ouch!

"Bloody blazes!"

The doctor had just poured a fiery liquid onto his wound that now had his body in flames, and not in any good way. That *burned*!

Of course, this was what the doctor had been trying to warn him about. He ought to have listened instead of gawking at Florence like a besotted idiot.

"Trajan," she said softly, putting a hand to his cheek.

He gave a groaning laugh. "I'm fine."

She smiled at him.

"Are *you* all right?"

"Yes, now that the doctor has taken care of you. Sebastian and I will help you into bed, and then I'll order some broth with marrow brought up for you. It is good for restoring your blood. You've lost quite a bit of it. Mrs. Palmer has beef stock already made for tomorrow's menu. It will do you good to have some now."

Who knew that Florence had any nurturing in her? He liked that she was fussing over him.

But what a week this had been, and it was only halfway done. Betrothed, threatened, and shot, when all he had meant to do that first day was take a morning walk. He should have walked in the opposite direction.

Well, no. That would have been disastrous. He would have found Florence dead in his woods because the girl did not know how to lie her way out of any situation. Frampton would have confronted her and killed her.

He shook out of the thought and concentrated instead on the splendid kiss they had shared on the beach. That kiss made up for all the turmoil that had ensued…almost.

There was no rest to be had until Florence was safe.

But would she ever be safe while Frampton walked free and his evil doings were not exposed?

Trajan had to give this serious thought. Frampton had to be stopped.

What were they to do next? And how could he think straight when Florence was staring at him with big, soft eyes?

"Your Grace," the doctor said, regaining his attention and proceeding to instruct him on the care of his wound.

Florence and Sebastian were listening attentively, too. Good, because Trajan realized those instructions were going in one ear and out the other. He was not at his best right now and could not seem to hold anything in his brain.

"How many stitches in all?" Sebastian asked.

"Twenty," the doctor said, surprising Trajan, for he did not realize the wound had necessitated that many. Well, he had been stubbornly ignoring his injury while off chasing that assailant.

Florence was tearing up again.

"I forbid you to cry," he told her in a soft and loving growl.

She laughed as she nodded and her tears still fell.

"The wound is clean," the doctor assured him, "and you

should make a full recovery within a few days. Get a good night's rest, Your Grace. Take it easy tomorrow. Cancel anything strenuous. No morning ride, no lifting anything heavier than a teapot. No driving a rig. You have plenty of staff who can help you with anything you require. If you must leave home, then have someone drive you wherever you need to go. Although I would urge you to remain in bed all day tomorrow."

Trajan nodded. "I've nothing urgent. I'll do as you suggest."

He hated to lie to the doctor, but could not risk his travel plans being reported to Frampton.

He cast Florence and Sebatian warning looks as he began to embellish. "I had planned to take Miss Newton and her aunt on a tour of Weymouth, perhaps a picnic and a fossil hunt, but this can wait for another day."

"Yes, put it off for a day or two. Summon me at once if you develop a fever."

Florence frowned. "Is it likely?"

"No, I believe His Grace's wound has been thoroughly cleansed. But this happens sometimes."

"I'll be fine," Trajan insisted.

Florence was still frowning. "I understand. Just do not be stubborn or needlessly heroic. Your healing is more important than anything to me."

"Give me a kiss, Florence. You're the best medicine any man can have."

She blushed. Sebastian and the doctor chuckled.

But this was the last bit of merriment Trajan felt, because the fact remained that Frampton had meant to kill Florence.

How was he to protect her?

CHAPTER SIXTEEN

FLORENCE KNEW SHE was being stubborn when refusing to leave Trajan's side.

There was nothing scandalous about her remaining in his bedchamber, because his cousins also declared their intention to camp out here overnight.

"I am not hosting a bloody party in my room," Trajan grumbled. "All of you, out."

"No," she said, holding her ground. Was it not right that they all should be worried about him?

It was well into the wee hours by the time the magistrate finished taking Trajan's statement. The doctor conducted a quick examination of the assailant's corpse and declared him to have died of a broken neck received due to an accidental fall.

The magistrate, an older man by the name of Lord Amos Charwood, seemed competent enough and also quite deferential to Trajan when asking his questions. He accepted the duke's account in full. "Your Grace, do you recognize this man at all?"

"No, and neither does anyone on my staff. We have no idea who sent him to cause this mischief."

"And you, Lady Florence? Have you ever seen this man before?"

"No, and I can assure you that my aunt has not either. Did you know that Lord Frampton had complained to us of trespassers just the other day? I recommend you question him and his staff about this man. I'm sure someone at Frampton Court must have seen him and may be able to provide a name to his blasphemous soul."

Trajan squeezed her hand. "Florence, no need to involve anyone else in this affair."

"Your Grace, your betrothed makes a good point," Charwood said. "I'll stop by Frampton Court tomorrow and have a chat with his lordship. Let's hope he did not have a similar incident."

"Do send him our warmest regards," Florence said. "And let him know we look forward to seeing him again shortly."

Oh, she knew Trajan would be scathing mad at her for the impertinent remark. But how *dare* Frampton send this man to hurt them! Should they not send a message right back to let him know they were not intimidated?

Lord Charwood walked out with the doctor. Andrew escorted the two men out.

This left Nathan and Sebastian in the bedchamber with her and Trajan, whose scowl was as thunderous as a summer squall. "Florence, are you purposely trying to goad Frampton?"

"Not at all. But is it not important to let him know that we do not fear him? And that we will not be stopped in our mission to right his wrongs."

"We?" He groaned as he stretched out on his mattress, his arm a hideous shade of red because it was inflamed and had black stitches poking out of it. He was obviously exhausted and in pain. "You might have given me a few days to recover before going at him again."

"He has to know that he has gone too far this time. He's just had his man shoot a duke, and the entire royal family will be in a livid rage when they learn of it. Besides, if you are well enough to travel to London, as you proclaim, then you are well enough to stand up to Frampton. You have been brilliant so far."

"Do not flatter me. I have not been so brilliant," he grumbled. "Did you not notice I was shot?"

"All the more reason to draw that horrible man out. As soon as we get to London and hand those letters over to the princess, we ought to stop by the Home Office and alert them about Frampton's activities. Or we can go directly to the prime minister. He'll want to hear about this, especially if he was the clot who wrote those letters to Lady Simmons."

"Let's just worry about getting to London at all," he said, yawning. "Go to bed, Florence. Your *own* bed. You're not sleeping in here. My cousins will look after me."

She reluctantly did as he asked, because he was hurting and she was to blame for it, no matter than he continued to deny it.

However, before leaving, she addressed his cousins. "Check his brow during the night. Summon me immediately if he turns feverish."

Andrew assured her they would.

She looked in on Hermia before retiring to her own chamber.

"Oh, my dear," Hermia said, stretching out her arms to her. "Come here and let me give you a hug. I'm so sorry I was out of your life for so long. I should have taken you from my brother when you were still a child."

Florence hugged her. "You couldn't have known. Besides, you were always kind to me whenever you visited."

"Which was never often enough."

Florence smiled. "You have no idea how little it takes to satisfy a child starved for love. A gentle pat on the hand. A smile. Taking me onto your lap. Those small gestures kept me going until your next visit."

"I'm glad, child. Although it really was not enough."

She kissed her aunt and bade her sweet dreams before returning to her own bedchamber. She had once asked Hermia if she knew the reason why her mother disliked her so much, but her aunt claimed she did not.

That was years ago, and she had not asked again. Perhaps when this Frampton affair was resolved, she would try once more. Florence sensed her aunt knew more than she was telling her about her family situation.

Would her brother or parents care that Frampton had tried to kill her tonight?

Fatigue overcame her once she was abed, and she fell asleep quickly.

She awoke amid the gray haze of approaching dawn, and was on her feet, washed and dressed in a gown suitable for riding, although it was not an actual riding habit, by the time the cock's crow marked the sunrise.

Most of the staff was not yet awake. There was not a sound in the house, although the scullery maids were probably rousing about now, since they had to light the kitchen fires.

Trajan had insisted they leave for London at first light, but she was not certain it would happen. She made her way to his bedchamber, knocked lightly, and, when she heard no response, quietly entered.

After all, why disturb his cousins if they were still asleep?

But the cousins were all awake, their clothes rumpled because they had slept in them, and sporting cowlicks and stubbles of beards, since they had not yet groomed themselves.

Trajan was also awake.

Dear heaven.

Magnificently awake.

He had just finished washing up and was now shaving, but what caught her breath was that he had nothing on save a towel wrapped low around his hips.

She had walked in on him while he was giving his cousins final instructions. None of them noticed her at first. She couldn't make a sound to alert them of her presence.

Nor could she breathe while gawking at Trajan's trim, muscled body.

"Florence," he said, turning toward her and frowning. "Are you all packed?"

She nodded, unable to stop staring at his broad shoulders or his sculpted torso.

Dear heaven. He was magnificent.

"Good, then wait for me in your bedchamber. I'll be along in a few minutes to get you and your belongings."

His cousins were smirking. She could not stop gawking at Trajan.

Sebastian rose and approached her. "Let me escort you back. Deucedly early, isn't it? Your eyes look like they are about to bug out of their sockets."

"I'll have the grooms ready your horses," Nathan said, also getting to his feet and trying not to chuckle at her.

Andrew stayed perched on the arm of one of the hearth chairs, no doubt remaining behind to assist Trajan in dressing. His valet, Reed, was also awake and assisting him.

Florence frowned, for Trajan's arm appeared even redder and more inflamed than yesterday. "Check his brow, Andrew. Does he have a fever?"

Trajan scowled. "Don't touch me. I am fine."

She strode over to him and put her hand to his forehead. "You are warm."

"Because I am hot for you," he said with enough heat to turn her cheeks to fire.

His cousins could not contain their laughter. Reed had turned away, but Florence saw his shoulders shaking and knew he also found Trajan's quips humorous.

Were all men so infantile?

Florence knew she should not be in his bedchamber, but was it not more important to make certain he was not burning up with fever? And he did have a fever, although it was a fairly mild one.

She looked at his eyes, and they appeared clear enough. She would have pushed him back in bed had they been glazed or unfocused. "Trajan…"

"I'm all right, love," he said more gently because he noted her distress. "Truly. We're only going to ride as far as Poole and then catch a mail coach directly to London. From then on, I can sleep the entire way to London."

"Is there not someplace closer that—"

"I dare not have us take the coach from Weymouth. That is the closest one, but Frampton might have his men watching for us."

She nodded. "All right, I see your point. But you know I am not a good rider."

"You'll have to do your best. We have to get to London fast, and this is the best I could come up with. It will take us a full day's riding just to get to Poole. Can you manage it?"

She winced. "Yes, I can manage. It is you I am worried about."

A light mist fell as they left the house a few minutes later and made their way to the stable. Nathan was standing by the saddled horses while Sebastian and Andrew followed with their travel bags. "We could come with you," Nathan said. "It won't take me a moment to saddle three more horses."

"No," Trajan insisted. "I need you to protect Gull Hall. Believe me, it is not an easy task. Frampton is going to be livid once he learns we are on our way to London. Your role is to delay his finding out as long as possible. You have my authority to dismiss anyone on my staff who gossips about our departure."

"No one will," Andrew said. "They like you. No one likes Frampton."

"Well, he has his spies. But this could also work in our favor. Let word spread that I was hurt. Exaggerate the rumors of my injuries. I want Frampton to think I am in my sickbed and Florence is racked with worry while tending me. Most of all, be ready for something to happen once he learns he's been tricked."

"He will figure it out in a day or two when he summons Dr. Pritchard for a report," Florence said. "I don't see how the doctor can lie to him. If Frampton does question the doctor or anyone on the Weymouth staff, then Andrew must proceed with the backup plan."

Andrew nodded. "Got it. I'll pretend I am Trajan, grab that

young maid, Felicity, and have her disguised as you, Florence. Then we'll take the Weymouth carriage and ride to Bath. You've said this is where Lady Simmons is right now."

Trajan nodded.

Nathan grinned. "You have a wonderfully devious mind, Florence. This makes perfect sense. Frampton will believe it, and this will get him running after you in the wrong direction."

Andrew gave her a mock salute. "Good idea. Bath it is. Got it."

"Your cousin is the brilliant one who thought it up," she said with a shake of her head. "I hope it won't be necessary. I'd much prefer all of you to remain safe here at Gull Hall."

"You just get yourself safely to London and don't worry about us," Sebastian said.

Florence released a shaky breath. "And watch over Aunt Hermia for me. She's all I have."

All three cousins nodded. "We've got her," Nathan assured her.

Sebastian helped her onto her horse, a big bay by the name of Centurion that looked hardy enough to gallop a hundred miles. Trajan's steed, a black stallion named Rubicon, appeared to be just as hardy.

Poole was less than thirty miles away. These horses were strong enough to make it there with hardly a lather.

She was the one who would slow them down with her inexperience riding. "What are we to do with the horses once we reach Poole?"

"They'll be left at the Redfern stable," Trajan told his cousins, who seemed to know the place well.

"I'll ride over with several grooms, but not before the week is out," Nathan assured him. "Don't want to give Frampton any hints about your whereabouts. Old Redfern can be trusted to care for those beasts until we arrive to pick them up. You'll be in London by then. Safe travels. Come back married."

Trajan laughed. "Will do."

The mist stopped shortly after they got underway, and they spent most of the day riding in sunshine. Dry roads and a light breeze off the water accompanied them for much of the ride.

Florence appreciated the good weather, because she struggled to keep up with Trajan, who appeared to struggle himself from time to time. But he was too stubborn to rest, and only agreed to stop when the horses needed to be fed and watered.

They reached Poole shortly before nightfall, having ridden for hours on end.

Florence's legs buckled when she finally dismounted upon reaching the Redfern stable, but she could match Trajan for stubbornness and refused to admit she had reached the limit of her endurance.

Redfern was the jovial owner and the one who ran out to greet them. He was quite a character, portly, with a bright-red face and sporting a stark-white beard. He spoke in a thick Cornish accent that Florence had to concentrate to understand. But she easily caught the gist of what he and Trajan were saying to each other.

Trajan handed over a fistful of coins and instructed Redfern to give their horses his finest care. "One of my cousins will come to pick them up in a week's time. Meanwhile, it is no one's business they are boarded here. Understood?"

"Aye, Your Grace. My lips are sealed." Redfern then called for his lads to take the reins and lead both horses to their stalls.

Florence had to admit the man ran an efficient and well-kept stable.

Their next task was to find lodgings, but Trajan did not appear worried about this either. "The Kenford Inn will suit," he said, before calling for one of Redfern's boys to follow him with their bags. "It's just around the corner."

Night was falling, but she was not worried. She could see they were in the finer side of town. The shops were elegant and the taverns they passed seemed to host a better class of gentleman drunk.

The Kenford Inn was indeed a beautiful lodging house that seemed to be a hub of activity.

"The mail coach to London stops here," Trajan explained.

"Truly? It seems too fine an inn to be on the mail route."

"There are several coaches that make their way along the seacoast route to London. This is one of the better ones. Fare is higher, so we will sweat and choke on dust with a better class of passengers," he jested. "I'll hire a private coach to bring us back to Weymouth once we finish our business in London."

Florence did not care if they rode donkeys back to Weymouth. She just wanted Frampton brought down, his hopes of high office dashed.

Surely the man who had written those letters to Lady Simmons would want his revenge. Perhaps she could convince that powerful lord to take action against Frampton.

Unfortunately, she did not know who he was, and had solemnly promised the Princess of Wales that she would not peek at those letters.

Drat. Being honest had its drawbacks.

The innkeeper seemed to know Trajan. "Your Grace! It is an honor."

But he cast furtive glances at Florence, no doubt wondering who she was. Since she felt weary to the bone and probably looked quite haggard, he could not possibly think she was some immoral seductress Trajan was taking to his bed for an evening.

"This is my wife," Trajan explained, surprising her as much as he surprised the innkeeper. "Newly wed, and perhaps we took on a little too much travel all at once. Didn't we, my love? Our baggage cart is days behind us. We'll require your best chamber, of course. And meals brought up for us."

"At once, Your Grace. I'll have my lads bring up whatever bags you've brought with you."

"We've only these small travel pouches. Make note for tomorrow that we'll have an early breakfast in our chamber, and we will require seats on the next mail coach to London."

"The mail coach?" The innkeeper appeared surprised by the last request. "Ah, but it leaves quite early in the morning."

"Then wake us in time to catch it. Are there seats still available?"

"Yes, Your Grace. It is often full, but you are in luck. You'll have only two riders with you to Bournemouth, and they have reserved the outside seats. I'm sure the coach will fill up at Bournemouth, though."

This meant she and Trajan would ride alone inside the coach for most of tomorrow. This was an acceptable compromise and would get them further from Weymouth in the fastest possible way.

They followed the innkeeper, an earnest-looking man by the name of Doncaster, upstairs. Florence was surprised by the luxury of their accommodations, although her heart was pounding because she and Trajan were to share the one room.

And the one bed.

"Your Grace," the innkeeper said, and it took Florence a moment to realize he was addressing her, "shall I send a maid up to assist you?"

"That is very kind of you, but my gowns are quite practical for travel. I'll take care of myself. And I am certain His Grace will not mind helping me with anything I cannot manage on my own." She smiled up at Trajan.

He took her hand in his and raised it to his lips. "Ever your servant." Then he dropped several coins in the innkeeper's palm for good measure.

"This is cozy," Florence said, letting out a breath once Doncaster had shut the door behind him. "You might have warned me about the sleeping arrangements. Not to mention the marital declaration."

"I should have," he admitted, "but we were riding hard and did not have time for a conversation about this. I intend to sleep on the floor, so you needn't worry."

She laughed lightly. "You will not. I'll take the floor, or we could share that ample bed. Sharing is the most sensible solution, don't you think? I long to fall asleep in your arms, Trajan. Is it wicked of me?"

"Not at all. We are as good as husband and wife."

"But not married yet." She shook her head. "We needn't discuss it. I am with you on this, since I am safest keeping close to you. I'll need to wash the dust off my hands and face, and change into my nightclothes."

He cast her a tender smile. "I can head downstairs for twenty minutes and have a drink while—"

"It isn't necessary. You can turn away or simply close your eyes whenever I need my privacy." She studied him a moment longer, noting the weariness in his eyes and wondering whether he still had a touch of fever. "Why don't you make yourself comfortable on the bed? You must be exhausted, although you are stubbornly trying to hide this from me. Will you let me take care of you?"

He arched an eyebrow. "Aren't I the one who ought to be taking care of you?"

"I've spent a lifetime doing things for myself." She nudged him onto the bed, and he offered little resistance. "Shall I help you take off your boots? You mustn't do it yourself or you'll strain the stitches. I can help you off with your clothes, too."

"Florence, are you seducing me?" he teased. "What's a shy fellow to think? Removing my clothes. Tossing me onto the bed."

She grinned. "You have found me out. I long to get at your body."

"And I ache to get at yours. Do you mind? But you have only to say the word and I will keep hands off you until we are married."

"Don't you dare. Is it not odd that I feel so comfortable around you? I am such a private person, and yet I am not shy about sharing everything with you."

"Because you trust me."

"I do," she said, studying his face. "I trust you and adore you."

He stretched out on the bed and clasped his hands behind his head. "I like where this is going."

"I thought you might. Trajan, you are very much in my heart."

"Mutual, Florence. It feels nice, doesn't it?" She saw the heat in his eyes and the tenderness in his smile as he watched her.

"Yes, I never thought such happiness was possible for me."

"Nor did I for myself."

She placed a hand to his forehead and breathed a sigh of relief when it felt cool to the touch. Nevertheless, she rose from his side for a moment to dampen one of her handkerchiefs in the ewer perched on a night table. After wringing it out, she returned to his side. "Keep this on your forehead for a little while."

He did not protest, so she suspected he might have had a headache even if there was no accompanying fever.

She stayed by his side and removed her boots, then did the same with his. "Do not help me," she insisted. "Your stitches, remember? I can manage this for you."

However, she did ask for his help in unlacing her gown. In truth, it was something she could have managed herself. But he appeared to be growing restless, not liking that she was taking on all the chores while he lay abed.

There was hardly anything to do. How was any of this onerous in the least?

But she liked the idea of having him assist her in removing her gown. Not only was it helpful, it was intimate as well.

He took his time with each lacing, and his touch felt wonderful. She tingled everywhere he touched her. She burned wherever he caressed her.

This man knew how to melt a lady.

She forced herself to tear away from his side in order to remove the packet of letters hidden in the secret pocket of her gown.

Trajan frowned. "What are you doing?"

"I thought to ask one of the inn's maids to freshen my gown.

It is so dusty. I'll choke if I have to wear it tomorrow." She held up the packet of letters. "I had better hide these elsewhere."

"Put them in your travel pouch for now," he said. "No one's going to touch them there."

"All right." She supposed it was more sensible than sticking them under the mattress and leaving them behind as they hurried to catch the mail coach.

After securing them in the pouch, she removed her gown and set it aside to hand over to the maid when their meal was brought in. The fabric was dusty and a little wrinkled. It only required the dust shaken off and a quick pressing. This should not take long. The maid could return the garment by the time she and Trajan finished dining.

"How about you? Anything you wish to give over for cleaning?"

"I'll think about it."

"All right." She was not going to insist, since tomorrow's ride would be just as dusty.

She thought to don her nightgown and robe, but wanted to wash up first. She wore only her shift, a practical cotton garment, but the material was thin and one could see through it under a bright enough light.

Perhaps he might think her shameless, but she really did not care if he saw all of her. In fact, it was time that he did, and she hoped he might do something about it tonight.

While Trajan watched her, she took a cloth, dampened it, and then applied soap to the cloth. She then ran it over her body to wash the layers of dirt off her skin.

This inn was of the highest quality, she noted. Where else would Farthingale soaps be provided for their guests? And they had a choice, no less. Lined up beside the basin and ewer were four cakes from which to choose. She put her nose to each one and inhaled. Sandalwood was the obvious choice for Trajan when he washed up. The next two were fruity scents. Peach and strawberry. The last was citrus. Lemon.

She felt like a peach.

Trajan looked quite comfortable as he watched her, his hands still clasped behind his head and the damp handkerchief still on his forehead.

When she was done, she donned her robe and dug out her brush from the travel pouch. She then unpinned her hair and was about to brush it when Trajan tossed the handkerchief aside and sat up. "Come here, Florence," he said in a husky murmur that had her insides melting. "Let me help you with that."

His smoldering gaze burned into her. By his wicked smile, Florence knew he meant to do more than merely brush her hair.

Her heart skipped beats.

She sat beside him and gave her back to him. He spent more time running his fingers through her hair and nuzzling her neck than actually brushing. Then he slipped the robe and the sleeves of her shift off her shoulders to bare them to his lips.

Dear heaven.

This was most exciting.

But how were they to get anything accomplished when he was so distracting?

A knock at the door had her bolting to attention. "That's our food."

He laughingly groaned and sank back onto the mattress. "Ah, yes. We did order a meal, didn't we?"

"Do you want your boots polished? The garments you wore today dusted off? These are quick chores, and we could request to have everything brought back before we fall asleep tonight."

"Florence, stop darting about. You are making me dizzy. Are you worried about something?"

She shook her head. "Not worried, just…uncertain. I like the way you were touching me. I've never experienced these sensations before."

"I know, love," he said gently, and rose to walk to the door. "But you'll like what's to come. I should not have started something when I knew we would be interrupted."

"I didn't mind."

"Good. This is to be continued after supper," he said, then gave her a quick kiss on the lips before he opened the door.

As the maid rolled in the cart, their room filled with a delicious aroma. Florence handed her gown to the girl, and Trajan did the same with his jacket and boots. He then gave the girl several coins. "We'll need them back within the hour."

"Yes, Your Grace." The maid scurried off with the bundle of garments and his boots.

Trajan shut the door and then turned to Florence. "Are you hungry? Or of a mind to continue what I started before we were interrupted?"

She melted at his wicked grin that also managed to be tender and endearing. "What do you wish to do? I've never done anything like this before."

"What? Eat?"

She laughed. "It's nice being here with you."

"Makes one forget we are on the run from a desperate, deranged lord that I hope will not be soon on our trail."

"Ugh, do not mention him. You'll spoil what I hope will be a most promising night for me. My first time. I've never been with a man before."

"I know, love. I promise you'll enjoy it."

She cast him a gentle smile. "I'm looking forward to it. But may we eat first? I'm famished."

"So am I."

He hastily washed up before sitting down to supper, choosing the sandalwood soap for himself.

Florence inhaled his scent as he sat beside her at the small table in their quarters. "Nice."

He breathed her in and gave her a heated kiss on the neck in return. "Even nicer."

She smiled as she dished out the simple repast of ham in a honey glaze and roasted potatoes that they both enjoyed.

As they were finishing the hearty meal, the maid returned

with his polished boots and their refurbished clothes. Trajan waited for the girl to wheel the cart out of their chamber, and then he latched the door and propped a chair against it for added security.

"The chair will topple if anyone tries to get in. I'm a light sleeper and will certainly hear the thud if it falls." He next tucked a knife under his pillow, set his boots beside him, and tucked a pistol in the lip of the right boot. "Probably unnecessary, but why take chances?" He took the letters out of her pouch and tucked them into the hidden pocket of the gown she was to wear tomorrow. "One less thing to remember as we scramble out of here in the morning."

She nodded. "What next?"

He cast her a breathtaking smile. "I kiss you."

CHAPTER SEVENTEEN

T RAJAN WAS EXPERIENCED in the bedchamber, but bedding Florence was proving to be more of a challenge than he expected because their hearts were involved, and hers was so fragile.

In all his years, he had never imagined himself falling in love with a big-eyed, slightly eccentric, and definitely stubborn bluestocking who trusted him, needed him, and loved him as no one had ever done before.

She cast him a smile filled with hope, heart, and sunshine.

"I love you," she said as he drew her close to kiss her.

With her words, she was also giving him permission to take her outside of the bonds of marriage.

But he was not certain she was truly ready for this yet.

As for him, he had been ready since first setting eyes on her. "Mutual, Florence."

Oh, he wanted her with an agonizing urgency.

He would show her pleasure tonight, but it hurt him to know that she would absorb his every kiss and caress, soak it all in like a little sponge because she had been denied love for so long. For this reason, he intended to wait until they were married to claim her as a husband should claim his wife because…well, taking her without that vow of marriage felt like a *taking* and not a *giving*. As though he were taking advantage instead of bestowing his heart, and it did not feel right.

Every time he thought of it, he was angered that she had been raised to feel lesser all of her life. Despite everything, she had accomplished so much.

And yet this notion of her being unworthy still haunted her. She carried it around like a great stone weighing upon her slight shoulders, waiting for the moment it would crush her.

To prove his point, she sighed and said, "I still do not see why you have feelings for me."

Trajan was impatient by nature, but he knew that healing Florence with his love would take a while. "I am not your parents," he said. "Whatever reasons they had for treating you like an outcast have nothing to do with the soul of *who* you are. I think this has to be our next investigation, something to be addressed once you and I are married and I can protect you from whatever we might learn."

He led her to the bed, stretched out beside her, and then took her in his arms. "I love you because you are beautiful and clever. You are also too independent for my liking, but that makes me like you all the more. Does this make any sense to you?"

She laughed lightly. "No, it doesn't."

"You think for yourself. You know who you are and what you believe in. And you care about *me*. Not the title. You would risk your life for me…not that I would ever let you do it. But it is nice to know you are always on my side."

"I am and will always be," she said with earnest ferocity.

"I know, love." He leaned over and kissed her with a soft crush of his lips to her own.

She sighed. "Lovely."

He kissed her again, a deeper kiss this time, and pressed his body lightly over hers because he wanted her to know how it would feel to have his body atop hers when they coupled. He wanted her to know that she was his mate and the one with whom he would spend a lifetime.

What came next felt natural and easy, for she responded to the touch of his hands and lips upon her body, accepting each new sensation and letting herself go because she trusted him to take her on this journey.

She closed her eyes and emitted breathy moans and soft purrs as he touched and teased her and aroused her.

She gasped when he put his mouth to her breast and suckled the bud.

He thought to draw away.

"No, Trajan. I like this very much."

All right, then.

He held back a chuckle when she clasped his head and held him to her so tightly that his nose was buried in her breast.

Well, who ever said the course of true love had to run perfectly smooth?

"Florence, ease up," he mumbled, lifting off her slightly to move to her other breast.

"Oh." She let go of him.

"Put your hands on my shoulders, love."

Her lips were pink and warm, and her eyes shimmered. She looked like a woman experiencing passion, which pleased him mightily. "All right, why?"

"Because I am going to send you soaring, and I want you to hold on to me."

She smiled. "I have no idea what that means, but it sounds thrilling."

"It will be. Do you trust me?"

Her expression turned earnest. "You know I do."

Yes, because her heart was as fragile as glass, and he was the only one she had ever dared trust to keep it safe and protected.

Perhaps this was why she was so completely wrapped in his heart. For all her independence and stubbornness, she wanted him and needed him.

He knew she would give every ounce of herself to him when he claimed her.

No hesitation. She was all in.

"Close your eyes, Florence," he whispered, and then kissed

her slow and deep.

His mouth sank onto her delicious lips and lingered there, lightly at first but with growing intensity. She took her cues from him and responded in kind, clasping his shoulders and drawing him close, as though afraid this moment might end if she ever let him go.

She seemed to like the press of his body upon hers, the warmth of it and the security of it. But he wanted her to know—and perhaps in time she would—that he would always be there for her even if she did let go.

Love was the string that bound him to her.

Of course, there was much to be said for the physical aspect, too. Their entwined arms, entangled legs, the friction of their bodies rubbing together and creating heat. Creating fire.

Her skin felt soft, and she quivered as he kissed his way down her body.

But she almost rolled off the bed in surprise when he put his mouth to the core of her parted legs and gave a soft lick. "Trajan!"

"Hush, love. The walls are thin."

"Oh, that is so unfair of you," she whispered, and gave a mirthful laugh, then clutched his head and drew him up by his ears. "Explain this. Why did liquid fire pour through me and set every pulse in my body throbbing?"

"May I get back to the task and explain later?" he said with a strained laugh.

His own body felt volcanic because he adored and craved everything about her. The softness of her skin, the scent and taste of it. The warmth of it. The lovely shape of her. The way she purred when he touched her.

"Can you not give me a quick hint now?"

He supposed this was what happened when one made love to an inquisitive bluestocking, so he moved back up and took her into his arms as he spoke. "There is no place more sensitive on a woman, Florence. Have you never read any books on this? Or spoken to friends about what takes place between a man and a woman?"

He knew her mother would never have explained this to her, since the woman had never done anything kind or helpful for Florence in her life.

"I did read a little about it, but never really bothered because…"

"Because you never thought anyone would love you," he said, quietly seething as he finished her thought. "But *I* love you."

She cast him a heartbreakingly tender smile. "Will you please continue? I did not mean to interrupt you."

He laughed softly. "Are you sure?"

She nodded. "Never more certain of anything in my life."

Trajan resumed his onslaught, thinking he had to start all over again to stir her passion. But he needn't have worried, for they were both lost to each other, ravenous and craving each other in less than the span of three heartbeats.

He once more kissed his way down her silky body, felt the rush of fire as he pressed his mouth to her core and tasted her sweet nectar.

She responded with exquisite innocence, and soon shattered in pleasure for what he expected was her first time ever.

He looked up and watched her, completely caught up and undone by the wild toss of her dark mane tumbling over her shoulders and partially covering her glorious breasts, and the breathtaking beauty of her face while in the throes of passion.

After a moment, she opened her eyes. Indeed, they flew open, and she softly asked, "Trajan, what in heaven's name was that?"

He cast her a conquering grin. "Did you like it?"

She nodded. "Was I not obvious? What did you do to me? Goodness, my skin is so hot. My heart is still beating too fast."

He rolled onto his back and drew her into his arms with a possessive growl.

But she wouldn't stay nestled in his embrace. She squirmed to her knees and hastily reached for her nightgown that was lost amid the sheets.

Praise heaven.

What a body she had. Gorgeous legs. Pert, sweet breasts. He was going to turn into a wild ape if he did not stop staring at her.

"Does it work the same way for you?" she asked.

"Yes, love. Possibly stronger. The male urges are pretty intense."

This seemed to surprise her. "What must I do to get you to respond to me in this way?"

"Nothing. Gad, Florence. Even now, I am desperate to roll you under me and have at your pink, pouty mouth and insanely luscious body. Do you have any idea how incredibly lovely you are?"

Once again, she appeared surprised.

"Just be you. My body will do the rest. But do not tempt me now. Not tonight. It's getting late and we need to sleep, or we'll be dead to the world come morning and miss the mail coach."

She said nothing, merely looked disappointed.

"Tonight was meant for you, love. We'll continue this biology lesson as soon as we reach London. But I'm going to marry you first. Then we'll arrange to deliver the letters to the princess."

"Shouldn't we go to her first?"

"No." He was adamant about this. "You are not to seek an audience with her until you are my duchess. And I intend to be there with you."

"Because you think she is going to cheat me out of the promised reward?"

"Saving your brother is not much of a reward," he muttered. "She may not cheat you so much as pile on another requirement. The point is, this needs to end. And she needs to be told of Frampton's retribution."

Florence lightly touched his bandaged arm. "Oh, I ought to have checked on your wound."

"No need. I tended to it before we rode off this morning.

You'll help me apply the salve and a fresh bandage tomorrow morning before we get on the mail coach. Come into my arms now, Florence."

"All right." She nestled against him without protest.

He thought she might take a while to fall asleep because her mind was awhirl with questions.

To his surprise, she fell asleep within five minutes.

He was bone weary, too. And lost in sleep within six minutes.

Trajan awoke with the approaching dawn, still half lost in a torrid dream of Florence. Perhaps his dreams of her were particularly hot because she was all over him, her legs entangled in his and her ample bosom pressed against his chest.

She looked so pretty in sleep. But dawn was approaching.

What time was it?

He quietly slipped out of bed to attend to his necessaries before waking Florence. She had slept like a log the entire night, not even flinching when he slid his arm out from under her.

What a sweet body she had.

He felt some remorse about waking her when she was obviously exhausted. But it was time. He heard the quiet hum of activity in the common room and knew the morning hour had to be approaching six o'clock.

Why had the maid not come to wake them yet?

The mail coach was due to arrive at the inn within the next thirty minutes, stopping just long enough to pick up the outgoing mail, drop off the incoming mail, and take on any waiting passengers before taking off for Bournemouth and then turning northward to London.

"Florence," he whispered, giving her shoulder a light shake. "Wake up, love."

She grumbled.

He gave her shoulder another light shake. "We'll miss the coach."

Her eyes flickered open. "I'm up. Good morning, Trajan. You're looking awfully handsome. That shirtless, divinely muscled look suits you."

He grinned. "Do not think to gain another five minutes of sleep by flattering me."

She cast him a sleepy but endearing smile. "I am found out. All right, I'm up. But you are still divinely handsome. Give me a moment to wash up and dress, then I'll help you with the salve and fresh bandage."

"I've already taken care of the salve. I just need your assistance with the bandage." He showed her his arm, which looked red and inflamed even in the dimness of the gray light of dawn.

"The doctor gave you a vial of laudanum, but you haven't used it. Why not? The gash looks awfully painful."

He shook his head. "No pain, love. I have but to look at your lovely face and I am soothed."

"Gad, now who is tossing compliments? Curb that silver tongue of yours. It is too early in the morning."

He turned away while she hastily tended to herself. She took another moment to wash her hands and face with the peach soap that now filled the air with a delightfully fruity scent. Then she tossed on her gown but did not take the time to lace it. He would help her with those laces after she bound his arm.

Within another few minutes they were both dressed and had donned their boots, and Trajan helped her pin up her hair so that she did not look like a wild thing freshly emerged from a primordial forest shrouded in the mists of time.

But she had looked so pretty last night with those dark waves flowing down her back and over her shoulders. Too bad she could not leave her hair long and loose.

But a duchess could not go out in public like this.

The innkeeper clomped down the hall and frantically knocked at their door. "Your Graces! My apologies. The fool of a lass forgot to wake you. I'll hold the mail coach until—"

Trajan opened the door. "We are up. No harm done."

The man let out a breath of relief. "I sincerely do apologize. I'll have the lass bring up your breakfast now."

"Are the salvers set out in the common room?"

The innkeeper nodded.

"Then my wife and I will have our breakfast downstairs." They did not need to wait another ten minutes for the lass to bring up the tray only to be told the mail coach had arrived and they had to run down to catch it without time to eat a morsel.

Nor was he particularly worried about their being seen in public, since it would take at least another day before Frampton realized they were gone. Then he would be running off to Bath instead of London.

Hopefully.

Trajan and Florence had just finished their breakfast in the common room when the mail coach rumbled up to the inn.

Doncaster came running in. "The coach is here, Your Grace."

Trajan had brought down their travel pouches and now tossed them over his shoulder. "Are you ready, Florence?"

She nodded. "I can carry mine. You should not be lifting anything heavier than a teapot."

She was reminding him of the doctor's words, which he had completely ignored. He had not spent yesterday resting in bed and was not about to allow Florence to carry any of their bags. "A duchess does not do heavy lifting."

"Nor should wounded dukes," she retorted, frowning at him.

Doncaster took their pouches. "I'll place these in the mail coach. You are the only riders booked for the interior seats, although there will surely be more passengers awaiting the coach at Bournemouth."

It would take them much of the day to reach Bournemouth, assuming they did not stop for more than a few minutes at a time along each post inn and met with no bad weather or accidents. The only reason to stop, whether day or night, was to exchange the worn-out horses for fresh ones and continue at breakneck speed to the next coaching inn, where those horses would be exchanged for another fresh team.

If they managed to travel thirty-five miles per day, a goal

easily accomplished along these better-maintained toll roads, this would have them reaching London within four days. The ride would be shortened to only two days if they stayed on the mail coach, since those coaches ran through the night as well as the day and could travel as much as seventy miles in a full day, weather permitting.

But Trajan could not imagine them staying on this coach beyond Bournemouth, for these public conveyances were often too crowded and the odor of unwashed, overheated bodies was too much to bear. He could hire a private coach in Bournemouth, if necessary.

In any event, no matter which mode of transportation they took, they would arrive in London in under four days. By the morning of the fifth day, at the latest, he hoped to have the marriage license in hand and be wed to Florence.

Their friends, the Duke of Durham and his wife, Fiona, ought to be in London. If so, he would invite them to serve as witnesses at their wedding. The same for any of the other Silver Dukes and their wives who might be present.

In truth, he would be honored if Bromleigh, Lynton, Camborne, Ramsdale, and their wives would attend their ceremony.

But not Florence's parents. He did not know them and could not trust them. They had been hurtful to Florence for most of her life, and being present at her wedding ceremony was more likely to cause tumult rather than joy. Better they be told of her marriage after the fact.

"Let me help you into the coach, love," Trajan said, placing his arms in proprietary fashion around Florence's waist. After last night, he'd grown quite familiar with her body.

Great body.

He checked that their travel pouches were secured in the coach, and then climbed in after her, sinking onto the bench seat beside her with a grunt. "All good, love?"

She nodded and smiled up at him. "Perfect."

The mail coach took off as though demons were on their tail.

Florence, being fairly light, almost flew off her seat.

He tucked an arm around her as the coach bounced along with reckless speed, and kept hold of her throughout the ride.

Not only Florence needed to be held secure. He was worried about those letters falling out of the hidden pocket in her gown. But she cast him a reassuring glance. "All's well."

"Good." He had not brought up the subject yet, but he intended to read those love letters before they were turned over to the princess.

How could he not? It was important for him to know who wrote them to Lady Simmons, if only to prevent the princess from piling more tasks onto Florence.

Florence might be angry with him, but he would smooth things over afterward. After all, she may have promised the princess she would not read them, but *he* had made no such promise.

Of course, he had no intention of ever revealing the name of the writer or the contents of those letters to anyone, not even Florence. But he needed to gather as much information as he could in order to better protect her. She was extraordinarily naïve when it came to matters of politics and power.

They made Bournemouth before nightfall. Trajan had no idea how the outside passengers had not flown out of their seats every time the coach whipped around a sharp curve or hit a rut.

He and Florence stepped out and reclaimed their travel pouches.

"Will ye no' be riding with us?" the guard who rode on the mail coach asked. As a security measure, each coach had a driver and armed guard because they traveled at night as well as day, and every highwayman recognized the distinctive red and black of these coaches.

"No, we'll be making private arrangements from here. My wife was bouncing around like a leaf in the wind. We'll take a more leisurely pace to London." Trajan gave the guard and driver their gratuities, knowing he had made the right decision as a dozen passengers climbed on, some elbowing their way inside and others atop the coach. This added load would probably slow the horses and tire them out faster.

He watched the mail coach rumble off, then entered the Bournemouth coaching inn and arranged for a private dining room for him and Florence.

After ordering their meals, Trajan took a moment to speak to the inn's proprietor and hire a private coach and guard. "Have them ready within the hour."

"Aye, Your Grace. You'll have my best."

Florence was surprised that he meant them to continue at night. "Isn't it dangerous?"

"It could be if we ventured off these toll roads. But we'll soon catch up to the mail coach and keep close to it as we travel through the night. We'll also have an armed guard with us. We should be all right, since I am also armed, and so is our driver."

"I ought to have a weapon, too."

"But you don't know how to shoot. Besides, you are too softhearted to take down a man in cold blood. He'll grab the pistol out of your hand as you stand there gawking at him and shoot *you*." He gave her a light kiss on the cheek. "I don't want to lose you, Florence."

She blushed. "You never will. You know I am hopelessly in love with you."

He smiled. "Yes, I know. Mutual, Florence. First thing I'll do once we are back at Gull Hall is give you lessons on the use of weapons. Is that a fair compromise?"

"Yes."

Their private coach was far more comfortable, and the inns and coaching stations where they had to pause every ten or so miles were clean and well maintained despite the amount of traffic that flowed through them.

There were enough carriages on the road even in the evenings to allow for a safe enough ride. Many stretches of the toll road were lit with torches, and the horses knew the route well enough by now to canter along without need for guidance by the driver.

They arrived in London on the morning of the third day, which was a day ahead of what Trajan had estimated. But these night coaches were faster than he'd realized, and this was a pleasant surprise. They could have spent last night at leisure at a coaching inn, but he was eager to reach London and marry Florence.

There was the matter of the letters, of course. Once that was addressed, he would turn his attention to the final matter that might prove more difficult to solve.

Why had Florence's family spurned this gem of a daughter?

✦

CHAPTER EIGHTEEN

FLORENCE COULD HARDLY keep her eyes open by the time they arrived at the impressive Weymouth townhouse situated in one of the more fashionable squares in Mayfair. It was shortly after sunrise, and the façade of the townhouse gleamed in the early morning light. It was quite a grand home, and she imagined the interior would be just as impressive because Trajan's granduncle had impeccable taste.

She felt like a duck out of water, having arrived bedraggled, covered in dust, and toting a travel pouch containing all of two muslin gowns practical for travel and one impractical silk gown suitable for afternoon tea.

What would the Weymouth staff think of their new mistress when they were better attired in their livery than she was in her wrinkled muslin?

To make matters worse, she had not thought to pack a proper pair of slippers to go with the silk gown, nor had she brought any jewelry with her. And what self-respecting duchess would travel without a lady's maid or her jewels?

Fortunately, the silk gown she had brought along was pretty enough to wear for her wedding. It was a lovely blend of aquamarine colors with a blue silk underlining and a sea-green sarcenet overlay.

The lack of slippers was a concern, however. She would have to wear her walking boots to the church. Perhaps no one would notice.

She sighed. Of course, everyone would. People always took note of such things.

"Ready, love?" Trajan whispered as they were let into the house by Bartlett, the longtime head butler who had served under his granduncle and seemed pleased to be serving under him now.

"Your Grace," Bartlett said with unmistakable good cheer. "A pleasure to have you home."

"Thank you, Bartlett." Trajan immediately introduced Florence as "his wife by sundown" and stated that she was to be given the duchess quarters adjoining his suite of rooms.

Florence tried not to cringe at the thought of what must be running through the minds of the Weymouth staff. She was a lady traveling alone with this handsome duke and there was the necessity of a quick marriage, as though she were some doe-eyed waif he had maneuvered into a compromising position and got caught.

A glimpse in the hallway mirror as they were led past the entry hall showed her hair to be an utter disaster—pins loose, wisps dangling from behind her ears and the nape of her neck. One fat curl had simply come undone and lay flat against her cheek.

"No fuss is to be made for us. Just bring up a tub for Lady Florence and assign a maid to attend her. Where is Mrs. Blake? Have her come up to the duchess quarters and assist Lady Florence in making a list of all she needs. Oh, and we'll need breakfast sent up for us. Just for today. We'll come down to the dining room tomorrow and the following days."

"Yes, Your Grace."

"And we'll need the house stocked with supplies for several small dinner parties that we plan to have while we are in residence. Close friends, that's all. No more than fifteen or twenty in an evening. Mrs. Blake can go over the menus with Lady Florence for those. We'll have a grand party once we have settled in. Isn't she lovely, Bartlett?"

"Quite so, Your Grace."

Florence rolled her eyes and smiled at the elderly man who had a jovial look about him. "We have done this all quite haphazardly," she said. "Forgive us if we have put the household in an uproar."

"Not at all, m'lady. We are pleased to have you with us."

Trajan tucked her arm in his as they started up the stairs to the duchess suite of rooms while his head butler bustled off to alert the housekeeper. "Bartlett lives to have his mettle tested. He is up to the challenge. So is Mrs. Blake. It is frightening how organized and efficient she is, and scary how she can read one's mind almost before one has even had the thought."

Florence laughed. "You seem happy to be here."

"It isn't that I enjoy London above the countryside—you know I do not. But I am relieved we have made it here in one piece and can now put an end to this ordeal in which you are embroiled." He opened the door to the duchess quarters and moved aside to allow her in.

Florence drew in a breath. "This is beautiful! Your granduncle truly had an eye for elegant design. Nothing is overdone or garish. Much like Gull Hall. It is impressive without screaming wealth and power, which actually enhances the image of wealth and power."

"Understated elegance," he said with a nod. "That was my granduncle."

The walls were a creamy white and trimmings were in a lighter shade, perhaps an ivory white. The curtains and counterpane were of a floral print, the colors of the seacoast to give it an airy feel.

"Want to see the ducal bedchamber?" he asked, smiling like a child given a new toy.

"Of course." What she cared about most was knowing the interior door between their bedchambers would never be closed to each other.

Her mouth gaped open again as she surveyed this distinctly

masculine room decorated in darker colors, with polished wood wainscoting that went around the entire room.

Mrs. Blake, a thin woman in her early forties who could best be described as a whirlwind, bustled into the duchess quarters and then poked her head into the duke's chamber. "Your Grace, I am here."

"Excellent." Trajan introduced Florence to the woman, who also had a kindly smile for her.

"The bath for Lady Florence will be brought up shortly, as will your breakfasts. Shall I set it out in m'lady's chamber or yours, Your Grace?"

"We'll dine in Lady Florence's chamber."

"Very good, Your Grace. Polly will be along to attend to m'lady's bath and grooming. I have taken the liberty of laying out a robe and some other useful items, since I noticed you were traveling very light. M'lady, do you wish to wait until after you have eaten and bathed to review the menus for the week?"

"Yes, I think the menus and list of supplies for any dinner parties we might have ought to wait until we have finished the two urgent matters of the day," Florence said, turning to Trajan to remind him of their wedding and seeking an audience with the princess.

"All right, business first. Parties later."

The breakfast cart arrived. Florence's new maid, Polly, set everything out for them on the small table in her chamber, and then left them to their privacy.

Florence and Trajan did not linger long over the meal, even though they were both famished. He was about to leave her to attend to his own grooming when her bath was wheeled in and footmen began filling it with buckets of warm water.

Then Mrs. Blake bustled in to deliver slippers, scented oils to go along with the scented soaps she had brought in a few minutes earlier, a fresh supply of hairpins, and a hairbrush. "M'lady, I noticed you are also lacking proper footwear for your finer gowns."

Florence sighed. "Yes, I did not think to pack even one pair."

"I thought that might be the situation and took the liberty of tracing your boots to record their size. I sent one of the maids to the local shoemaker to obtain suitable slippers for you, a pair in white and a pair in black I thought might be most practical. She ought to be back shortly. The size may not fit exactly, but we can stuff cloth in them if they are too big or stretch them if they are too small."

"Do you think he will have those available for the mere asking?" Florence asked with much surprise.

Mrs. Blake smiled. "I know he does, for he had an order from Lady Westcomb for those exact slippers, and her feet are about your size. He'll give them to us, though."

"He will?" Florence glanced at Trajan to see if he approved of such duplicity.

He cast her a smile and winked.

Mrs. Blake continued. "I have standing orders from His Grace to overpay if we need something done fast. Is this not so, Your Grace? These were his granduncle's instructions and have never been rescinded by His Grace."

"It is a most practical arrangement," Trajan said. "Do not frown at me, Florence. You cannot wear scuffed boots to your own wedding."

Florence admitted he was right, and was not remorseful for their housekeeper's bit of subterfuge, because she really needed proper slippers.

In truth, she could have made do for their wedding because it would take place only with a minimum of witnesses. But she could not show up looking lesser when visiting the Princess of Wales.

"Lady Westcomb will not need hers for another week, and the shoemaker can do up another two pairs for her by then," Mrs. Blake added.

Problem of her footwear solved.

If only the rest were so easily resolved.

As it turned out, the matter of their wedding went just as smoothly.

Both of them were fed, washed, and elegantly attired—she with her new slippers—by the time they took the Weymouth barouche for their short ride to the residence of the Duke of Durham and his wife, Fiona. As it turned out, they were home and delighted to learn of the wedding plans.

"I knew there was something between the two of you from the moment you were introduced last year," Durham said, slapping Trajan on the back.

Florence gasped. "Oh, do be careful with him."

She quickly explained what had been going on, but omitted specific mention of Lady Simmons. It was sufficient to relate that a certain lady's intimate letters had been reclaimed at the princess's urging.

Durham and Fiona listened attentively.

"Ramsdale and Bromleigh are both in Town," Durham said. "Unfortunately, their wives remained at their country estates. They have both been growling bears and insufferably ill-tempered because they miss their better halves so much. This is exactly the distraction they need. Let's gather them and then head to church. No prelate is going to say no to four dukes demanding a marriage license and an immediate wedding thereafter. Besides, you'll need some powerful friends to back you up if Frampton thinks to cause you trouble."

"Or the princess decides to alter the terms of your arrangement," Fiona said, frowning. "We won't let her get away with it."

Florence laughed at the look of stubborn resolve on Fiona's face. Did she not often have that same look when arguing?

She thanked them both and was pleased they were going to witness their wedding, but was adamant about their not interfering with respect to the princess. "It is bad enough Trajan might face her wrath. I'll not have anyone else hurt in this matter."

Within the hour, Trajan had obtained the license from a most obsequious parish prelate who, indeed, could not do enough for these four Silver Dukes, and agreed to conduct the wedding ceremony immediately thereafter.

Florence felt so emotional while standing before the altar alongside Trajan during the brief ceremony.

She never thought she would marry, much less for love. Or marry anyone as handsome, thoughtful, and kind.

If she had a thousand hearts, she would give them all to this man who stood beside her. As it was, she had only the one heart to give him, and she did so fully and completely.

She was sorry her dear friend, Jocelyn, Duchess of Camborne, was not here with her, for her husband was also one of these legendary Silver Dukes, and Florence had hoped they might be in Town. But Camborne's estates were in Scotland, and she did not think they would often make the long trip south.

However, it was so very nice to have Fiona beside her. She had experienced her own heartaches and found happiness with Durham. Florence and Trajan had been there to see that lovely moment last summer. It was right that Fiona and Durham should now be here for their moment.

A wealth of recollections flooded Florence as she stood at the altar, the years of anguish and frustration in trying to figure out why her family did not love her, all her attempts to win them over. But they thought her worthless no matter how hard she had tried to please them.

Trajan insisted she was not to blame and seemed to think there was something more behind her family's behavior.

She dreaded finding out the truth.

But she was also coming to believe the fault was never with her.

Then what was the cause?

She could endure the truth because Trajan was beside her. He loved her and would stand beside her because he loved her.

What a miracle this was. He thought she was someone remarkable and special.

Tears streamed down Florence's face as she said, "I do."

Trajan's smile was beaming as he repeated his vows.

"I now pronounce you husband and wife," the prelate said.

Trajan let out a highly inappropriate whoop that was met with a frown from this man of the cloth, but Trajan did not seem to care. He lifted Florence up in his arms and twirled her in front of the altar. "Your stitches!" she cried.

He laughed. "Let every one of them burst. I have a wife who will tend me if I bleed."

"Put me down, you wonderful fool! I do not want you bleeding to death on our wedding day." But she wiped her tears and smiled with radiant happiness, for this marked the start of a happy, new life.

They shared a kiss once he set her down, and then their friends rushed forward to offer their congratulations.

Ramsdale, Bromleigh, and Durham all signed as witnesses, lest there be any questions raised about the hasty marriage.

Florence was floating on air, never happier…until she noticed several royal guardsmen darkening the church's entry.

As though acting on warrior instinct, the Silver Dukes immediately surrounded her, Trajan—or Weymouth, as she had better get used to referring to him—standing in front of her.

A squawking Fiona was shoved protectively behind all of them, although Florence thought her friend was as fierce as any warrior and was glad to have her on her side, even if it was to take up the rear.

Nor was Florence the sort to back down from any confrontation.

In truth, she wanted to be at the forefront. If there were to be a fight, she did not want Trajan or any of their friends involved or hurt.

One of the guardsmen stepped forward. "Your Graces," he said, addressing her and Trajan. "Her Royal Highness requests that Her Grace attend her immediately."

Trajan had sent off their request for an audience just before they left to collect their friends for their wedding ceremony. That the Princess of Wales should respond so urgently meant something was wrong.

But what?

Florence had tucked the packet of letters in the secret pocket of this gown she was wearing. Perhaps she ought to have listened to Trajan when he suggested locking them in his safe at home. But she had insisted on keeping them with her at all times.

Had she made a grave tactical mistake?

CHAPTER NINETEEN

"FLORENCE, SEND WORD as soon as your audience with Her Royal Highness is over," Durham said, scowling and tense as he faced down the royal guards. "If we do not hear from you by nightfall, we are storming the palace."

The guard who had approached them heard the threat and his eyes widened. "Your Grace, I would reconsider—"

"They are not really going to do it," Florence interjected. "He is merely expressing his desire for our wedding celebration to start. He is talking about parties, not rebellion. I am pleased to cooperate, as any good and loyal subject would be."

Trajan placed her arm in his. "As she is newly married and now the Duchess of Weymouth, I am certain Her Royal Highness will expect to meet her new husband. I am coming with you."

"But you were not summoned," the guard said.

"Are you going to risk her wrath when she learns you have insulted me?"

The guard considered the matter and then nodded. "Follow me."

Their barouche was escorted to Kensington Palace by a dozen horse guards. The crowds they passed gawked at their procession, as though they were people of importance.

Well, they were.

But perhaps not for long.

Was there more to these letters than she had realized?

In this moment, Florence was glad she was now a duchess. Trajan had insisted on it, no doubt thinking ahead to all the possibilities and concluding she needed his considerable power as the Duke of Weymouth.

Florence knew it would take some getting used to before she adjusted to being his duchess. The duties did not overwhelm her, for she was never one to shirk from work. It was the pomp and circumstance that often surrounded the title that she did not care for.

And the political maneuvering. This was her weakness. She had no sense of political posturing or strategies.

Trajan was very good at this, however. He could discern a person's character almost on first impression.

But she had not been trained for this. How was she to spot the liars and manipulators? The last thing she needed was an entourage of false friends.

Instead of being led to the receiving hall, she and Trajan were taken to a back entrance and escorted up a flight of private stairs. He kept tight hold of her hand until the moment they were led into the parlor of the princess's private apartments.

A man stood beside the princess, an older gentleman who appeared to be in his early fifties. He was tall, and had a full head of snow-white hair and a commanding bearing. This man had an unmistakable aura of power, and Florence sensed he could be ruthless and dangerous in his dealings.

She had no idea who he was.

But Trajan suddenly stiffened. He knew the man.

Who was he?

"Do you have the letters?" the princess asked Florence after polite introductions were made.

The man turned out to be one Lord Peregrine Althorpe, perhaps the most influential peer in all of England. Florence had heard his name mentioned before, often in hushed tones, but had never met him until now. He was a kingmaker, wielding power over noblemen of the highest ranks and government ministers all the way up to the prime minister. They all bowed to him.

Why was *he* here?

"The letters?" She did not want to admit she carried them on her person, but could not lie to the princess. "Yes, I do."

"Give them over," Trajan said with a surprising tone of confidence.

"All right. Um…they are tucked in a secret pocket of my gown and I will require a little privacy to slip them out."

The princess smiled. "Gentlemen, turn your backs. That includes you, Weymouth. You may have your intimate moment with your wife tonight in your own bedchamber, but not here in front of me. Congratulations on your nuptials, by the way. However, I must rebuke you, for you are an important personage in the realm and ought to have sought our approval and done it up properly."

Trajan maintained his composure as he said smoothly, "We shall have a grand party in celebration in the upcoming months. Rest assured, it shall be quite lavish, no expense spared. You will be the first invited."

With that said, he and Althorpe turned their backs.

Florence lifted her gown and unfastened the fabric that covered the hidden pocket. She removed the packet, smoothed out her gown, and then held the letters out to the princess. "Here they are."

The princess did not take them. "Turn around, Althorpe. You as well, Weymouth." She then motioned for Althorpe to take possession of the letters. "You are to burn them, as my foolish friend ought to have done years ago."

The princess cast this man an admonishing look, as though to blame him—

Dear heaven.

Had *he* been the one to write those torrid letters to Lady Simmons? No wonder the lady refused to burn them. This man could have been an original Silver Duke and must have been impossibly handsome in his younger days.

Yes, irresistible as sin.

Florence would not have been surprised to learn he had been born with that aura of confidence and ruthless authority, a child able to stare down a nanny or governess by the age of four.

She now expected she would be dismissed and the princess would carry on with her next bit of business. But there was the detail of her brother's fate that also needed to be resolved. She had risked so much, and placed Trajan's life in danger for that worthless scoundrel. Would the princess live up to her part of the bargain? "Your Royal Highness…my brother…"

Althorpe stepped forward. "He will be cleared of all debts and charges against him, given a clean slate. But he will not be protected from any new misdeeds that may arise."

Florence nodded. "Understood, my lord. Nor will my husband allow me to take on such risks to save his unworthy hide again. It is up to my brother to make what he will of his opportunities."

Instead of dismissing them, the princess rang for tea. "Stay, Florence. You too, Weymouth. The four of us have more to say to each other."

Trajan nodded. "It will be our pleasure."

Florence could not imagine why the princess would ever want to share an afternoon tea with them, but here they were.

On the one hand, she was honored for her notice. On the other, she was quite confused as to the reason and dreaded another assignment in the offing.

Trajan's expression revealed nothing. She needed to learn this trick of hiding one's thoughts. A wealth of feelings had to be showing on her face, ranging from dread to hope, one extreme to the other like the swing of a pendulum.

Althorpe surprised her by smiling as they all sat down to tea. "How did you manage to retrieve those letters from Frampton?"

With Trajan's encouragement, she told them everything. The fake bird watching, falling out of the tree onto Trajan, even their kiss on the beach.

Her face was crimson as she told them that part.

"Dear girl," the princess said, stunning Florence with her friendly informality, "Weymouth was right to kiss you and keep on kissing you. You are one of those rare people, genuine and honest to a fault. You could never have talked your way out of trouble, so he had to keep you quiet."

Florence was aghast, but Trajan was grinning at her.

She acknowledged his courage and quick thinking. "He saved my life that day, and then again just before we left Gull Hall."

She told them the last of it, of the search for duplicate parchment and ribbons, of Hermia's grand acting abilities, and Lady Frampton's assistance that was vital to the success of their plan.

Florence then spoke of Trajan's injury. Both Althorpe and the princess took the news with sincere concern.

Of course, Florence dared not make mention of their sharing a bed in Bournemouth, since that was nobody's business.

As she related the details of her retrieval of those letters, she sensed something was going on beyond their mere curiosity in her plan and how it was carried out.

However, she was not politically savvy enough to understand these undercurrents, so she merely told the truth and hoped it would be enough.

Althorpe and the princess remained silent a long moment once she had finished.

"Had I been aware of Frampton's taking possession of my letters," Althorpe spoke up, confirming Florence's suspicions that he was the writer, "I would never have allowed you to undertake this task. He is an extremely dangerous character and has been under watch by the Home Office for several months now."

"Those letters should have been burned years ago," the princess confided. "But my dear friend simply could not bring herself to part with a single one. They were her treasures. Please believe me when I say we had no idea the dangers you were facing, or we would never have considered asking you to get those letters back."

"But you were quite brilliant and brave," Althorpe added. "We are all very much relieved to see you safely back in London."

The princess turned to him. "Lady Simmons was afraid to tell you. She ought to have gone to you first and admitted all, but she was so terrified you would be angry with her. Of course, we had no idea what a fiend Frampton was, or she would have swallowed her pride and told you at once."

"Weymouth, I am very much in your debt," Althorpe said, "for I think the result would have been tragic had you not protected your wife so ably. Frampton will be dealt with now, and quite severely."

"And what of Lady Frampton?" Florence asked, concerned for her friend.

Althorpe handled this response as well. "No charges will be brought against her. Obviously, she had to do her husband's bidding for fear of the dire consequences to herself. But she showed bravery in helping you get them back. I hope she will continue to cooperate with us, for I know he is holding similar damaging information on others."

"He is," Florence said. "I considered grabbing everything I could, but that would have given us all away, and I could not risk our plan failing."

"A wise decision," Althorpe said. "This is a task better left to agents of the Home Office. They will gather and destroy whatever else he has."

She wasn't sure if the information on others would be destroyed or used for Althorpe's gain. But he had the trust of the entire royal family, which said a lot about his honor and intelligence, because many in the family despised each other and would not trust another's ally. Althorpe seemed inclined to work for the good of England rather than for his own personal gain.

But what did she know? She *hoped* that he wielded his power far more wisely than Frampton ever had.

"Frampton worked his way up to his position of authority by

threats and extortion," Althorpe went on to explain, as though reading her expressions that were much too transparent. "But he overstepped all bounds when he killed one of our Home Office agents last month. Well, we suspected he was the one who gave the order, but we did not have the direct evidence to prove it. And now it appears he tried to kill you, too. This must be beyond what even a loyal wife would support."

"It is," Florence assured him. "Lady Frampton will cooperate. I am certain she will. Her life is as much in danger as any of your agents. She will need the protection of the Home Office against her husband's retribution."

"She will have it," Althorpe replied.

Florence was relieved her friend would be safe. And even more relieved that the Home Office would now come down on Frampton and take away his claws.

With matters resolved and their tea finished, the princess dismissed them.

Florence was never more relieved to be sent packing. They returned to the Weymouth townhouse, and she was too drained to say much on their ride home. Nor did Trajan appear to want to talk as his barouche made its way through the bustling London streets.

To their surprise, Durham, Fiona, Bromleigh, and Ramsdale awaited them in Trajan's study.

"Thank goodness!" Fiona cried, rushing forward to greet Florence. "Tell us everything!"

Florence hugged her. "I'll let my husband tell you, for he understood the nuances of our royal meeting. Much of it went over my head."

"It was extraordinary," Trajan admitted, settling Florence in one of the plump leather chairs beside the hearth and then taking a seat beside her on the fat, padded arm of it. "But we are not at liberty to tell you who was in attendance along with the princess."

Florence looked up at him. "You peeked at those letters,

didn't you? You knew who had written them. This is why you were not surprised when you saw him beside the princess."

"Yes, and I'm glad *he* was there."

"You aren't referring to Althorpe by any chance, are you?" Fiona asked.

Florence groaned. "Why did you mention him?"

Fiona gasped. "Oh my goodness! It *was* him!"

Trajan slapped a hand to his forehead and muttered an oath. "You cannot repeat this to anyone, Fiona. Nor can any of you. How in blazes did you know?"

"It is an open secret," Fiona said. "Everyone is aware he was Lady Simmons's first love. They wanted to marry, but her family thought he was a man of little merit at the time. He proved them wrong, didn't he?"

"I'll say," Bromleigh said with a snort.

Fiona nodded. "But sadly, to what purpose? By the time he'd risen to sufficient consequence, she had married Lord Simmons, who then inherited an earldom, and she became a countess. To divorce an earl and marry her true love would have ruined her *and* Althorpe."

"They chose power and *ton* acceptance over love," Florence remarked. "That is sad."

"But practical," Ramsdale noted. "Such choices are not easy ones to make. Would their love hold up if they were cast out and Althorpe lost all his power?"

Trajan went on to relate the rest of what was said.

When he finished, all the dukes were gaping at him.

Durham shook his head and laughed. "Althorpe actually said he was indebted to you?"

Trajan nodded.

Ramsdale whistled. "You have made a powerful ally. Rest assured, we will keep everything you have told us in strictest confidence. That man will cut us all off at the knees if word of those letters or his presence at your afternoon meeting with the princess ever gets out."

Florence nodded. "So, we are all in agreement? Not another mention of Althorpe, Lady Simmons, or those letters."

They all vowed to maintain their silence to the grave.

It was almost suppertime now, so she and Trajan invited their friends to stay.

Fiona answered for all of them. "Oh, no. It is your wedding day, and time for us to leave you lovebirds to yourselves."

Durham winked at his wife. "But first we are stopping at White's, because I intend to collect my winnings. I think I was the only one who wagered Weymouth would marry you, and the odds were astronomical. I'm about to reap a fortune."

"Which we are going to give to charity," Fiona said as she dragged him out the door.

Bromleigh and Ramsdale bade them a good evening and followed their friends. "Let's have supper at the Carlton Hotel," Bromleigh said, referring to one of London's finest establishments. "Durham's treating."

Florence was relieved to finally have time alone with Trajan. She was exhausted and looked forward to sleeping in a real bed tonight. Hopefully Trajan's bed.

Yes, of course it would be. This was their wedding night. Trajan was not going to leave her alone tonight.

They had made the trip from Weymouth to London in record speed, been jostled night and day, unable to close their eyes for more than a few minutes at a time while riding inside a hired carriage with leather seat benches that had retained the sweat and pungent odors of prior passengers.

Her earlier bath with fragrant oils and scented soap had fully expunged the offensive odors from her body, thankfully.

Her anticipation of her wedding night had given her a second wind. She was not going to miss a moment by falling asleep.

Trajan requested their supper be served in his bedchamber. "Do you mind?" he asked her.

"No, it's practical. A quick meal and then bed. I long for it."

He laughed. "So do I, although we are thinking of the bed for different reasons. You wish to sleep, and I wish to keep you awake and howling with pleasure."

"Trajan! Hush. What will the staff think if they hear you?"

"That I love my wife and wish to have her in my arms."

She smiled, even though she was embarrassed and her face was in flames because of his remark.

He had given her a taste of pleasure at the inn at Bournemouth, so she knew he could elicit those howls from her.

Well, they were mostly moans and purrs.

The real question was, could she elicit those howls from him?

CHAPTER TWENTY

T RAJAN DID NOT rush Florence through their meal, but noted she had hardly eaten anything. Well, it had been an upheaval of a day for her. But also a good day, and so much had been accomplished. She was his wife now, and he felt such great contentment knowing she would be his from this day forward, his with which to share hopes and confidences, and always give him honest answers.

A beautiful confidante.

He hoped to be the same for her, the one in whom she chose to confide her deepest yearnings.

She looked up from her plate and cast him a breathtaking smile. "Trajan," she said in wonder, "can you believe it? We are now husband and wife."

He took a sip of his wine and nodded. "How does it feel to be my duchess?"

"Oh, it feels nicest to be your wife. The duchess part will take a bit of learning on my part. I'll seek Fiona's help, or that of Mrs. Blake, if ever I am uncertain. Fiona was born to the role, don't you think? She always handles everything so effortlessly. Did you see how happy she and Durham were together? Have you ever seen smiles so filled with love?"

"Yes, it was the first thing I noticed. This is what I hope for us."

She poked her fork around the remains of a potato. "I think I am there already. My heart swells to bursting whenever I am near you."

He chuckled. "Florence, that sounds like a dangerous, adverse reaction to me."

"All right, then I'll merely say that my heart swells with happiness. No bursting or rupturing."

"Much better. Mutual, my love."

She smiled and set down her fork. "I'll never tire of hearing your endearments."

He took her hand in his. "Then you shall hear them often from me, for you are quite easy to love."

Her smile faltered. "Am I?"

Ah, her childhood deprivation rearing its ugly head again. "Yes, and this is among the things we will address in the upcoming days. But not tonight. Tonight is about us, and if I am very lucky, lots of naked sex."

She gasped and then laughed. "Oh, I think you shall be a most lucky fellow."

He grinned, but then sobered. "Never more than you are comfortable doing, all right?"

She cast him an impish smile. "My goal is to make *you* howl. I just haven't figured out how to do that yet."

He leaned back in his chair and groaned. Gad, if she only knew how easily it would be accomplished. Had he not been irresistibly drawn to her from the very first?

"Are you done? Shall I have the dinner cart taken away? And do you want a maid to assist you in preparing for bed?" he asked.

"Yes to both, I think. Do you mind?"

"That you prefer a maid to me?" He grinned. "No, I'll patiently wait my turn. Just knock on our interior door whenever you are ready."

He had his routine as well. And an eager valet inherited from his granduncle waiting to assist him.

This would likely be their routine from this night on, so why not keep to it now? The only thing he did not wish to compromise on was sharing a bed. He did not care which bed he and Florence shared, so long as they remained together.

He had just donned his banyan and dismissed his valet, who strode off happily with an armload of clothes to refresh and his boots for polishing, when he heard a soft knock at their shared door.

He opened it to find Florence in her ever-practical nightgown and robe, her silky hair long and loose, and her emerald eyes wide and sparkling.

Buying her a new wardrobe was also an item on his list of things to address—certainly the addition of a few silk nightgowns was warranted, even if he would be slipping them off her the moment they got under the sheets. "Ready, love?"

She nodded.

He lifted her in his arms and carried her to his bed.

"Trajan, your arm! The stitches! The doctor said not to lift more than a teapot for this first week."

"My arm is fine. And you weigh little more than a teapot."

She laughed. "That is utter nonsense."

"Fine, but you are still light as a feather. Or perhaps it is that my heart feels light as a feather because you are now my wife," he said, making her laugh again as he set her down gently on his bed.

The room was fairly dark, save for the soft glow of three candles on his nightstand casting an amber light upon the bed.

"I love you," she said with a vulnerable ache of feeling that tore straight through to his heart.

"Mutual, Florence."

Those were the last words they spoke as he kissed her and slipped the nightclothes off her to reveal the beauty of her body. He removed his banyan as well, wanting nothing between them.

He took it slow, at first doing nothing more than sliding his roughened hands over her soft curves as she became accustomed to his touch.

In the meantime, she asked her questions about *his* body, *his* arousal, and what all of it signified. "It means I desire you, Florence."

He then proceeded to show her with his kisses and his mouth on her skin, his tongue on her breasts, and his fingers that would ready her when he claimed her as his wife. She tasted as sweet as a peach, which was the scent of the soap she had used on herself, apparently her favorite. It suited her skin, the warmth of it and the refreshing sweetness of it.

He shifted atop her as he aroused her and felt her passion mounting along with his. He entered her, slow and gentle thrusts at first, hardly intrusive until she became used to his body inside hers and he embedded himself fully.

He wrapped her legs around his hips. "Like this, Florence."

Although her instincts were just fine and he did not have to explain any further. She went with her feelings, arching to meet his thrusts and clinging to his shoulders that were taut as he felt the heat and pressure of his own impending release.

He kissed her lips with urgency, deep and long, and felt the lovely press of her breasts against his chest as he moved with greater urgency, his body undulating in shifting rhythms and bringing her along with him.

His thrusts were now more urgent. Longer. Deeper.

He saw her passion rising. Felt her on the precipice.

But so was he.

Then all exploded at once, Florence shattering in the throes of her release, her body quivering as his own liquid force spilled into her in wave upon wave of hot desire, his spasms ungentle and unrefined.

Just raw craving. Both of them lost to this scorching need to be one. Lost to passion and, most of all, love.

He watched her exquisitely expressive face as she soared and then slowly floated down to rest in his arms. She embraced these new sensations and embraced *him*.

"We both howled," Florence said, casting him a triumphant smile as they calmed and he rolled off her to collapse on his back atop the mattress.

She turned on her side to face him, her hair spilling over her shoulders in silky, dark waves, and her body as smooth as cream and deliciously warm.

Once again, he drew her into his embrace and lightly brushed his hand along the silken length of her hair. "It was nice. Really nice. Great, actually."

She kissed his shoulder. "I thought so, too." Her lips were rosy from his kisses.

They lay together in silence for a long moment, each of them needing time to absorb what had just happened between them. She was so soft and sweet, meant to be in his arms.

Meant to be *his*.

Yes, they surely had been destined to meet and fall in love. One heart recognizing the other. Their bodies recognizing their mate.

He expected Florence would begin to toss him questions about what they had done, but she lay quietly huddled against him, her breathing smooth and even.

He smiled and kissed the top of her head. She had fallen asleep in his arms.

This was nice. Really nice.

He blew out the candles and fell asleep soon afterward, too.

Trajan awoke a few hours later when a sudden chill replaced the cozy warmth at his side. He blinked, for it took a moment for his eyes to adjust to the predawn light, and soon made out the shape of Florence as she searched for something within the rumpled folds of their bedcovers.

She *eeped* as he put a hand on her sweetly rounded rump, and turned to him while at the same time drawing the sheet up to cover herself. "I did not mean to wake you. I was searching for my nightgown."

"Are you cold, love?"

"No, I was comfortable against your heat. But…I wasn't sure if you wanted me to stay."

"You were going to leave me?"

"No, just be prepared if you wanted me gone."

"I don't want you gone," he said, drawing her back to his side and taking her in his arms, the sheet still tucked around her. "Not ever. I thought you understood that we are to share a bed."

She nodded. "Well, we discussed your *taking* me to bed. I wasn't quite clear on the specifics afterward."

He kissed her softly on the lips. "Specifically, I wish to wake to your lovely face each morning and fall asleep to your smiles and kisses each night. Workable for you?"

"Yes." She curled up against him and purred.

They made love again by the early light of dawn.

Florence fell asleep once more and remained contentedly sleeping even when his valet knocked at his door.

Trajan rose from the bed, groped about the covers and found his banyan, then made certain Florence was safely covered before he allowed Higgins in. He took the freshly pressed clothes and polished boots from his valet's hands. "Come back in an hour. Knock first. My wife might still be in here."

The man's face turned crimson.

Yes, they were going to have to figure out a better schedule. It was bad enough the man knew Florence was naked beneath the covers. He might pass out if he ever caught a glimpse of her leg or—egads—her breast.

Trajan would have to pound on the man's heart to revive him. He'd also have to kill him.

Higgins had been his granduncle's valet. But Trajan could not bring himself to discharge Higgins, so he'd kept him on in London and Reed, his own valet, on at Gull Hall.

Now that he was married and meant to share a bedchamber with his wife, they needed to figure out a workable routine here and in Weymouth.

"Yes, Your Grace. One hour, knock first," Higgins repeated, and quickly backed out of his bedchamber.

Florence stirred shortly afterward. Trajan helped her don her nightgown and robe, doing more to undress her than assist because she had a truly gorgeous body and he could not get enough of her. He wanted to toss her back on the bed and claim her for a third time.

But they had a lot to accomplish today, and they would never get anything done if they did not get moving now.

The first item on his list was the matter of her clothes. Much of her wardrobe was at her parents' townhouse, but little of it would be suitable for a married duchess. Fiona had given him the name of her modiste yesterday, and generously mentioned that Florence could borrow any clothes she needed from her in the meanwhile. But Trajan wanted his wife to have her own things, for he could easily afford the best.

Visiting her parents was on his list, as well.

He wanted to understand their behavior toward their daughter. Why did the mother treat Florence as though she did not exist? Was it some odd family custom to ignore the girls and adore the sons? Did that practice not die out along with medieval fiefdoms? And girls were useful to give away in marriage to form alliances.

But her family was more intent on disowning her or fobbing her off on the wastrel son of a friend rather than matching her in any useful alliance.

He had also considered that Hermia might be her real mother, that Florence was adopted by her parents to protect Hermia from ruination, especially if she bore a child out of wedlock.

But Hermia was forthright and spoke her mind. She would have said something to Florence by now. Nor did Trajan get the feeling that Hermia was a mother looking after her secret child.

Instinct told him that Hermia was exactly who she claimed to be, a loving maiden aunt.

He told Florence what he wanted to do and why.

She did not look happy, but agreed to the plan. "I will need new clothes. But believe me when I say that I won't need my family."

"Would you mind if I went to them on my own?"

She shrugged. "If you think one visit to my parents will clear up something I haven't been able to figure out in my entire lifetime, then you are welcome to try. We lose nothing by it, and they do need to be told I am married to you. I might come with you."

"I hope you will, but I am not going to force you."

"I think I must go with you. But if the visit becomes too much for me and I want to leave, then you must promise not to stop me."

"I promise," he said, placing a hand over his heart.

"If I do walk out, I'll wait for you in our carriage. All right?"

"Yes." Trajan did not know if this was helpful in any way to Florence, but he hoped it might be. He doubted her parents would suddenly open up to him and reveal the dark secrets surrounding their treatment of her. But it was important for him to get a sense of them and the friction within the family.

Frampton may have been a physical threat, soon to be squashed by Althorpe, but Florence's family was just as bad. They had landed some heavy emotional blows on her and left deep bruises on her soul.

Florence went to her duchess quarters to prepare herself for the day while he remained in his bedchamber and did the same.

They met downstairs. He smothered a grin when he saw her, for she wore one of her sturdy muslin gowns and her walking boots. She looked ready to climb trees.

Well, she had little choice in what to wear, since she had only brought along three gowns for the journey. This was why they required an urgent visit to Fiona's modiste, one Madam de Bressard, who seemed to be popular with the fashionable set.

They left immediately after breakfast for the modiste's shop. Fiona, to Trajan's relief, joined them, arriving only a few minutes after they had. "Here I am. Shall we get started?"

Florence groaned.

"You can do this," Trajan teased. After all, she had just

brought down one of England's most vicious lords. Selecting fabrics for new gowns could not be all that difficult.

He was glad Fiona was with them. Florence liked her and trusted her fashion knowledge.

He also happened to know what looked good on a woman and what would suit Florence specifically, but she was not likely to accept his opinion, since he was a man and would choose what pleased *him* and not necessarily conform to current fashion standards.

They spent hours selecting an extensive wardrobe, for Florence could no longer wear her spinster gowns or her sturdy, bird-watching muslins with their secret pockets and utter lack of style.

Well, in his opinion—again, which did not count—Florence would look pretty wearing a potato sack. As far as he was concerned, she could wear whatever she liked when in residence at Gull Hall. But Fiona was right to insist on elegant gowns for London, since Florence was going to be watched and talked about everywhere they went.

The *ton* could be cruel. He did not want her ridiculed.

They made good progress, and arranged for a handful of gowns to be rushed so that Florence had something decent to wear these next few days they would remain in Town.

"I'll arrange for the others to be forwarded to Weymouth once they are ready," the modiste said in a crisp French accent. "I'll match each gown to your precise measurements from these first gowns fitted for you, so no alterations should be necessary. Do not give them over to some local seamstress to butcher."

Florence smiled and promised she wouldn't.

Fiona next led them to the shoemaker and haberdasher for all the shoes and accessories Florence needed.

"This is too much," she protested. "I have a wardrobe full of clothes and shoes at my family's house."

"Florence, you dress to attract chickens and squirrels," Fiona said, which was what Trajan was thinking but would never dare say it because Florence looked lovely, and her fashion sense, or lack thereof, suited just fine in the countryside, which was where he preferred to reside.

He next took the ladies out for lunch at a local hotel known for its elegance and fine dining. Durham joined them. "How did it go? Did Fiona exhaust you?"

Florence laughed. "Yes! I think we bought every bolt of fabric, glove, parasol, and shoe in London."

"Well, you are the wife of a Silver Duke now, as I am sure Fiona explained," Durham said. "This means people will look at you wherever you go. You've bought yourself a little time because word has not spread yet about your marriage. Everyone still thinks Trajan is a dashing, silver-at-the-temples bachelor on the prowl."

"Not after today," Fiona remarked. "I'm sure my modiste is already spreading the word to her clientele. It is a coup for her, being among the first to learn of Weymouth's marriage, and to be given the task of an entire new wardrobe for his duchess."

Florence sighed. "Perhaps this will take a little more adjustment on my part than I thought would be required."

They finished their meal in pleasant conversation, and then Durham took Fiona home.

Florence turned wistful once they were in Trajan's barouche on their way to her family's residence. "I look forward to returning to Gull Hall. It already feels like home to me. The Newton townhouse never felt like a home."

"I know, love." He was also eager to return to Gull Hall, but he dared not do so for another few days yet. Althorpe and the Home Office agents needed time to deal with Frampton and remove him as a threat.

Trajan took Florence's hand and kept hold of it as they arrived at the Newton home and marched up to the front door. It was an elegant house, well maintained on the outside, and appeared to be properly staffed. He noted a head butler, who met them at the entry, and two footmen were passing by.

The butler stared from one to the other, apparently confused.

"Lady Florence?"

She smiled at the man. "Good afternoon, Halliwell. I believe my parents are expecting us."

"They were expecting His Grace and his mother," Halliwell explained. "But it is nice to see you, Lady Florence. Are you back to stay? Or will you be traveling again?"

"Traveling again soon, I hope."

Trajan noted that she made no mention of her new title, no doubt preferring to reveal the news to her parents before saying anything to the staff.

By the sudden brightening of Halliwell's eyes, he must have caught on that the duchess reference was to Florence and not his mother. His expression immediately softened. "Come this way."

He led them to the family parlor, a formal and elegantly designed room, and then left to advise her parents of their arrival.

"Is this where you grew up?" Trajan asked, surveying the well-appointed room that nonetheless felt cold and uninviting.

She nodded. "For much of my life."

"It is nicely maintained. I'm not sure what I was expecting."

"Yes, my mother loves everything about this house except for me," she said with a snort. "If she could expunge my presence, she would. Will you stay close? I'm not sure I'll hold up throughout this visit."

He gave her a light kiss on the cheek. "Just take my hand whenever you feel the need to scream."

"Or I'll just bolt if it becomes too unbearable."

Trajan was surprised by the extent of Florence's struggles, but this was his fault. He had been raised in a happy family and did not fully appreciate the depth of harm done to her because she was so deceptively strong.

Florence was not merely strong, but also smart, capable, and had a big heart for loving. She had overcome her mother's cold rejection in so many ways.

He cursed himself for a fool, for this meeting could turn agonizingly painful for her. He should have understood and left it alone, contacted her parents later on his own. But he'd thought to address this problem as he did every other and approach it like a charging bull. Only it wasn't Florence's parents who would end up gored, but her.

Her father walked in first and seemed genuinely pleased to see his daughter. "Florence," he said, giving her a hug, "how have you been? We've been so worried about you."

"We?" She returned his hug before slipping out of his embrace.

He sighed. "*I* have been worried about you. And where is Hermia? I thought you were traveling with her."

"I was. I am. We were in Weymouth." She then took a deep breath and introduced her father to Trajan. "He's my husband."

Her father's mouth dropped open. "Florence, I am delighted, of course. But…is this a jest? When did you marry? Why did you not tell your mother and me?"

"It all happened very quickly," Trajan said.

"Not out of necessity," Florence hastened to explain. "Ours is a love match."

"I've known Florence for a little over a year now, and we happened to meet in Weymouth recently. That is my seat. I was delighted to see her again. I have loved your daughter since the moment we met and could not allow her to slip away from me this time."

They heard a bitter laugh from the direction of the doorway.

Florence's mother.

Gad, she sounded like a witch.

But she looked very much the elegant lady as she strolled in and held out her hand for Trajan to bow over.

He saw a look of caution flash in the eyes of Florence's father, a warning aimed at his wife.

Bloody blazes.

Was this what Florence had faced every day of her life?

Trajan felt a palpable anger radiating from this woman, although she kept her words polite.

Well, moderately polite.

"Why did you not tell us, Florence? Are your father and I not good enough to share in your happy day?"

"It is a long story," Florence said evasively. "We shall hold a party to formally celebrate, and all shall be invited. Should anyone ask you for details, you may tell them we were married in a quiet ceremony in London yesterday."

Her mother's eyes rounded in obvious surprise.

"The ceremony took place at St. Bridget's in the presence of several Silver Dukes," Trajan said. "They served as our witnesses and were the only ones in attendance, save for Durham's wife, who was also present. She is a good friend to Florence."

"Seems Florence values fleeting friendships over her own parents." Her mother tipped her chin up. "We also have good news. Your brother has been absolved of all his legal difficulties. I knew he was innocent of those preposterous charges. Thank goodness I was there to help him out. His sister certainly did not care."

Trajan laughed incredulously. "Are you serious? Or deluded? Your daughter is the one who saved him, at no small risk to her life, I might add."

Florence took his hand, no doubt to calm him. She was used to this nonsense, but he wasn't.

Nor would he stand for his wife being insulted.

"Pray tell, madam. What do you think *you* did to miraculously free your wastrel son?"

"I gave reference as to his good character."

"Did you also provide him with a false alibi?" Florence asked. "Because that would have put you in prison for perjury. Do you think any judge would believe your word over those of a marquess and a dozen other lords who witnessed the duel? Not to mention the gambling debts he ran up, also in front of a dozen witnesses of rank. You have only to ask the Princess of Wales herself if you wish for confirmation about which of us truly saved him."

"Am I supposed to believe you?" Her mother laughed. "When would you ever be admitted to see her?"

"We had tea with her yesterday," Trajan replied. "Florence is a favorite of hers."

"Florence? That is a jolly jest." If this woman could spew snake venom, she would have done so. "Weymouth, do you have any idea what you have married?"

Florence's father shot his wife another furious look.

The woman excused herself and stormed out.

Florence remained surprisingly calm as she watched her mother leave. "Papa, it is time. My husband needs to know the truth. I can step outside if you do not wish to tell me. But he has the right to know. What did she mean? *What* am I? She has despised me all of my life. What does she see when she peers into my eyes?"

CHAPTER TWENTY-ONE

FLORENCE'S FATHER BOWED his head. "I feared this day would come."

An ill feeling came over Florence, and she shuddered.

Dear heaven. What was he going to tell her?

Trajan remained beside her and kept firm hold of her hand.

"I prayed it would never come to this," her father said with such aching, Florence was afraid to hear what promised to be worse than even she had imagined.

She turned to Trajan. "I have to leave."

"Stay, Florence," her father pleaded. "You deserve to learn the truth."

Tears welled in her eyes. She'd wanted this moment to arrive for all of her life, but now that it was upon her, she dreaded it.

What was the adage? *Ignorance is bliss.* Perhaps it was.

This revelation was going to be ugly and horrible because her mother hated her.

"All right, I'll stay," she said with trepidation, as she had never been a coward and knew she needed to face whatever would be revealed. But she felt scared and was shaking.

Trajan wrapped his arm around her. "Go on, Lord Newton."

Tears streamed down her father's face as he finally spoke. "What she sees whenever she looks at you is the mirror image of the woman I love…loved. *Her* cousin."

Florence paled. "What?"

"No one ever knew. Not even Hermia."

"I don't understand." What was he suggesting? Was the cousin her true mother?

"Claire," he said, referring to the cousin, "died in childbirth."

Florence's head began to spin. Not only was she another woman's child, but she had killed her mother. The breath rushed out of her. "Giving birth to me?"

Her father's eyes widened, but he nodded. "Dear heaven, Florence. You are innocent. No child can be at fault for an act of nature. We wanted you so badly, and I have never regretted you. You are my blessing. You've kept my Claire alive for me."

Florence's head was now in full reel. All these years, she had blamed her mother… No, her father's wife, for the woman who had just stormed out of the room had never been a mother to her. She now understood why.

Growing up, she had thought of the woman as a monster.

But who was the real monster? Weren't they all tainted? Hadn't they *all* committed a wrong?

What would she have done if Trajan had brought home a child belonging to the woman he loved and insisted she raise it as her own? How would she have responded when having to face this child who resembled her real mother day after painful day? And knowing Trajan loved this other woman above her?

This could have been him and Eden.

Of course, it wasn't. Eden had chosen another and Trajan had gotten over her.

But what if he hadn't? What if he was only telling her that he loved her because he could not have Eden?

She was going to be ill.

"Florence, I am not the villain you believe me to be," her father insisted, although she did not care to hear his attempts to explain. "Claire was the one I always wanted to marry, but our families refused to allow it. If you and Weymouth are a true love match, perhaps in time you will understand the heartbreak and desolation of two bound hearts being torn apart. Celeste," he said, referring to the woman he'd married, the one she always thought had been her mother, "never loved me. Not once, not for a moment did she ever care about me. I tried so hard to make our marriage work. I promise you, I did. But she never wanted anything to do with me after she gave me a son. I endured four years of her loathing."

"Because your heart always belonged to another," Florence shot back.

He shook his head. "No, she never had it in her to love. Look at how your brother turned out. She *obsessed* over him. She put him up on a pedestal and worshipped him. She indulged him and protected him. She shunned everyone else. Is this a healthy way to love?"

Florence knew it wasn't. But it did not make what her father did any more right.

"You were my child, Florence. I was not going to give you away."

"But what you did to her... She had to see me every day, a constant reminder."

He shook his head vehemently. "No, she was this way before you ever came along. I would have left her before I ever abandoned you. I hadn't seen Claire, my one true love, in over four years because I wanted to make our marriage work. But I could take it no longer and finally gave up. I began a liaison with Claire, and you were the result of it."

"And when she died?" Trajan asked, his own voice racked with pain.

"I brought Florence home and struck a bargain with Celeste. I would never leave her. I would never look outside our marriage. But you were to be ours now, Celeste was to be your mother, and no one would know otherwise. It was easy. Our home at the time was in the countryside, and Claire kept mostly to herself. For all her supposed devotion to our son, Matthew saw little of her. When she did pay attention to him, she spewed her poisonous words in his ear."

Perhaps she was behaving like a coward, but Florence could not stomach to hear another word and ran out.

She had told Trajan she would wait for him in the barouche, but how could she? Why would he ever want to see her again?

She was the daughter of Claire and her father.

Claire.

She was a child born out of wedlock.

What had she done to Trajan? He was the Duke of Weymouth and had just married the offspring of an unmarried woman and a lord of little account.

She ran down the street, having no idea where she was going, just needing to get away from that suffocating house and all its secrets and lies.

Someone grabbed her by the arm and drew her into his muscled embrace.

Trajan.

"Love, where are you going?"

"Away. What have I done to you?" Her tears flowed uncontrollably. "You've married a bas—"

"Don't you dare say it, Florence! Don't you dare," he said with a wealth of anger and frustration, but she knew it was not directed at her. Still, she felt such a wrenching ache because this was what she had brought to their marriage. "You are my wife. Do you think I care where or how or to whom you were born? Do you love me?"

She nodded. "With all my heart. Which is—"

"No! That's all I want to hear. I love you too. You are the one who is *first* in my heart, and no one will ever replace you."

"But Eden—"

"Did not love me. Did not choose me. And I got over my infatuation with her the moment I met you. I have been mad, demented, crazy in love with you since first meeting you. And here's something I vowed never to tell you…"

She looked up at him through her veil of tears. "What weren't you ever going to tell me?"

"Last year, at the Bromleigh house party…"

"Yes?"

He let out a heavy breath. "I took my binoculars, climbed a tree, and spent an entire night peering at you through your bedroom window."

"What!"

"Not while you were undressing or anything sick like that. I thought you were a thief attempting to rob the Milbury house, and wanted to see if you had any tools designed to break into people's homes. In my heart, I knew it was not possible. But what if my feelings for you had clouded my judgment? You ignored me, frustrated me to no end, and yet I could not stop looking at you or thinking about you. I resolved to stop you and make you reform your wicked ways."

"Because you thought I was a thief?"

"You were acting strangely. Do you dare deny it? And how was I to know what you were doing? All I could think of was to save you from a life of crime. And you were so impossibly beautiful. I would have lied to give you an alibi had you turned out to be a thief. Of course, I would have made you give back everything you had stolen."

Florence found herself laughing and crying at the same time.

"Gad, I should not have told you this. It is deranged, I know. I have never done anything insanely mad like that before. Nor will I ever again. But I was in love with you. My lovely, fake bird watcher who turned out not to be a jewel thief after all."

He kissed her, and she did not resist.

"But you were a thief of hearts. *My* heart. You had quite stolen it. Then you crash landed back in my life, and I knew I could not lose you. I love you, Florence. *You*. Because of your big heart. Your strength and your softness. You could have been born a bird and fallen out of your nest, for all I care. My love for you is without conditions. It is unbreakable. And it is forever."

She hugged him and cried some more as he led her to their carriage, lifted her in, and climbed in after her.

He wrapped his arms around her as the carriage rolled away from the Newton townhouse. "I'll be meeting your father tomorrow to discuss this further. He and I alone."

"And then we need to discuss *us* and where we go from here. What will your mother think once word is out? Your sister? Your cousins?"

"Are you serious? First of all, word is not getting out. Your father and Celeste are not about to say anything and ruin their social standing. As for my mother, we are talking about a woman who named her children Trajan and Persephone, and loved and supported my father's eccentric ways. Make no mistake, he was eccentric."

She could not help herself, and laughed.

"Persephone is going to love you because you make me happy," he said gently. "My cousins already adore you. They think you are Queen Boudica reincarnated, a dazzling warrior who managed to single-handedly bring down Frampton when England's Home Office had tried for months and gotten nowhere."

"But I am nobody."

He growled. "You are *everything* to me."

"You are acting on impulse. We don't have to resolve anything right away, although we should not take too long to come to an agreement."

"Florence," he said sternly, "I am playing my duke card here."

"What do you mean?"

"The matter is resolved. I order it so by ducal edict. We stay married. We remain deliriously happy being married to each other. There will be no talk of ending this marriage. There will be no talk of separate sleeping arrangements. We are going to share the same bed. We are going to share everything until the moment we take our last breaths."

She wiped her tears and stared at him.

He cast her the softest smile. "We are going to kiss each other each night before we fall asleep and do whatever else of an amorous nature we are of a mind to do. In the morning, I shall wake to your happy, smiling face. No frowns allowed, even if you are peeved at me."

"I must still smile?"

"Yes, even if peeved. Do you accept these terms?"

"Need I? Are they not decreed by ducal edict?"

"Yes, but I still want your willing acceptance."

She leaned her head against his shoulder and let out a shuddering sigh. "You have my willing acceptance and my gratitude. You have my heart for always. I love you beyond measure. But—"

"That's all I need to hear. Edict, remember? High-handed duke here. Discussion is over."

"But not our marriage?"

"No. That is unbreakable and unconditional. We stay married." He arched an eyebrow. "Just how grateful are you?"

"Seriously?" She laughed again. "Very, very grateful. I will show you tonight."

"You will?"

She nodded. "Better have a libation for your throat."

"Why?"

"Because I shall have you howling until you are hoarse."

"Tucker!" he called to their driver with a hearty laugh. "Get us home fast!"

EPILOGUE

Gull Hall
Weymouth, England
December 1819

T RAJAN SMILED AS he glanced up from his desk in the library at Gull Hall where he had been reading crop reports. His gaze fell upon Florence, who sat curled up like a kitten on the settee, reading a letter she had just received from Fiona. "Fiona has decided to sell her townhouse on Duchess Square."

"Is that so?" Hermia asked, looking up from her embroidery. She was settled in a plump chair by the window working on her latest sample as the snow fell lightly outside the window.

Florence tucked her shawl more securely about her shoulders and nodded. "Yes, but she is in no hurry and wants to find someone nice to purchase it. Someone her neighbors will like."

"Another spinster?" Andrew remarked, looking over at Florence. He was seated in one of the leather wing chairs beside the hearth, reviewing warehouse ledgers.

"Who's a spinster?" Nathan asked, striding in.

He and Sebastian had been in the billiards room having a game before supper was announced, but now both marched in to join the others in the library. After pouring brandies for themselves, they sank into the other wing chairs beside Andrew and soaked in the warmth of the fire blazing in the hearth. It was an unusually cold and blustery day even for this time of year, and they had been up since before dawn to attend to a minor disruption at one of the Weymouth dairies.

Sebastian was just back from university, home for the yuletide holidays, and had immediately set about helping Nathan with this Weymouth dairy. He was campaigning to defer his studies for a term in order to participate more in the family businesses. Trajan saw no harm in keeping him here for the term because Sebastian wanted to learn about the Weymouth properties, and this was just as useful as his reading the Greek classics that he had declared were dreadfully dull, and he would fail the class if he were forced to take it.

"Lady Berengaria and Lady Miranda are the spinsters in question," Florence said. "They are Fiona's lovely neighbors on Duchess Square."

"Berengaria," Sebastian said, putting on the Upper Crust accent of an elite Oxford don. "She must be sixty years old and an utter dragon."

Florence laughed. "Not at all. She is very pretty and about my age, I would say. Maybe a year or two older. Her friends call her Lady Berry. She's sweet as can be."

"Is she rich? Does she like younger men?" Nathan teased.

Florence laughed. "I'll ask Fiona when I write back to her."

Trajan set aside his reports and listened to the banter among his cousins, Hermia, and Florence, his heart full as he watched his family, one that he had almost lost because Florence had been so devastated when her father revealed the truth about her parentage.

But the four of them—him and Florence, her father and Celeste—were the only ones who knew the truth. No one else—not Hermia, nor Florence's brother Matthew—had been told or ever would be told.

And if the secret ever got out? Trajan knew they would weather the scandal.

Florence's father had taken Celeste and their son on a Grand Tour. He hoped their travels on the Continent might help to repair these damaged souls. New places. New beginnings.

Trajan's gaze rested lovingly on Florence, his wife who

showed incredible strength, compassion, and resilience.

She was just beginning to show now, although he did not think she was more than three months along.

He was more in love with her than ever.

She looked over at him and smiled.

Her sunlight poured into his heart. "Are you cold, Florence?" She was fussing with her shawl.

Andrew grinned. "Why don't you sit beside your wife and warm her?"

Nathan and Sebastian giggled like idiot schoolboys.

Florence patted the seat cushion beside her. "I am perfectly fine, but you are welcome to join me on the settee, if you wish."

Trajan did just that, putting an arm around her as he settled back and stretched his legs before him. "How's the planning for the holiday party going?"

"All is well in hand. The rooms for your mother, and sister and her brood, are all ready." She turned to his cousins. "Your father will have the guest suite next to you three boys."

"Oh, joy," Sebastian remarked.

Their father, Trajan's uncle, was a very good man and his sons adored him.

Trajan liked him, too. He was as eccentric as his own father had been. However, he was aging and could not help out with the Weymouth properties. It was of no matter, for his sons were smart, hardworking fellows and were up to the task.

Those three, Andrew, Nathan, and Sebastian, were as close as brothers to Trajan.

"Will Lady Frampton be joining us for the holiday party?" Sebastian asked.

"Haven't you heard?" Hermia replied. "Now that her husband has died, she—"

Sebastian jerked upright in his chair. "Frampton's dead? When and how? And why was I not informed about this?" he grumbled. "See why I should not return to university? I have obviously learned nothing while I was away."

Trajan laughed. "Stop campaigning for the deferral of your studies. I have agreed to it."

"But what about Frampton? And his wife?"

"That toad made many enemies," Hermia intoned. "The circumstances are hazy, but it seems a disgruntled business partner shot him in broad daylight on a busy London street, and then fled to parts unknown."

Trajan said nothing, but he expected Althorpe might have had a hand in it. One did not cross England's kingmaker without dire consequences.

Well, Frampton had made many enemies, extorting people and ruining careers for years. Half of London's elite probably wanted to kill him.

"Dear Sylvia is a merry widow now," Hermia continued. "Of course, she is dutifully in mourning for the moment. But she has made a few appearances around Town. No parties. Just a few quiet events, escorted by Lord Peregrine Althorpe."

Trajan exchanged a look with Florence.

"She'll do just fine for herself," Hermia added. "She's a lovely lady, gentle in heart but strong in spirit. Few women could have survived marriage to that horrible man. But Althorpe's a gentleman. Who knows if anything will come of it?"

"I hope it does," Florence said.

Trajan was not certain what to make of Althorpe and Sylvia. Was it not another bit of a mess? And what would Lady Simmons say if they were to become an item? Well, she had made her choice and chosen to remain the wife of an earl. It was likely Althorpe had gotten over her years ago, just as Trajan had gotten over Eden.

Even ruthless men were permitted to fall in love, he supposed. Why not?

Florence regained his attention with a light poke to his side. He glanced down at her.

I love you, she mouthed.

Life felt perfect for him in this moment. A gentle snow was

falling outside. A crackling fire kept them warm inside. The woman he loved to the depths of his soul was seated beside him and loved him.

He put his lips to her ear and whispered, "I love you too, my beautiful bird watcher. I'm glad you crash landed on me."

THE END

Also by Meara Platt

FARTHINGALE SERIES
My Fair Lily
The Duke I'm Going To Marry
Rules For Reforming A Rake
A Midsummer's Kiss
The Viscount's Rose
Earl of Hearts
The Viscount and the Vicar's Daughter
A Duke For Adela
Marigold and the Marquess
The Make-Believe Marriage
A Slight Problem With The Wedding
One Night With Tulip
If You Wished For Me
Never Dare A Duke
Capturing The Heart Of A Cameron

BOOK OF LOVE SERIES
The Look of Love
The Touch of Love
The Taste of Love
The Song of Love
The Scent of Love
The Kiss of Love
The Chance of Love
The Gift of Love
The Heart of Love
The Promise of Love
The Wonder of Love

The Journey of Love
The Treasure of Love
The Dance of Love
The Miracle of Love
The Hope of Love (novella)
The Dream of Love (novella)
The Remembrance of Love (novella)
All I Want For Christmas (novella)

MOONSTONE LANDING SERIES
Moonstone Landing (novella)
Moonstone Angel (novella)
The Moonstone Duke
The Moonstone Marquess
The Moonstone Major
The Moonstone Governess
The Moonstone Hero
The Moonstone Pirate

DARK GARDENS SERIES
Garden of Shadows
Garden of Light
Garden of Dragons
Garden of Destiny
Garden of Angels

SILVER DUKES
Cherish and the Duke
Moonlight and the Duke
Two Nights with the Duke
Snowfall and the Duke
Starlight and the Duke
Crash Landing on the Duke

LYON'S DEN
The Lyon's Surprise

Kiss of the Lyon
Lyon in the Rough

THE BRAYDENS
A Match Made In Duty
Earl of Westcliff
Fortune's Dragon
Earl of Kinross
Earl of Alnwick
Tempting Taffy
Aislin
Genalynn
Pearls of Fire⋆
⋆also in Pirates of Britannia series

DeWOLFE PACK ANGELS SERIES
Nobody's Angel
Kiss An Angel
Bhrodi's Angel

About the Author

Meara Platt is a USA Today bestselling author and an award winning, Amazon UK All-star with over seventy books published. Her favorite place in all the world is England's Lake District, which may not come as a surprise since many of her stories are set in that idyllic landscape, including her award winning, fantasy romance (romantasy) Dark Gardens series. If you'd like to learn more about the ancient Fae prophecy that is about to unfold in the Dark Gardens series, as well as Meara's lighthearted, international bestselling Regency romances in the Farthingale series, Book of Love series, and Silver Dukes series, or her more emotional Moonstone Landing series and Braydens series, please visit Meara's website at www.mearaplatt.com.